FOR YOU, FOREVER

(THE INN AT SUNSET HARBOR—BOOK 7)

SOPHIE LOVE

CHAPTER ONE

The windows in the nursery wide open, their lace curtains billowing in the breeze, Emily folded baby clothes, placing them neatly into the chest of drawers. She sighed with contentment. The beautiful weather—unseasonably warm for post–Labor Day—was most welcome.

Feeling a little tired, Emily sat in the nursing chair and rested a protective hand on her belly. Baby Charlotte was squirming around inside.

"Do you like the Indian summer?" Emily asked her. "Ninety degrees at this time of year isn't the norm. You'll have to get used to the cold at some point."

Baby Charlotte was due in December, on the cusp of winter, in just three short months. Emily could hardly believe how quickly the pregnancy had gone, and how fast the time had flown by. The weather they were enjoying at the moment made winter seem very far away, and Emily certainly wanted to keep it that way. Because with each new season that dawned, Emily thought of her father, of the fact that it would be the last time he'd ever experience that particular season.

She'd tried very hard to keep his terminal illness from her mind. Every time she spoke to him—which was daily—he didn't mention it, instead telling her of all the fun activities he had planned. And the letters were starting to stack up now. They'd promised to write each other a lifetime's worth of correspondence. Roy wasn't wallowing in his impending demise, so Emily wasn't going to either.

The door flew open then and in waltzed Chantelle. She was carrying a packet of diapers in her arms.

"Where should I put these?" she asked.

"On the changing table, please," Emily said, smiling at her sweet daughter.

She and Daniel were going out of their way to make Chantelle feel included. At the moment, that took the form of her buying a practical item of her choice from the grocery store on each trip. Today it was diapers. Yesterday had been binkies. She'd also purchased bottles, burp cloths, teething rings, and a rattle. Emily loved the way Chantelle found purpose in her task. She took it *very* seriously.

Chantelle walked over to the changing table and dumped the diapers down. Then she turned and faced Emily.

"Have we had any news yet?" she asked.

Emily knew Chantelle was referring to the island that she and Daniel had put in an offer on. She asked every day.

Emily checked her cell phone for what must have been the millionth time. She saw no missed calls or messages from the real estate agent.

She looked at Chantelle and shook her head. "Not yet."

Chantelle pouted with disappointment. "When will we find out?" she asked. "Will it be before Charlotte arrives?"

Emily shrugged. "I don't know, sweetie." She stroked her soft, blond hair. "You do know we might not definitely get it, right?" She'd been preparing Chantelle for the worst from the get-go but the little girl had a tendency to get carried away at times. She talked about the island as though it were a definite, bringing up in conversation how great it would be once they could go and play on the island, or how pretty it would look once Daniel had finished the construction work there.

"I know," Chantelle said, a little glumly.

Emily smiled brightly then, seeing that the child needed cheering up. "Come on, let's go downstairs and have some lunch."

Chantelle nodded and took her hand. They headed into the kitchen together.

To Emily's delight, Amy sat at the kitchen island. She'd been in Sunset Harbor for weeks now, staying with her new boyfriend, Harry, dipping her toes in the water of domesticity. Emily loved having her nearby, and Amy was certainly making the most by dropping around whenever she had time between conference calls and remotely managing her business. She was drinking coffee and chatting with Daniel, who was busy putting away the last of the groceries. He kissed Emily as she entered.

"Hey, gorgeous," he murmured, fix one of his intense looks of love on her.

Emily smiled and stroked a finger along his firm jaw line. She murmured, "Hey."

Just then, Amy coughed. Emily tore her gaze from Daniel and looked over her shoulder.

"Hi, Ames," she added to her friend, rolling her eyes jovially.

It still felt unusual for Emily to have Amy so readily accessible. Her temporary move to Sunset Harbor had been wonderful for them both, bringing back the easy friendship they'd shared before Emily disappeared from New York City without telling her. And Amy's organizational skills were certainly useful when it came to planning the logistics of Charlotte's birth.

"I didn't know you were coming over today," Emily said to her friend.

"I just came to speak to Dan about the checklist," Amy replied.

Emily took a seat opposite her, frowning with curiosity. "What checklist?"

"Of baby things," Amy said in a tone that suggested it should have been obvious. "You need your night bag ready for the hospital, a plan for how to get there, where to park, who to call. We've written a communication hierarchy, where Dan calls me and I'm responsible for passing it on to Harry, Jayne, your mom, and Lois. Harry does the announcements for Sunset Harbor folk, Lois tells the rest of the staff at the inn, et cetera. Honestly, Emily, I'm shocked you haven't gotten this stuff down yet."

Emily laughed. "In my defense, I'm not due for three months!"

"You have to be prepared," Amy said, knowingly. "If Charlotte felt like coming tomorrow, that's a very real possibility."

Chantelle's eyes widened. "She could come tomorrow?" she asked, looking thrilled at the prospect. "I could have a sister *tomorrow*?"

Emily touched her stomach protectively, a nagging worry growing in the back of her mind. "I hope not."

Daniel came and sat next to them. "Don't give Emily nightmare scenarios to worry about," he said to Amy. "And don't get Chantelle's hopes up, either. She's desperate to meet her little sister." He turned to Chantelle. "Charlotte will stay in Mom's tummy until December. There's only a very, very small chance she'll come sooner than that."

"So you mean she could come on my birthday?" Chantelle asked, grinning from ear to ear at the prospect.

Daniel laughed and shook his head. "Halloween and *two* birthdays?" he joked. "I don't think so!"

"It would make it easy to remember," Amy said with a chuckle.

Just then the doorbell rang.

"I'll get it," Emily said, wanting a distraction from the thought of Baby Charlotte being born prematurely.

Out in the foyer, the inn was a flurry of activity. The busy summer period was over but there was always plenty to organize, especially now that the dining room served three meals a day and the speakeasy was open every night. Once the restaurant and spa opened they would never get a moment's peace, Emily thought.

She hurried past Lois and Marnie, who were busy at the reception desk, then opened the door. A smartly dressed gentleman stood there. He looked to be around fifty years of age, with salt and pepper hair and a smattering of laugh lines around his eyes.

"Paul Knowlson," he said confidently, holding his hand out for Emily to shake like their meeting was some kind of business transaction.

She took it and shook. "I'm sorry, Paul, I don't think I know you," she said.

"I've booked an apartment," he said, pulling a slip of paper from his inner suit jacket pocket. "In Trevor's House," he said, reading off it.

"Oh!" Emily exclaimed. He was their first guest in the new apartments! "That's in the house across the lawn," she said. "Here, I'll lead the way."

"Fantastic," Paul replied.

Emily led him along the pathway. She felt a thrill of excitement knowing this would be the first time of many she'd be doing this. It was wonderful to see all their hard work on Trevor's House come to fruition, and to know the gift he'd left them was being utilized rather than left to languish.

"Now, I think I heard a hint of a New York City accent," Paul said as they walked. "Is that where you're from?"

"You're right," Emily replied, smiling. "Born and bred. Do you know it well?"

Paul nodded. "Yes, I grew up there. But I'm based in Florida now."

"And you're in business?" she added.

Paul laughed, gesturing to his expensive-looking suit. "What gave it away?"

They reached Trevor's House and Emily led him inside. The main area downstairs was now completely open plan, with just a hip-high glass partition between the brand new, sparkling restaurant and the route to the staircase that led up to the apartments. The restaurant hadn't yet opened its doors but it wouldn't be long now until that happened, Emily thought with excitement.

"You're in apartment four," Emily said, gesturing toward the stairs. "It's got a lovely balcony looking over the ocean."

"Sounds perfect," Paul replied.

Emily led him up the stairs to the mezzanine floor, then gestured to a Parisian-style wrought iron gate with a sign in gold reading *Guests Only*. She showed him the large key that opened the gate, and then they headed along the corridor and stopped outside apartment four.

Emily remembered the excitement she'd felt the first time she'd looked around the new apartments. They'd been masterfully designed by the Erik & Sons triplets. She hoped that Paul would be as impressed on first sight of the apartment as she had been.

She unlocked the door and pushed it open, then gestured for Paul to enter.

"This is fantastic," Paul said with a nod.

He seemed like a nice man, but Emily could get the sense of a business-savvy sharpness about him. It was the same quality that Amy had, an almost hawk-like ability to sniff out money and quality, to assess one's surroundings and make an instantaneous judgment. It was a huge compliment that someone like that would want to even book into her humble inn!

Emily handed him the key. "Meals are served in the main house at the moment," she explained. "So please join us whenever you wish. The restaurant downstairs isn't open yet so everything will be very quiet."

They said goodbye and Emily headed back out toward the main house. She caught up with Lois in the foyer.

"I forgot we had a guest in Trevor's," she said. "Is everything arranged for him? Clean bedding, bath robe, coffee pods for the machine?"

Lois nodded seriously. "Yes," she said, sounding a touch insulted by the insinuation she might have forgotten something.

Emily blushed. "Sorry, of course you're on it."

It wasn't always easy for Emily to remember that Lois wasn't the flustered, over-emotional scatterbrain she'd once been. She'd really flourished recently, probably due in part to her promotion and pay raise, and Emily knew she could trust her to run the inn perfectly. She'd even taken well to dealing with the suppliers and putting in grocery and goods orders. In fact, Emily realized, she could probably leave the country for a month and entrust the inn to Lois's capable hands; something she'd once have never thought possible!

Emily went back into the kitchen. Daniel, Amy, and Chantelle were still sitting around the kitchen table, chatting animatedly. No doubt Amy was using her business brain to force Daniel into planning every last detail of Charlotte's birth down to a tee, employing the sort of organized precision that babies paid little heed to.

5

"There she is." Daniel beamed when he saw her enter. "I've got some news."

"You do?" Emily said, taking a seat. "But I was only gone a minute."

"Jack called," Daniel said, referring to his boss at the carpentry workshop where he'd been working for the last year.

"Oh? And what did he say?" Emily asked, curiously.

"It's his back again," Daniel said. Jack had injured himself at work not that long ago and hadn't been back to normal since. "You know how it gives him problems. Well, his wife has finally managed to convince him to reduce his hours at work. She's inherited some money and wants them to take an early retirement, cruise around the Caribbean, that sort of thing."

Emily frowned. "Your exciting news is that Jack and his wife are going on a cruise?"

Daniel laughed. "Yes!"

"I don't get it," she added, looking with bemusement at Chantelle's and Amy's excited expressions. "What's the joke? What am I missing?"

Daniel continued. "Think about it," he encouraged her. "He'll need someone to run the wood store in his absence. Someone to deal with the shop."

Emily gasped. "You mean… you?"

Chantelle couldn't contain it anymore. She burst out her joyful exclamation. "Daddy's getting promoted!"

Emily clapped a hand over her mouth. "That's amazing!" she cried. "You deserve it."

She couldn't believe the good fortune and hopped off her stool, going around behind Daniel and hugging him tightly.

Daniel blushed shyly. He wasn't one to readily take compliments.

"He's going to give me a raise and a new title. It will mean longer hours though," he added, sounding very serious. "I'll need to be the first in to open up and I'll need to be the last there at night to lock everything up properly. There's expensive equipment and products in there and Jack never lets anyone else lock up, so it's kind of a big deal for him to release the reins on that front. My shift pattern will be really odd as a result. Jack never minded driving to and from the woodshop at all hours, but now that I'll be expected to do the same it will be an adjustment."

Emily didn't want to think about any of the possible downsides to the good news yet. Long shifts, extra responsibility over safety and security, and the inevitable stress that would cause him were all things she would deal with at the time. Right now, she wanted to ride the high of the good news.

"I'm so proud of you," she said, pressing a kiss into the crown of his head.

"You should do something to celebrate," Amy said from the other side of the breakfast bar.

"Definitely," Emily agreed.

"I think we should go down to the beach!" Chantelle suggested.

"Well, while the weather's like this, I don't see why not," Emily said. "We shouldn't waste it."

Chantelle punched the air. She loved the beach, the outside in general. Any opportunity to run and sprint in nature she took greedily.

"Amy?" Emily asked. "Are you joining us?"

Amy consulted her watch. "Actually, I'm supposed to be meeting Harry soon so I won't have time."

Emily couldn't be sure, but she thought she heard an undertone in her friend's voice, a kind of exasperation. She wondered if there was an issue between her and Harry.

But there was no time to discuss it now. The Morey family was in full action mode, Chantelle hurrying off in search of the dogs' leashes, Daniel flinging open cupboards and pulling out bags, juice boxes, and snacks.

Emily touched Amy's hand across the counter. "We'll talk later," she said.

Amy nodded, her expression a little downcast. Then Emily was swept up in the chaos of her family, like a tornado spinning around her pulling her in.

"Let's go! To the beach!"

CHAPTER TWO

The beach was stunningly beautiful in the sunshine. Emily could hardly believe it was so sunny at this time of year. It was as warm and bright as any summer day.

They strolled along together, letting both the dogs off their leashes so they could run ahead and bark at the breaking waves.

Once they'd found a good spot to settle, Daniel helped Emily down to the ground. She sat crossed-legged, her pregnant bump nestled comfortably within her legs. Chantelle bounded off, filled with exuberance for what felt like their last chance to enjoy the beach this year.

Daniel reached over for Emily's hand and stroked it tenderly.

"How do you feel about my promotion?" he asked. "Are you worried about the extra hours taking me away from home?"

"Well, how much time are we talking?" Emily asked. She was ready now to know more of the intricacies, to consider the challenges that they may face.

"Jack opens the store at eight," he began. "That's not the issue, really. I'm used to early starts and it will fit in with the school run. It's the woodworking shop that's the bigger issue. There are times when we get a big order and not a lot of time to do it. Before, when I was just a worker, I'd be one among many and at most it would add an extra hour or two to each work day. We could share the burden. But since I'll be the one supervising the equipment use and be solely responsible for quality assurance, I'm going to need to be on site through each order, seeing everything through to completion, just like Jack used to. You know how long the hours could get anyway. Well, now I won't be part of the shift pattern anymore. I'll be in charge of it, and expected to be there during the busy periods."

The more Daniel spoke about it, the more Emily could feel her anxiety increasing. The promotion was pretty bad timing. The thought of Daniel not being there when she went into labor worried her. And what about paternity leave? Would he even be able to get any?

But more than her anxiety, she was bursting with happiness for him. She was also extremely proud of Daniel and didn't want to bring down his mood in any way. He had achieved so much since she'd known him. And besides, she had Amy there to catch the slack.

"I'm just so happy for you," she said. "You deserve it, after all your hard work."

"We could certainly do with the raise," Daniel replied, his spare hand touching Emily's stomach gently. "Since we'll soon have more mouths to feed."

Emily smiled and sighed with contentment. Despite the hardships she was facing, she was still looking forward to the future, to meeting Baby Charlotte.

When Daniel spoke again he sounded a little melancholy. "More responsibility means more stress. I hope I still have enough energy to spend time with the kids."

"You'll do amazingly," Emily encouraged him. "I know you will."

Though able to play the role of supportive spouse on the outside, Emily was still quite anxious about Daniel's changing role. He had a tendency to let stress affect him, or to feel weighed down by perceived expectation. It was something she admired in him. But it could also be to the detriment of the family, because sometimes it felt like he'd put everything else in the world first before them. It wasn't always easy for Emily to remind herself that the very reason he sometimes put other things first *was* for them—for her, and Chantelle, the inn, and of course, Baby Charlotte.

"I do wonder why Jack didn't promote one of the others," Daniel wondered aloud. "I'm relatively new there compared to some of the old hats."

"Probably *because* you're young," Emily said. "Because you'll work hard for your family. Or maybe because he knows that you have the talent to make it on your own."

Daniel frowned. "What do you mean?"

"I mean that you could easily open your own wood shop. It's not like we don't have the space for one on site somewhere. We could convert one of the barns, after all. And now you have tons of expertise with making furniture. I mean, you made the crib for Charlotte in your spare time and it's phenomenal! People would pay loads for something like that, a unique crib for their baby. You only have to look at the price tag on my nursing stool to see that!" She laughed, remembering the thousands of dollars Amy had splashed out on the rocking armchair and footstool for her.

Daniel, on the other hand, was quiet. His expression was sort of dreamy and far away.

"What are you thinking?" Emily asked him.

9

He snapped back to attention. "I'm just thinking that you might be right about Jack promoting me to keep me there instead of losing me."

"Might be right?" Emily joked. "I'm definitely right! You could run a bespoke kids' furniture business. Or you could even make boats if you want. You have the talent to do anything you put your mind to."

It was so obvious to Emily but Daniel looked stunned, as though the thought had never crossed his mind.

"I never really thought about it that way," he said. "It's just a job to me, you know."

"Just a job! You're too humble for your own good sometimes," Emily continued. "How many people do you really think have that kind of skill? You have a talent, Daniel. You just have to think bigger sometimes."

Instead of her words encouraging him, Daniel seemed to retreat then.

"I do think big," he mumbled, defensively. "I'm just not as good as you seem to think I am."

"It's not just me," Emily told him, gently. "Jack clearly thinks so, too."

She hadn't meant to push so hard. She'd only meant for Daniel to understand he had a talent and that it could take him far. But he seemed to be shrinking, deflating under the weight of her perception.

Quietly, he turned his face down to the sand, picking pebbles up and throwing them across the beach.

Just then Emily's cell phone began to ring. She sighed, on one hand relieved to have been saved by the bell but on the other frustrated to be robbed of the chance to get to the bottom of Daniel's apparent mood change.

She rummaged in her purse and plucked her cell phone out. With surprise, she saw that the caller ID was the real estate agent for the island. It flashed at her like a beacon.

"It's them!" she exclaimed aloud, feeling excitement warble in her chest.

Daniel looked up sharply from where he'd been flinging pebbles. From the shoreline, Chantelle turned at the sound of Emily's voice.

"It's the broker!" Emily called across the beach to Chantelle.

The two dogs mirrored Chantelle's movements, all three pelting across the beach toward Emily, kicking up clouds of sand behind them.

Once Chantelle reached Emily, she skidded to a halt, and the dogs ran around them in circles, salty sea water clinging to their fur, yapping with their instinctive understanding that something exciting was about to happen.

With uneven breath, Emily answered the call and put it straight onto speakerphone. The family crowded forward, looking down at the cell phone expectantly. It was as if the little block of plastic held their entire futures in its power.

"We're all here," Emily explained. "On tenterhooks. So, what's the news?"

Ever since they'd put the offer in, Emily had prepared herself for the worst. In fact, she'd pretty much convinced herself that it wouldn't come to fruition, that they wouldn't get the island. It just wasn't the sort of thing that happened to normal people. But despite telling herself over and over that it just wasn't going to happen, she'd been unable to dampen the small glimmer of excitement inside of her, that sliver of hope that challenged the pessimistic part of her mind with the simple mantra, *what if...*

The broker spoke, her voice coming through the line in crackles.

"It's good news," she said. "Your offer was accepted. The island is yours!"

Emily couldn't believe what she'd just heard. Had static on the line made her hear what she wanted? But when she looked up into Daniel's eyes, she saw them sparkling with surprise and elation. When Chantelle leapt up in the air and jumped up and down, waving her arms, Emily knew there was no doubt.

The dogs began barking at Chantelle's commotion, leaping up with soggy paws, making wet sand marks all over her clothes.

"Really?" Emily stammered, straining to hear the crackly line through the din. "We really got it?"

"You really did," the broker replied. Emily could hear the smile in her voice. "Of course there's still some paperwork to sign and file. But you're very welcome to go and visit in the meantime." She finished with a chuckle.

Emily was so stunned she couldn't find her voice. Daniel took over, leaning closer to the cell phone between them.

"You mean we can actually go there now?" he asked, his gaze fixed on Emily rather than on the phone. "As the official owners?"

From the speaker, the broker's voice came, tinny and robotic, "You can indeed."

Chantelle crouched down then and threw her arms around her father's neck, so exuberant she almost knocked him clean to the ground.

"We're going to the island now?" she cried in his ear.

Daniel winced, but he was grinning broadly. Chantelle's arms were wrapped around his neck like an octopus's tentacles and he brought his hands up to loosen her grip as he raised his eyebrows at Emily.

"What do you think? Shall we go and look at it through the eyes of its owners?"

Emily touched her stomach, feeling Baby Charlotte's form inside. She was growing increasingly protective as the weeks passed, not wanting to subject her growing child to any unpleasantness. But the sea was calm today, and she felt certain that she wouldn't experience any seasickness on the ride over.

"Let's do it," she said.

Chantelle screamed with joy.

Daniel leaned down to the phone, almost yelling now over the noise of dogs and children, straining as Chantelle yanked him roughly around with her excitement.

"You've made us extremely happy," he said to the broker. "Thanks for everything."

"You're welcome, Mr. Morey," the broker replied.

They ended the call and Emily and Daniel sat back with matching stunned expressions, both looking as dazed as the other as their new reality began to sink in. Chantelle whizzed around, throwing their things haphazardly into a bag, moving as though on fast forward.

"Come on," she cried. "Let's go!"

Daniel snapped into action, standing and helping Emily to her feet. The harbor was a short walk away but Emily knew she'd have to take it slowly. Chantelle ran on ahead with the dogs, stopping periodically to hurry back, effectively doubling the distance she was covering in comparison to Daniel and Emily.

On the way they passed Cynthia and Jeremy out on a bike ride.

"We bought an island!" Chantelle called out to them as they passed, waving.

Cynthia frowned. "It sounded like you said an island?" she called back.

"I did!" Chantelle cried, jumping up and down.

Emily laughed. No one was going to believe what they'd done, that they'd bought themselves an island off the coast of Maine! She could hardly believe it herself.

"Look, it's Amy and Harry!" Chantelle cried then.

Emily squinted ahead and saw that the loved up couple were sitting together on a bench at the harbor's edge, deep in conversation. It looked as though it might be somewhat intense, with Amy leaning in and gesticulating widely, Harry shaking his head emphatically with what looked like a stern expression on his face. Emily wondered again what was going on with the pair. It really looked to her like they were arguing.

"Do you think they'll want to come and see our island?" Chantelle asked.

Emily was about to tell her to leave them be, but before she had a chance to reply, Chantelle had already hurried off. Chantelle was on a mission and Emily's waddle was too slow to catch up to her.

She saw Chantelle reach them, and watched as they sprang apart, shocked by the interruption. She couldn't hear anything from this distance, but she could see the false smiles on each of their faces, and the strained looks hidden in their expressions.

By the time she and Daniel made it to the trio, Chantelle had already broken the news. Amy turned and hugged Emily.

"You're crazy, you know that?" her friend said. "An *island*?!"

"It's an extension of the inn," Emily tried to explain.

"But you only just fixed up Trevor's House." Amy laughed. "And there's still the spa to open, and the restaurant."

She gestured at Harry, who would be the manager of the new restaurant once it opened. They caught one another's eyes, their smiles clearly put on, then Amy looked away again quickly. Not quick enough for Emily not to perceive it though. She knew her friend inside out. There was definitely something going on between her and Harry. The easiness that usually existed between them felt strained. She wondered what it might be.

Suddenly, Chantelle interrupted the conversation with impassioned cries of, "Come on, come on, come on!" She'd clearly lost patience for the adults' "boring" conversation, and was tugging on Amy's hand. "Please can we go to the island now?"

Daniel addressed Harry. "You're both welcome to come along with us. Since you're pretty much on the payroll now, it makes sense for you to be there!"

Harry grinned. "I can't wait for the grand opening of Trevor's," he said. "I'm ready to sink my teeth in!"

"Glad to hear it," Emily replied, beaming. "So what do you think? Island excursion?"

She wasn't sure the invite would be welcome, especially since she'd deduced that they'd interrupted an argument, that Amy at the least was clearly not in the mood, but Harry spoke first, muting her before she had a chance to turn them down.

"Absolutely," he said. "We've got nothing else to do today, do we, Ames?"

Amy glanced quickly at Harry, and Emily saw the exasperation in her eyes over whatever it was that had been left unresolved between them.

"Sure," Amy replied, her tone overly jovial, like she was acting happy for everyone else's sake. She grinned at Emily, but couldn't hide the trouble in her eyes from her best friend. Her smile faltered as though she'd realized she'd been caught faking. At least her happiness appeared genuine when she slung an arm around Chantelle's shoulders, Emily thought. "May as well see what crazy thing you've gotten yourself into now!" She peered over Chantelle's head at Emily.

"You okay?" Emily mouthed to Amy.

Amy nodded once, decisively, then mouthed back, "Talk later."

Whatever atmosphere Emily had picked up on between Harry and Amy, she'd been right in thinking there was something wrong. She was concerned for her friend and determined to get Amy alone in order to get to the bottom of it.

But for the time being, Emily chose to focus on her own happy moment; a boat trip with friends and family to the island of their dreams.

CHAPTER THREE

The sun sparkled off the surface of the water as the boat cut through the small waves. They bobbed up and down, and Emily held onto her stomach protectively. Luckily, she didn't feel seasick.

"I don't think we've ever had this many people in the boat before," Chantelle remarked. "Four adults, one child, two dogs. And a baby in Mom's tummy, of course."

Emily laughed. "It's quite the adventure," she agreed.

Amy was quiet as they went, her arms crossed about her middle, her face turned out to the ocean. She wore an expression of deep contemplation. She was clearly lost in her thoughts, and Emily wondered again what they were. Being out on the ocean, Emily herself had discovered, invited quiet reflection at the best of times, and could easily lead the mind toward an existential crisis. She watched her friend anxiously.

Harry, on the other hand, either had nothing on his mind or was very good at hiding it. He was chatting openly with Daniel and Chantelle about the types of fish that could be caught in the ocean, about their plans for the island and boating in general.

"Now that we have a destination to boat to this will happen much more often," Daniel was saying. "We'll be ferrying people over here all the time, for parties and picnics."

"Sounds awesome," Harry said in his usual cheery manner.

Chantelle was looking up at her father with rapt attention. "Can we have Thanksgiving here?" she asked, wide-eyed.

"I doubt it," Daniel replied. "It will take a long time to get the well installed, figure out the plumbing and the solar generators for power. It's much more work than a few months, and the winter weather that's coming soon won't help. Sorry, kiddo, there's just too much to do between now and Thanksgiving for it to be a possibility."

Chantelle pouted, looking downcast.

"But we can definitely visit the island as much as the weather allows us," Emily told her. "And since we won't be sailing around in circles anymore, but have a place to head to, I think we'll be able to come out more often than we used to."

Chantelle pondered her words for a moment, then returned her expression back to happy.

Emily smiled at Daniel. He seemed relieved that she'd handled the situation so well and Emily felt a surge of pride. Her maternal instincts seemed to be sharpening as her due date grew closer.

After a while, they reached the island and the ancient jetty that was barely still standing. The faded sign that proclaimed the island was for sale was still there.

"You can start by kicking that down!" Emily told Chantelle.

Chantelle didn't need telling twice. She leapt off the boat, ran at the sign, and yanked it out of the ground.

As he tethered the boat, Daniel gestured to a stack of old, rotting fishing crates. "Put it here. We can have a bonfire."

The idea of a bonfire seemed to thrill Chantelle. She jumped up and down with excitement.

Emily stepped carefully from the boat onto terra firma, trying to absorb the strange reality that she now owned this island, that it was hers. Unlike the inn, which she'd inherited, and Trevor's, which had come into her possession through his will, this was the first thing she'd truly ever bought, she and Daniel together. It was theirs, and the overwhelming relevance of that struck her even more deeply now that she was standing on its shoreline.

Behind her, Amy and Harry stepped off the boat. They were both wearing bemused expressions as they glanced about them at the scraggly, overgrown island, the strewn debris from years past. Amy in particular must have thought Emily had gone crazy buying this deserted plot of land, surrounded by ocean, filled with squirrels and birds. If she thought Sunset Harbor was uncivilized, what on earth must she think about the island?

"I know it's not much to look at, at the moment," Emily confessed. "But there's so much potential."

"Of course," Amy said, looking perturbed as she stepped lightly along the uneven ground. Her high-fashion clothes looked more out of place here than usual.

"Do you guys want the tour?" Emily asked.

Harry nodded enthusiastically, but Amy made only a lackluster noise of confirmation.

"I'll show you!" Chantelle cried.

She led the way, heading into the trees with Harry and Amy in tow. Their footsteps and noisy voices disrupted the black squirrels that inhabited the island, making them scurry up the trees.

As Emily trekked after them, slower because of her pregnant waddle, she could hear Chantelle excitedly making announcements.

"We're going to have a tree house here," Chantelle told them. "It will be a pirate ship for me and Charlotte to play in. And that will be where the magical fairy castle ballroom will be."

Daniel, having finished securing the boat, came up beside Emily and helped her through the thickets. They drew up beside the others, Emily panting slightly from the effort and exhilaration she felt from being here.

Amy raised her eyebrows as they approached, surprised and interested.

"Are you doing all the work yourself?" she asked Daniel. "It sounds like there's a lot to do. Too much for one man, especially a soon-to-be father."

Emily smiled to herself; her friend always had her best interests at heart and knew how difficult Emily found it whenever Daniel was away from home.

"No!" Daniel exclaimed with a chuckle. "We have great contractors for it. Two kids, straight out of college. They're desperate to add to their portfolio so we're expecting really great things from them."

"And other than pirate ships and magic castles," Harry said, "where will the actual inn parts be?"

"Well, there will be a three-room cabin which we want to start as a sort of writer's retreat. Tracy is also going to do some yoga workshops on the island, like day-long well-being retreats."

"It sounds fantastic," Harry said. "How much do you think you'll get done over the winter?"

"Depends on the weather," Daniel said. "It's a shame it took so long to get the sale through, really. This Indian summer could have given us a head start, but I'm sure it will be over by the time we've organized all the machinery and materials."

Thinking ahead made Emily worry. No longer was the island a fantasy or a dream. It was real. Now everything had to be practical. There was so much to organize and pay for, so many components that had to be in place. They'd barely finished the renovations at Trevor's. It felt a bit like they'd jumped from the frying pan and into the fire!

But still, Emily was thrilled. She couldn't quite believe she and Daniel had had the guts to buy the island. Not only had they been brave enough to make a child together, they'd been brave enough to follow their dreams, no matter how crazy they may seem. Emily smiled to herself, knowing that above all else, they were a team, and that together they were indestructible.

"Now, let's go start a fire," Daniel said, rubbing his hands eagerly. "Chantelle, can you collect all the pieces of wood on the beach?"

She nodded and hurried off, always in need of a task, always wanting to do her part to help. Then Daniel pulled a package of marshmallows from his jacket pocket. Emily laughed with delight, knowing how happy Chantelle would be when she got back from her trip to the beach to discover Daniel's plan to toast marshmallows around the bonfire.

"You should have brought your guitar!" Emily said.

But Daniel just smiled and kissed her tenderly. "There will be so many more opportunities for songs around the bonfire," he said, his eyes going dreamy. "You, me, and the girls."

Emily gazed at him, awed by the man he was, the gorgeousness of him, and so excited for their future together, for all the adventures that lay ahead.

*

Mouths sticky with melted marshmallow, bellies and cheeks aching from laughter, the small party headed back to the boat. Daniel had called it, saying that the light would soon fade. And besides, there was no plumbing on the island yet and Baby Charlotte had a tendency to kick Emily's bladder on a regular basis, so she'd be relieved to be heading back within the vicinity of a restroom.

When they reached the main lane, Daniel found their spot in the harbor. There were very few vessels in the water now, though many more than usual at this time of year. Everyone was making the most of the warm weather, eking out as many trips on the water as they could before winter came along and robbed them of that pleasure.

"Thanks for that impromptu trip to your island," Amy said, hugging Emily farewell. "I don't think I'll ever get over how crazy that is."

Emily smiled at her, tucking loose strands of her hair from her eyes. "When can we hang out just the two of us?" she asked.

Though Amy was often around, they were always surrounded by people. Emily couldn't actually recall the last time the two of them had gotten together for a good chat, and she could tell that Amy needed someone to talk to right now.

"Chantelle's back at school tomorrow," Emily added, "so we'll be able to find some privacy more easily. How about coffee at Joe's once we've dropped her off?"

Amy nodded and Emily noticed the look of relief in her eyes to know she'd finally be able to offload whatever was on her mind.

They parted ways with Amy and Harry, everyone hugging and waving goodbye, then strolled slowly back to the inn, exhausted from the long day. Even the dogs were dragging their paws.

"I'm tired," Chantelle said through her yawn as they idled up the driveway.

Ahead of them sat the inn, silhouetted against a deepening blue sky. Its windows beamed out yellow light, looking like twinkling stars from this distance. Emily smiled, content. Seeing the inn always gave her a sense of peace, and made her feel like she was home.

"Let's have some dinner first and then you can head up to your room," Emily said. "It's your first day back at school tomorrow so you need a good night's sleep."

Chantelle looked a little sad. "The summer's over already?"

Emily nodded. "I'm afraid so, sweetie. But don't worry, you love school! You'll see Bailey and Toby every single day again. And Gail."

"Will Miss Glass still be my teacher?" Chantelle asked.

Emily shook her head. "You'll be in a new class with a new teacher. Does that worry you?"

Chantelle paused, her expression showing that she was thinking about it. "No," she said, eventually. "I'll still see Miss Glass on the playground sometimes."

Emily smiled, then caught Daniel's eye. He was smiling too.

They went inside the inn, the foyer bright, warm, and welcoming. Bryony was in the side lounge on her favorite couch, surrounded by half-drunk coffee mugs as usual. She leapt up when she saw them, her metal bracelets jangling as she did, and hurried over. Her perfume smelled of spices.

"Guys, I can't believe it!" she gushed. "An island!" She hugged Emily. "Do you know how few islands there are in the hospitality world? This is going to be a gold mine!"

"I'm glad to hear that," Emily replied. "Or else it might have been a very expensive mistake."

Daniel and Chantelle went into the kitchen to make food. Emily decided to head up to the nursery while they were cooking. She wanted to look through another one of Charlotte's boxes to see whether there were any toys she could pass on to the baby.

She went inside the nursery and sat on the floor beside one of the many boxes that contained her sister's old toys and clothes, which had been brought down from where they'd been carefully stored in the attic.

This task was always tinged with melancholy. Though Emily felt that Charlotte's spirit was with her in this house, smiling down on her and the family she'd built, it always felt a little bit like she disappeared more with each day that passed. Time was supposed to make pain lessen but for Emily she felt that the more days that went by without her sister the more she missed her, because the last time they spoke was that little bit further in the past.

She opened up the cardboard box, a smell of dust wafting out with it. Like most of the boxes, this one was filled with cuddly toys. It surprised Emily to see that Charlotte had owned so many stuffed toys. She hardly had any memories of her sister playing with bears or dolls. They spent most of their time imagining worlds and acting out plays. Other than their twin rag dolls and Charlotte's favorite bear, Andy Pandy, Emily couldn't recall them ever playing with such toys at all.

But as she reached in and pulled out a faded pink toy, Emily felt a sudden surge of a memory. She turned the toy over in her hands and saw it was a unicorn, its once shimmery sequined horn now dull.

"Sparkles," she muttered aloud, the name of the toy appearing on her tongue before her mind had even kicked into gear.

Then suddenly she felt a familiar swirling sensation, one she had not felt for a very long time. She was slipping back into the past, into her old memories.

The flashbacks had begun once she'd first returned to the inn. They'd been terrifying at first, frightening memories such as the night Charlotte had died, and the raging arguments between her parents. But then as time had passed, as she processed those repressed memories, Emily had started to experience some of the more pleasant ones. Times when she and Charlotte had played together; had been carefree. This memory filled Emily with a sense of calmness, and she knew it was going to be a nice one.

She and Charlotte were in the attic, in one of the rooms her father had filled with antique items. On the floor beside them was a bronze globe, and Charlotte was spinning it idly with a finger. Sitting next to Charlotte was Sparkles, the beautiful unicorn toy. Brand new, fluffy pink, with a sequined horn.

"Sparkles is sad," Charlotte told Emily.

"Why?" Emily asked, curiously, hearing a child's voice coming from her throat.

"Because she's the last unicorn," Charlotte explained. "She doesn't have any other unicorn friends."

"That's sad," Emily replied. "Maybe you should take her on an adventure to cheer her up?"

Charlotte seemed to perk up at the suggestion. "Where do you want to go, Sparkles?" she asked her toy. Then she spun the golden globe and stopped it with a pointed finger. It was a small island to the east of the continent of America. "Sparkles wants to go to an island," Charlotte informed Emily.

Emily nodded. "In that case, we'd better get in the boat."

They pulled out old chairs and coffee tables, disturbing the dust and stirring the smell of mildew, then configured them in such a way that satisfied their imaginations that they'd constructed a boat. Then they used a threadbare curtain as a sail and clambered into their boat with Sparkles.

Emily could almost feel the wind in her hair as they sailed across the ocean to a distant shore. Charlotte used a kaleidoscope as a telescope, scanning the room as if searching.

"Land ahoy!" she suddenly cried.

Emily threw the anchor—which was in fact a wooden coat hanger tied to a curtain cord. Then they leaped from the boat and swam to shore.

Panting from exertion, the two girls began exploring the island, poking through the piles of antiques, pretending it was a volcano.

"Look in here," Charlotte cried to Emily. "Down in the volcano!"

Emily peered behind the hat stand that Charlotte was pointing at. "I don't believe it!" she exclaimed, playing along.

Charlotte's eyes were wide. "It's the rest of the unicorns," she said. Then she spoke hurriedly to Sparkles. Her face dropped. "Sparkles wants to go down the volcano to be with them," she said to Emily.

"Oh," Emily said, a little sad. "Even though that means leaving us?"

Charlotte looked at her dear unicorn friend and nodded. "She says this is her home island. She misses it a lot, and all her friends. She wants to live here. But we're allowed to come and visit."

"That's okay then," Emily said.

They tied their cardigan sleeves together to make a sling for Sparkles. Then they lowered the unicorn down the back of the furniture and left her there.

"Are you sad to say goodbye?" Emily asked Charlotte as they climbed back into their makeshift boat.

Charlotte shook her head. "No. Because I know I'll see her again."

Emily suddenly snapped back into the present day. She was holding Sparkles tightly against her chest, and the toy's head was wet with her tears. On one hand she felt desperately sad, because she knew Charlotte had never had the chance to see Sparkles again. But the other part of her felt buoyant with joy. The toy was a sign from Charlotte, Emily was certain. Sparkles had been left on that island, down the back of the furniture, completely forgotten about until this moment, perhaps even specifically for this moment.

She hugged Sparkles tightly, then placed her, poignantly, on the shelf overlooking Baby Charlotte's crib. She felt the circle of life continuing, and smiled knowing that once Charlotte arrived she would have a guardian angel watching over her as she slept.

*

Emily snuggled up into bed beside Daniel. It had been a long and tiring day, and she found herself quickly drifting off to sleep.

"I can't believe we own an island," she murmured into the darkness as she began to fall asleep. "My future is looking nothing like I thought it would once."

Daniel let out a sleepy laugh. "How so?"

"Well, I never thought I'd be married and pregnant. I never thought I'd have Chantelle, or this inn." She stroked Daniel's chest as it rose and fell slowly.

"I never thought I'd have Chantelle or the inn either," he replied.

"But you're happy you do?"

"Of course."

"Are you happy we're having another girl?"

He kissed her forehead. "I'm very happy," he assured her.

"And that our daughter is going back to school tomorrow where she's doing fabulously?"

Daniel laughed again. "Yes. I am glad that Chantelle is doing well at school."

Emily smiled, contented. Sleep seemed ready to take her.

"I'm only sad about one thing," she said.

"What's that?"

"That my dad won't be around to enjoy it all with us."

Daniel fell quiet then. She felt his arms tighten around her.

"I know," he said. "I'm sad about that too. But let's just make the most of the time we have with him now. Let's make sure every day is as good as it can be. Let's make each day count."

Emily nodded with affirmation. "I think we made today count," she said, yawning. "We bought an island, after all. It's not every day that happens."

She felt Daniel's chest shudder with his laugher. She squeezed herself even more tightly against him, overjoyed and welling with love. Wrapped in one another's arms, their heartbeats synchronized. They fell asleep in unison, in perfect harmony, two people united by love.

CHAPTER FOUR

Emily took a final sip of her decaf coffee and put the mug down on the kitchen table. She'd slept deeply but had awoken feeling groggy—partly because of the alarm clock being set a whole hour earlier than she'd gotten accustomed to over the summer—and she really could have benefited from some actual caffeine. It was probably the thing she was most looking forward to once Baby Charlotte arrived, the thing she missed the most and yearned for the most. She watched Daniel enviously as he drank his across the table from her.

"Right, darling," Emily said at last, looking at Chantelle. "It's time to head to school."

Chantelle was sitting with her head bowed over a pile of clock pieces, her tongue sticking out the corner of her mouth in concentration. Her empty bowl of cereal was beside her, discarded haphazardly so she could pursue her task.

"Can't I have five more minutes?" she asked, so absorbed in her task she didn't even look up. "I just need to work out where to put this cog."

Since their return from England, Chantelle had been determined to make a clock like Papa Roy. Emily thought it was very sweet that Chantelle was so inspired by her grandfather, but it also broke her heart at the same time. She and Daniel had not yet told Chantelle the news of Papa Roy's illness; the girl would be utterly crushed when she lost him. They all would.

Daniel took command then. "Nope, sorry, sweetie. You need to get in on time to meet your new teacher and new classmates."

Chantelle put her screwdriver down with a reluctant sigh. "Fine."

Emily wished she could convince Chantelle to do her mucky, oily work somewhere more appropriate—the garage, or shed, or just about anywhere that wasn't the kitchen table, really. But Chantelle wouldn't hear of it. Papa Roy did his clock fixing at the breakfast table so Chantelle had to as well!

They all headed out to the truck together, Daniel taking the driving seat since Emily was finding it too uncomfortable to fit her growing belly behind the steering wheel. Chantelle hopped in the back into her car seat.

"I can't wait until Baby Charlotte comes on the ride with us to school," she said, glancing across at the baby seat they'd recently installed (at Amy's instance, of course, because you never know when the baby might decide to come and the last thing you'd want to be doing is fiddling with a complicated seat while in the painful grips of contractions).

"Me too," Emily said, resting her hands against her tight belly. It seemed to be becoming more uncomfortable with each day that passed.

"First she'll just be coming along for the ride, but it won't be long before she'll be walking through those doors with you," Daniel said with a chuckle. "She'll be in kindergarten before we even know it."

Emily felt wistful at the thought. She knew what Daniel meant, that time went by quickly, that they should appreciate every moment because it would disappear from them like sand sifting through a timer. But the future Daniel was alluding to was also one in which her father had long passed. He would not be there when Charlotte started kindergarten. He'd never see the numerous photos that Emily would take of the two girls heading into school together, hand in hand. That future, though she couldn't wait to be living it on the one hand, would also be fraught with grief on the other. She'd be a different person, changed irreparably by losing Roy.

They drove along the familiar Sunset Harbor roads and turned into the parking lot at the school. It was already very busy with parents eager to deposit their children after the long summer break.

"It's Bailey!" Chantelle cried, pointing to where her best friend played on the grass. Bailey's normally unruly auburn hair had been styled into two long plaits. Emily had never seen her look quite so presentable. "But who is she with?" Chantelle added.

Bailey was playing with an unfamiliar child, a very skinny, pale girl with long, straight blonde hair.

"I don't know," Emily said. "I've never seen her before."

Daniel parked and they got out of the pickup truck. Emily noticed Yvonne leaning against her four-by-four, chatting with Holly, another one of the moms they were well acquainted with.

"Why don't you go and say hi," Daniel told her. "I can supervise Chantelle and do the teacher handover."

Emily deliberated. She wanted to meet the new teacher but she felt a yearning to reconnect with the friends whose company she'd missed over the summer.

"I'll be super quick," she told him, one hand clicking the passenger door catch and pushing it open.

Daniel chuckled and headed off in the direction of the steps where all the teachers were congregated supervising the morning play session.

Emily went up to Yvonne and gave her friend a big hug. Then she hugged Holly as well.

"How was your summer?" Emily asked.

Holly blushed then. Yvonne seemed to be holding back a smirk.

"It was great," Holly told Emily. "Logan and I took the kids to Vancouver to visit family."

"And…" Yvonne prompted.

Emily frowned, looking from one woman to the other.

"And…" Holly said, her blush deepening. "We're pregnant."

Emily's eyes pinged open. "You're kidding!" she exclaimed.

Holly shook her head. She looked shy, but thrilled.

"I'm so happy for you," Emily cried, hugging her again. "Our babies will be able to have playdates."

"With Robin," Holly added, referring to Suzanna's new son who was just two months old.

"They can be a little gang," Emily added with a laugh.

Yvonne pouted then. "Ugh, I'm jealous. I wish I was having another."

"Was it planned?" Emily asked Holly. "You're blushing like it wasn't!"

"No," Holly told her. "It was a surprise. A welcome one, but Minnie's not even one yet so we didn't think anything was possible! But in Vancouver the kids were doted on by relatives and we were able to get rest and go on dates and, well, one thing led to another."

Everyone laughed. Emily felt happy to be back in the company of some of her other school parent friends. Though Yvonne was very much one of her best friends, and Suzanna to a lesser extent, the wider circle of parent friends was very much context dependent. She realized then that she'd missed their company, she'd missed having people to share the trials and tribulations of parenthood with.

"Look at my little Bailey," Yvonne said then, glancing over at the playground. "She's taken the new girl under her wing."

Emily looked over and saw the two of them zipping around the playground. Chantelle, she noticed, was not playing with them. Instead, she was with the boys, Toby, Levi, and Ryan, engaging in a much more rough and tumble kind of game. She wondered why they weren't all playing together.

Under her breath, Yvonne whispered, "I hope she doesn't invite her over for playdates though. I met the mom this morning. She's as sour-faced as her daughter. And the kid's name is *Laverne*."

Emily couldn't help but giggle. It felt so good to be back with her parent friends, back at the school gates. Last time she'd done this it had all been new and strange. Chantelle had appeared out of nowhere and knocked Emily's life for six. But she wouldn't change a thing now. Becoming a mom had been the best experience of her life, and she loved the feeling, the opportunities it had given her, and the people she'd met because of it.

She looked over and saw Suzanna approaching, baby Robin strapped to her chest, his little feet bobbing along with each step she took. That would be Emily soon, she realized, her heart swelling at the thought—both from excitement but also anxiety. Charlotte was going to change everything again, just like Chantelle had. And Roy would not be there to support her through it all. But as she looked from Suzanna to Yvonne to Holly, she knew that she had the best people in the world beside her, watching her back. She could do it. She could do anything with her friends supporting her.

She realized then that she'd gotten so absorbed in catching up with all her friends that she'd lost track of the time.

"I'd better go and meet the new teacher," she told them, turning to head toward the steps.

But at the same moment she did so, she noticed Daniel approaching. He was looking at his watch with an expression of alarm.

"Daniel!" Yvonne cried enthusiastically.

"Hello, everyone," he said, sidling up to the group of moms. "I'm afraid I can't stop to chat, I have to get to work." He turned to Emily. "Am I still dropping you at Joe's?"

"Can I introduce myself to the teacher first?" Emily asked.

Daniel looked tensely at his watch. "Um… well…" he said, sounding a bit flustered.

Emily could sense he was clearly eager to make a good impression in his new elevated position at work. She decided to drop it and not cause a fuss.

"Don't worry," she told him, relenting. "I can meet the new teacher at pickup."

She said goodbye to each of her friends, sad to be torn from their wonderful company, and headed toward the pickup truck with Daniel.

"We'll catch up soon," she called over her shoulder, waving as they climbed back inside.

Slamming the car door, Emily turned to Daniel. "Remind me not to do coffee dates with Amy on school days. At least not until I'm back in the driving seat of my own car!"

She missed the freedom she'd had before her pregnancy. Missing out on meeting the teacher made her feel terrible. She hoped she hadn't made a bad impression because of it. She didn't want to look like an uninterested parent, distracted and self-centered.

Daniel drove out the lot, heading toward town.

"So how was the teacher?" Emily asked him.

"Miss Butler," Daniel informed her. He shrugged, as though he hadn't been paying much attention. "She seemed a bit more stern compared to Miss Glass. A little older, a little less soft around the edges."

"I wonder how Chantelle will take to her," Emily mused. The little girl struggled at times with authority figures. The soft approach worked well with her, but the main thing for Chantelle really was boundaries. As long as she knew what was expected of her she could excel. She just hoped this new, sterner teacher had the patience needed to reach that point.

"Gail was there as well," Daniel said. "She's going to be Chantelle's counselor again this year."

"That's a relief," Emily replied, thinking again of her father. Chantelle would need Gail's help more this year than ever. Not only because of the consistency Gail gave her, but because of the life experiences she'd need to be guided through this year.

"So what are you and Amy chatting about today?" Daniel asked.

His question jolted Emily out of her anguished reverie. "I'm not sure, but I think Harry. Did you notice anything odd between them on the island?"

"Not at all," Daniel said, bemused.

It didn't really surprise Emily that Daniel wouldn't have picked up on the nuances of Amy's behavior. Amy was her best friend after all; she knew her inside and out and could read the smallest signs in her expression.

"They'd better not be breaking up," Daniel said sternly as he turned into a side road. "We're about to open the restaurant. I don't want Harry over-salting the soup with his tears!"

Emily chuckled. "I'm sure it's not that. It's probably the opposite, I think. Amy's ready to marry him but wants me to tell her she's not moving too fast. You remember what happened with Fraser?"

"How could I forget," Daniel said with a wince.

They made it to Joe's diner, and Daniel pulled over. He kissed Emily, and she slid from her seat out of the truck, no longer able to hop sprightly like she'd done before gaining fifteen pounds of pregnancy weight.

"Have a good day at work," she told him.

He smiled and waved, then drove away. Emily headed inside the diner.

"Well, if it isn't Emily Mitchell," Joe exclaimed as she entered. "I haven't seen you in a long time!"

She hugged him hello. "It's Emily Morey now, don't forget," she told him.

"Of course," Joe laughed. "And to think you had your first date here." He beamed. "Coffee?"

Emily patted her stomach. "Decaf please."

Joe went off to make a fresh batch of coffee while Emily found the booth that Amy was already sitting in.

"This is just like old times, isn't it?" Amy said as she kissed her friend hello. "Grabbing coffee before work, whenever we could, of course. Breakfasts and lunches and cocktails at night."

"Cocktails!" Emily exclaimed, patting her stomach. "Don't remind me." She laughed. "It is wonderful to have you around more often. And you're right, it is like the old days, except without the high rises or rows of yellow cabs." She smiled as she recalled their old lives in New York City. It seemed so long ago now. "So, what's the deal?" she asked Amy. "How are things?"

Amy chewed her lip as though deliberating opening up. She clearly decided against holding back and launched straight into the heart of the matter. "It's Harry. We're arguing."

"Oh," Emily said, sadly. "That's a bummer. I'm sorry."

Amy shrugged and pushed her sleek blond bob behind her ears. "It's inevitable, isn't it? The distance. The fact we're from different worlds. I mean, I joke about things being like they were back in New York City, but they couldn't be more different. I just don't know if I can commit to living here. How did you do it?"

Emily pondered the question. "Honestly, I think New York City didn't have anything left to offer me."

"Oh thanks," Amy said with a pout.

"I don't mean you!" Emily exclaimed, backtracking. "I mean career wise and relationship wise. Things with Mom were terrible. Then Ben was a jerk and it just felt right to get away. Coming here forced me to confront a lot of things. You know, with my dad and Charlotte's death. It just made sense that I'd find myself here. Then there was Daniel." She smiled to herself as she recalled meeting him for the first time. Of the hesitation she'd felt, the resistance at letting herself fall for someone new. But the risks had all paid off.

"So basically you're saying I need to fix up an old house, start a business, and find myself," Amy said with a giggle.

"And fall in love," Emily added. "So you've ticked one box."

Amy sighed. "I know. That just makes it harder. I don't want to walk away from what I have with Harry but I just don't know if I can be happy here."

Emily reached across the table and held her friend's hand. "Is this because of what happened with Fraser? I really don't want that one bad experience to taint this. Because I'm sure you can tell it's completely different. What you and Harry have is a thousand times better than what you and Fraser did."

"Is it though?" Amy said with a strained voice. "At least Fraser and I were from the same worlds. We wanted similar things. Holidays and careers and property. Kids, but there'd be a nanny to help, obviously. Harry is the opposite of that. He's … I don't know. Rustic? He's…"

"….he's Sunset Harbor," Emily said with a decisive nod. She knew exactly what Amy was getting at. "But need I remind you that Fraser was a cheat? Harry would never do that. He's honest and kind and loyal. That's what you get with a Sunset Harbor man."

Joe arrived with their waffles and Emily's coffee. The two friends hunkered down, continuing their conversation.

"The thing is," Amy added, "you never had to worry about this stuff. Like, you and Daniel didn't have to debate about long distance or who would move where. It was always going to be here. But Harry and I seem to talk about it endlessly. Could we be long distance? Can I really leave my life behind, my *business*, for a man? It's against everything I stand for!"

Emily smiled and sighed. "Amy, is that really what's holding you back? Or is it something else?"

Amy chewed her waffle slowly. "I honestly don't know. I'm so on the fence."

"Do you think you might just be scared?" Emily asked. "I know you don't get scared, that you're a confident, no-nonsense businesswoman, but is there just a small chance that perhaps you're scared of the fact that Harry adores you and that he might be the One, and that if you move your life here and take that risk you might be happy?"

"I guess," Amy said. "But it's not happy I'm scared of. It's content. It's… bored."

She looked at Emily apologetically. Emily knew Amy was suggesting that life in Sunset Harbor was boring, but she didn't care. She wouldn't change it for the world. If this was boring she'd take it over exciting any day!

"Maybe I should go back to the city for a bit," Amy said. "Clear my head. Check in with the business. Remind myself of my roots, you know?"

"If you think it will help," Emily said. She forked some waffle and put it in her mouth. "Man, I haven't been back to New York City in ages."

Amy's eyes widened then. "Oh my God! Come with me!"

Emily looked at her, surprised. "Um…"

"Please, Em," Amy added. "We can have a long weekend together. I'll throw you a layette shower, since the last shower was a bust."

Emily blushed as she remembered how she'd awkwardly run out on the baby shower Amy had arranged for her. She couldn't help but hesitate.

"Please, please, please," Amy continued. "You deserve some time off. And the rush of the summer is over. I'm sure the inn can survive without you for a few days." Amy snapped her fingers then. "And if we have the shower in New York City, your mom can come!"

Emily instantly recoiled. "Okay, now I definitely don't want to come," she said, remembering the huge fight she and Patricia had been in last time they spoke. Indeed, every time they spoke.

"Em," Amy said with a maternal tone. "She's about to become a grandmother for the first time. How long is this rift between you going to last?"

"Forever," Emily said glumly. "You have met my mom, haven't you?" she added wryly.

But as she thought it over, she realized there was one very important thing she needed to speak to her mom about, something that couldn't be done over the phone. And that was Roy's illness. She needed to know.

"Actually," Emily said, "I am overdue a trip to New York City. Maybe my mom will be less of a handful in her own territory."

Amy clapped her hands. "Really? This weekend?"

Emily shrugged. "I guess so."

When was a good time to tell your mom her ex-husband was going to die? There didn't seem like a solution to Emily, so the approaching weekend was as good a time as any.

Amy bounced up and down in her seat, excited. "This is going to be so much fun. I'm going to tell Harry."

She grabbed her cell phone and punched in his number. At the same time, Emily's cell began to ring.

She pulled it from her pocket and answered it at the same time as Amy. It really *was* like their old New York City days!

"Is this Mrs. Morey?" the voice on the other end asked.

"Yes, who's this?"

"It's Miss Butler, Chantelle's teacher. I'm sorry to disturb you but there's been an incident. I think you should come in."

Emily leaped up. "What kind? Is Chantelle okay? Is she hurt?"

"She's fine," Miss Butler replied. "It's a behavioral incident."

Emily frowned. What did that mean?

"I'm on my way," she said, hanging up and slinging her cell into her purse.

Amy was chatting with Harry on the phone, but she looked up at Emily, using her amazing multitasking abilities to carry on a wordless conversation with her friend without missing a beat in her telephone call.

"Chantelle," Emily mouthed. "School." She mimed a driving motion. Daniel had the car so Amy was her only way of getting there.

Amy nodded and pointed at their waffles. They'd barely eaten them. But Emily shook her head. She had to go right now.

Without questioning her at all, Amy stood, collected her purse and, still chatting with Harry, headed out of the restaurant toward her car, Emily in tow.

As they went, Emily hoped everything worked out between Amy and Harry, because it was in moments like this one, when Daniel was busy and life had thrown a spanner in the work, when Emily needed her friends more than ever.

CHAPTER FIVE

As Amy drove Emily back to the school, Emily felt her nerves increasing. She hated it when Chantelle had a behavioral outburst because it felt like a step backward, and reminded her of the terrible start the girl had had to life, the scars that she still carried despite her happy demeanor.

"Do you want me to come in with you?" Amy asked, glancing over at Emily's pale face in the passenger seat.

Emily didn't usually bite her nails but the anxiety was making her do so. "No, no, it's probably best if it's just me," she said, feeling flustered, her face stiff with panic.

They reached the parking lot, now empty, and Amy swung into the closest space to the school doors. "Well, I'll wait here and drive you home when you're done."

Emily already had a hand on the door handle, and she shook her head. "Thanks for the offer but I have no idea how long this will take."

"How will you get home?"

"I'll figure it out later. Back of Raj's delivery truck? Handlebars of Cynthia's bike?" She was cracking jokes, but only as a way to distract herself from her anguish.

Amy smiled tenderly. "Are you sure?"

"I promise," Emily said, shoving the door open and quickly getting out.

She slammed her door shut and blew Amy a kiss before hurrying as fast as her pregnant belly would allow her up the stone steps. She pressed the intercom button and the receptionist answered, crackling out a greeting.

"Mrs. Morey," Emily said into the silver speaker. "Chantelle's mom."

There was buzz. She heaved the door open and hurried to the desk. It was the same girl as last year, Emily realized, young, freckled, with a sweet smile that showed off a gap between her teeth.

"Hi, Emily," the receptionist greeted her as she hurried in.

Emily realized—feeling a little distressed at the thought—that she was well known enough at the school for the receptionist to recognize her and remember her name.

"Here's your visitor badge," the girl added.

She handed the pass to Emily and Emily saw that she'd written her name in a red marker pen, in cursive, surrounding it with stars. It was a sweet gesture, but Emily was too flustered to appreciate it. Her focus was solely on Chantelle. But she did notice the girl's name badge: Tilly. She made a point to commit it to memory so that at least the next time she saw the girl, hopefully in less stressful circumstances, she could be kinder.

"They're down the hall in the counselor's office," Tilly said. "Do you know the way?"

"Unfortunately I know it all too well," Emily replied.

Tilly gave her a sympathetic smile, and Emily hurried off down the hallway to Gail's office.

Through the small window in the door, Emily saw the familiar bright red couches, the play table, reading nook, dolls house, and art station. She recognized Gail right away, sitting on one of the grown-up-sized chairs with her hair in a neat bun on top of her head. The other two women Emily didn't know. And Chantelle was nowhere in sight. She could hear her, though, hear her yelling and screaming even through the thick pane of glass in the reinforced fire door.

Emily knocked quickly and saw Gail turn toward the window. Through the glass, she beckoned Emily in.

It was only once she was inside the room that Emily got her first glance of Chantelle. The child was curled up in the corner, crying desperately, surrounded by ripped up pieces of paper.

"What happened?" Emily asked.

"Take a seat," Gail said. "You've met Miss Butler."

"Actually, no, we didn't get a chance to meet earlier," Emily said. She shook the teacher's hand. It was a terrible way to first meet her, Emily thought. She was a bag of nerves and felt completely frazzled. "You spoke to my husband, Daniel."

The young teacher smiled politely, giving Emily a glimpse of the sternness that Daniel had noted. "Yes, I remember."

"And Mrs. Doyle you'll know," Gail added.

Emily did a double take then. In her haste, she hadn't really noticed the third woman in the room, but she realized now that it was the principal. Things must be serious if she was involved!

"So?" Emily said. "Was it the new class that triggered this?"

Gail nodded. "I think we were all aware this might happen. But maybe we should ask Chantelle to explain it to us. Chantelle?" Gail had an incredibly soft, gentle voice. It was the kind of voice that could coax anyone out of a tantrum.

The little girl was sobbing furiously in the corner. "I HATE her!" she yelled.

Emily looked up at Miss Butler, assuming she was the one Chantelle was referring to, and gave her a sympathetic look. She didn't want the teacher to think it was her fault in any way.

"Who is it that you hate?" Gail continued.

"LAVERNE!" Chantelle screamed.

Emily remembered from Yvonne's gossiping at the school gate that Laverne was the name of the new girl, the brittle-boned blonde girl whom Bailey had taken under her wing. She'd never heard Chantelle's voice sound so shrill and piercing, so drenched in hatred. And she'd never seen so much passion in the young girl's face, so much pain and anguish. Even in her past meltdowns over Sheila, Chantelle had never looked this distressed. Laverne had really gotten to Chantelle. Emily couldn't begin to fathom what she could have done to cause Chantelle to perceive her to be worse than Sheila.

"Can you explain what happened with Laverne?" Gail asked softly. "We all want to understand why you're feeling so unhappy."

Chantelle looked up then, her face red with fury. "She stole Bailey."

Emily frowned with confusion at the mention of Bailey's name. She and Chantelle were as thick as thieves.

"What do you mean?" Gail probed.

Chantelle's expression was one of unfathomable pain and hurt. It upset Emily just to see her that way.

"She said that I have a stupid accent," Chantelle shouted. "And that Bailey was only allowed one friend with blond hair. Then Bailey told me that Laverne is her new best friend." Chantelle's face cracked. Instead of anger, she dissolved into tears, dropping her head onto her knees and weeping bitterly.

Emily's hand fluttered to her heart. This was too much to bear.

"Can we do something?" Emily asked, looking up at Gail. "You understand how important it is for Chantelle to have consistency in her life."

"Of course," Gail replied diplomatically. "You're good friends with Yvonne, Bailey's mother, aren't you? Perhaps you should speak with her about this?"

35

"I'm not sure how that will help," Emily replied. "Bailey's strong-willed. Just because her mother tells her to do something it doesn't mean she would. Wouldn't it be easier to just move Laverne into another class so they naturally grow apart?"

Mrs. Doyle looked aghast. "Absolutely not."

"But look what it's doing to Chantelle," Emily exclaimed.

Mrs. Doyle spoke frankly. "Laverne is new here, just like Chantelle was once. She's made a friend in Bailey and it would be cruel to take that away from her."

Emily felt her maternal instincts sharpen. "With respect, Laverne doesn't have the same kind of history as Chantelle. She hasn't been through the same hardships. Wouldn't the easiest solution be to switch their classes now? To nip it in the bud before it gets any worse? If Laverne is this mean now, how much worse will she be tomorrow or the day after?"

"I'm sorry," Mrs. Doyle said, shaking her head. "But they will have to work through their problems. Gail can guide them, and of course Miss Butler will be overseeing everything in the classroom. There are no quick fixes in these situations, Mrs. Morey. Chantelle's circumstances don't come in to it."

Emily looked appealingly at Gail. "You're on my side, aren't you?"

"It's not about sides," Gail replied. "I'm here for Chantelle and what's best for her."

"Let me guess," Emily said. "What's best is for her to come into your office once a week to hash out her feelings? She's a seven-year-old child. She acts on her emotions, on her feelings. Sitting here talking to you endlessly won't help with bullying."

"Our sessions are very valuable," Gail replied calmly.

"I don't think we should be so quick to label this bullying," Mrs. Doyle interjected.

Emily was furious. She felt like everyone was abandoning Chantelle. How was this not bullying?

"Chantelle's been mocked for her accent. She's had her best friend taken from her. This new girl has ostracized her. How is that not bullying?"

"Emily," Gail said softly.

But Emily was exasperated. She felt like no one in the room was prepared to do anything concrete about the situation. All they were offering was more of the same wishy-washy conversations, which felt useless to her right now, like marriage counseling for a couple of kids barely old enough to tie their own shoelaces!

"What?" Emily said furiously to Gail, so close to losing her temper it scared her.

"I have a great deal of experience dealing with these situations," Gail continued. "I will have Chantelle, Laverne, and Bailey here together. There's no blame. We just need to work out a way for them all to occupy the same space together."

Emily had heard enough. "This is absurd. You're bending over backwards to protect a bully. Come on, Chantelle, we're leaving."

Chantelle looked completely surprised. She blinked, her lashes wet with tears, then pulled herself to standing. Emily felt a great sense of relief when the girl rushed to her and wrapped her arms tightly about her middle. She'd done what she was supposed to as a mother; support her child unconditionally. None of this was Chantelle's fault and the last thing she wanted was for the child to think that she'd done something wrong. Together, they marched out of the office.

"Mommy, you're shaking," Chantelle said as they walked along the corridors, passing Tilly at the reception desk and out onto the stone steps.

"I'm sorry," Emily replied, taking a deep breath. "I didn't mean to lose my temper."

But Chantelle seemed to have been entirely distracted from her tantrum. "Don't say sorry," she said, her eyes wide. "It was cool!"

Emily couldn't help but feel a little tug at the corner of her lips. "Well, thanks. But don't go getting any ideas. Shouting at people is not a good way to behave."

"Okay, Mommy," Chantelle replied.

But Emily could see the twinkle of respect in her eye. When Chantelle had needed someone on her side, Emily had been there for her. Though she felt terrible for her outburst, at least Chantelle could see firsthand that this Mama Bear always had her back.

Once standing out on the steps of the school, Emily remembered that they didn't have any way to get home. She deliberated calling Daniel but knew he was extremely busy today with his work at Jack's. She wasn't sure whether she should disturb him over this. Although on the one hand he'd want to know what had happened, she was Chantelle's mother as much as Daniel was her father, and she felt certain she could handle this situation without him. They could discuss it once he was home from work.

She dialed the inn. Lois answered.

"I don't suppose Parker is around, is he?" Chantelle asked Lois, an image of Parker's battered little wholesale truck in her mind's eye.

"He is," Lois said. "I'll fetch him."

The line went silent. A moment later Parker's voice sounded through the receiver.

"Boss-lady," he quipped, "what can I do for you?"

Emily looked down at Chantelle, who was sitting on the step fiddling with her shoelaces. She looked so glum. Emily felt confident that she'd made the right decision in not bothering Daniel. She wanted to be back on safe ground, in the comfort of their home, before the issue of Chantelle's school day was broached.

Emily spoke into the phone to Parker. "I have a favor to ask of you…"

*

That evening, the family relaxed together in the lounge. Finally, Emily felt like enough time had lapsed and she was ready to tackle the topic of Chantelle's first day back at school.

"So, Chantelle didn't have a good day today, did you, sweetie," Emily said. "Can you tell Daddy what happened?"

Daniel raised his eyebrows and looked at Chantelle. She squirmed in her seat.

"You're not in trouble," Emily explained softly. "It's just that Daddy doesn't know that I had to come into the office and speak to Miss Butler and Mrs. Doyle."

Daniel's surprised expression grew stronger. "Mrs. Doyle, the principal?" he asked.

Emily could tell he was fighting to keep his tone even.

Chantelle nodded with shame.

"I wanted to change class because of a horrible girl," she said, her gaze fixed on her lap.

"What horrible girl?" Daniel asked.

"She's new," Chantelle said. "Her name is Laverne. And she's Bailey's best friend."

Daniel looked over at Emily. She flashed him a sad look.

"I'm sure that's not true," Daniel said. "I'm sure Bailey is just trying to be nice to her because she's new and doesn't know anyone."

"It's not like that," Chantelle said, hitting her fist against the armrest of the couch. "Laverne told Bailey that she's only allowed one friend with blond hair and because Laverne's is blonder than mine, Bailey chose her!"

Emily could see the little girl was in pain, and she was growing irate as she recalled the painful events of the day.

"Have you spoken to Yvonne?" Daniel asked Emily.

She shook her head. At the same time, Chantelle shouted, "No!" She seemed panicked. "Please don't speak to Yvonne about it. I don't want her to tell Bailey off or force her to be my friend again. I only want her to be my friend if she wants to, not because her mom told her to."

Emily felt so bad for Chantelle. The world of seven-year-olds could be just as complicated as the grown-up one. She desperately wished she could take all the hurt away from the little girl, but that wasn't possible. And it wasn't right, either. It was her job as a mom to guide Chantelle through these unpleasant experiences, not shield her from them or eradicate them.

"Do you also remember what Laverne said about you?" Emily prompted. She knew Chantelle didn't want to talk about it but it was important that they worked through her emotions. She was almost eight years old and the people around her would soon lose patience with her tantrums. She had a steep learning curve ahead of her and a lot of time to make up for. She'd already made remarkable progress but there was still so far to go.

"She said I had a stupid accent," Chantelle said. Then glumly, she added, "She's right. I wish I had your voice, Daddy. Why do I have to sound like Sheila?"

"There's nothing wrong with your voice," Daniel told her. "Your accent is beautiful."

"But it makes me different. And it makes people think I'm stupid."

"You're not stupid," Daniel said sternly. "Don't ever let anyone make you feel like you are. You're perfect the way you are."

Emily loved the amount of warmth in his voice. His speech was very touching. But Chantelle did not seem to be buying it at all. She looked just as glum as ever.

"May I be excused now?" she said quietly.

Daniel looked at Emily. She shrugged, unsure what the best thing to do was.

"I'd like to watch cartoons in my room," Chantelle added.

"Sure," Emily said. Everyone deserves a cheer-up routine, she thought. If cartoons in bed could self-soothe Chantelle then that was better than having her melt down.

Chantelle slid off the couch and left the room. Once she was gone, Daniel looked sadly at Emily.

"You should have told me," he said with an exasperated sigh. "As soon as it happened. Why didn't you call?"

Emily frowned. She'd been so sure of her decision to get Parker to pick them up before, but now seeing Daniel's expression she felt her resolve weaken. "You were at work," she told him softly. "I didn't want to disturb you."

"But this is my little girl," he said, sternly. "I need to know if she'd being bullied."

Emily touched Daniel's hand. She knew him well enough now to understand that it was the stress from his new work that was making him grouchy and short with her. It wasn't meant to be personal and so she tried not to take it as such.

"Honey, I handled it," she told him calmly but firmly. "Having you there wouldn't have helped matters. In fact, having us both show up like that at the school could have been quite intimidating for Chantelle. I don't know if it's always the best thing for her to have all these adults peering down at her evaluating her behavior. I dealt with the school, then we came home and spent the rest of the day quietly working on our respective activities. Giving her space is just as important as talking through these things." She folded her arms triumphantly. "I actually think I did a great job."

Daniel looked a little pained. "I'm not saying you didn't do a great job," he said. "You know I think you're an awesome mom." He ran his hands through his hair. "I just hate having responsibilities that pull me away from you, from our family."

Emily nodded, understanding. She'd been right in thinking it was the stress of the promotion compounding Daniel's response.

"I'm sure it will settle," she told him, reassuringly. "Once you've adjusted to the new responsibilities and found your feet."

For the first time, Emily saw a smile return to Daniel's eyes.

"Thanks, babe," he told her. "I'm sure you're right. It's just so hard, not being there for Chantelle. Especially after missing the first six years, you know?" He sounded wistful.

"I know," Emily replied meaningfully. "But you would have lost your temper if you'd been there. The school was useless! They wouldn't even consider switching Laverne into a different class. The principal may as well have just shrugged and said she didn't care. She actually said they had to figure it out amongst themselves. Seven-year-olds! Like they can sit down and have guidance counseling? I was furious. I unleashed the Mama Bear."

Daniel laughed. "I would love to have seen that."

Emily shook her head, recalling the fury she'd felt. "It completely ruined my coffee date with Amy."

"Oh yeah," Daniel said, remembering. "How was that? Did you find out what's going on with her and Harry?"

Emily nodded. "It's the obvious really. Commitment. She's not sure about throwing herself headfirst into the relationship. Especially after Fraser. I can't convince her. You know what she's like, stubborn. I'm just dropping gentle hints that Harry is the One and that she needs to take the plunge."

"It would be wonderful to have her here full time," Daniel said. "For you. And Chantelle, of course. I think it's important she has grown-ups to rely on and look up to."

Emily nodded, but became a little quiet as she thought of Roy. His was the kind of adult relationship that Chantelle needed so badly, but it was going to come to an untimely and unjust end very soon. She and Daniel had agreed not to tell Chantelle her beloved Papa Roy was dying and she was glad of it now. The child clearly wouldn't cope with it. But she'd need to be told at some point.

"I almost forgot," Emily said, trying to force the dark thoughts from her mind. "Amy wants her and I to spend the weekend in New York City. She misses it and needs a bit of space from Harry to get her thoughts in order. Plus the baby shower was a bit of a disaster and she thinks a layette shower in New York City should happen, with Jayne."

"This coming weekend?" Daniel asked, sounding a little surprised. "That's a bit sudden."

"I know," Emily said. "Do you think Chantelle will be okay if I go? I won't if it's going to upset her more."

"You have to," Daniel said, surprising her. "Our baby should have a proper party. And I think Amy's right, it would be good to do it in New York City."

"Really?" Emily asked, surprised.

He nodded. "I want you to be happy and have as many fun experiences as possible, especially with your friends and Jayne. Things will be different once Charlotte's here. You need as many happy moments as possible for when you're exhausted after sleepless nights."

Emily laughed. "Well, okay. If you think it's a good idea. I don't mind postponing until Chantelle's feeling less fragile."

Daniel kissed the top of her head. "By the time this week's over, I'm sure this whole Laverne thing will be over and done with. And anyway, I can cope with Chantelle. You go. Have fun."

They kissed, deeply and tenderly.

"Thank you, sweetheart," Emily said, gazing at her loving husband with adoration.

Just then, the sound of distant piano music interrupted Emily's thought process. She frowned, quirking her head to the side in confusion.

"Am I imagining that, or can you hear a piano too?" she asked Daniel.

"It sounds like one of Owen's pieces," Daniel replied, confirming her suspicion.

They both looked at the piano in the corner. The music definitely wasn't coming from that! It seemed to be floating toward them from a distance.

Daniel stood from the couch and went over to the window, drawing back the curtains.

"Oh!" he exclaimed

"What is it?" Emily asked, getting up as fast as her bump permitted and going over to join him.

To her surprise she saw people walking up the path, not toward the inn, but toward Trevor's house. Light was streaming from the windows. The piano music was emanating from that direction, too.

"The restaurant!" Emily cried.

Daniel looked shocked. "It's opening tonight?" he said. "How did we forget?"

Emily couldn't believe something so important could have slipped her mind.

"Baby brain," she suggested, referring to that well-known phenomenon that caused forgetfulness in pregnancy.

"That explains it for you," Daniel chuckled. "But what about me?"

"Well, you've been focusing on your promotion," she said. "And I guess we did pass all the responsibility over to Harry. He must be so good at managing things he didn't even need to check in with us about anything."

She watched all the people heading toward the house for the opening night. It looked like it was going to be a popular new haunt for the people of Sunset Harbor and Emily was relieved. Missing the Labor Day business had been a worry for Emily but the restaurant just hadn't been ready in time to open then. She'd been certain that local folk would be too tired from all the celebrations to want *another*, but she saw now that she should never have doubted them. The good people of Sunset Harbor were always there to support her!

"We need to get ready and head over," Emily said. "Do you think Chantelle will want to come?"

"Of course," Daniel said. "I don't think there's a bully in the world that can keep our little girl from a party!"

He seemed excited to get going, and Emily was glad to see him so enthusiastic, especially after all the hard work he'd put into it.

They left the living room and headed in the direction of the bedroom, excited to get glammed up for the night.

"Oh shoot," Emily said suddenly, as she hurried up the steps. "None of my formal dresses are going to fit over my bump!"

CHAPTER SIX

Once they were dressed for the evening, the family hurried across the lawns, toward the twinkling piano music floating out of Trevor's. The doors were wide open, letting the light from inside spill out and the unseasonably warm air in. Long white lace curtains that framed the door blew in the light breeze. Emily felt like she was in the Mediterranean!

Harry was standing in the door, dressed in a suit. Emily had never seen him look so smart. Like George, he was rarely in anything other than jeans and a shirt. He looked even more dashing all dressed up.

"I wasn't sure if you guys were coming," Harry said, accepting a handshake from Daniel and hugs from both Emily and Chantelle.

"Of course!" Emily exclaimed. "We just got a little sidetracked." She flashed Daniel a knowing look.

Peering inside the restaurant, Emily was pleasantly surprised to see that it was incredibly busy. Amongst the patrons she noticed many of her local friends—Karen and her husband, Vanessa and Jason on a date night without baby Katy. Even Mayor Hansen was there, with Marcella and other people on the zoning board.

The place was decorated beautifully. It was even classier than Emily had imagined it to be. The chandeliers lit the space with dazzling white light, and the floor gleamed. At the far end of the large open-plan space was the traditional wood-burning oven, and several chefs in white coats were busy expertly flinging pizza dough into the air.

In the corner, Owen was playing the piano, solo without his jazz band. Serena was sitting alone at a table nearby, sipping a cocktail. Emily hadn't seen Serena in a long time and was glad for the opportunity to catch up.

Chantelle looked enchanted, and Daniel seemed lost for words.

"Wow," Emily gushed. "It looks magical in there."

"Come in," Harry said. "We have a seat for you on the mezzanine level." He gestured to the half floor above, where Emily could just see the faces of people peering down.

They climbed the staircase. On the mezzanine level there was a long banquet-style table. Amy was already sitting there, next to

George. Wesley and Suzanna were also in attendance, with Toby and baby Robin, who was fast asleep. Bryony, and Raj and Sunita Patel were also amongst the group. Everyone had made the effort to dress up and looked dazzling.

"I didn't know you guys were coming!" Emily gushed as she rushed toward each of them and greeted them with kisses.

"Of course," Suzanna said. "We want to support you."

"And Harry," George added. "It's great to see my little brother realize his dreams!"

Amy nodded in agreement.

Everyone took their seats. Chantelle sat next to Toby. She still seemed to be in a bit of a bad mood, but at least she was with one of her closest friends. Emily wondered whether Yvonne, Keiran, and Bailey's absences were pointed. It wasn't like them to miss big social events.

The waitress came to take their orders, and Emily opted for a buffalo mozzarella salad to start and lasagna for the entrée. When the waitress returned with wine and soft drinks, she produced a bottle of alcohol-free champagne for Emily.

Emily laughed, delighted by the gesture.

From her seat, she had a view over the whole restaurant. It filled her heart with joy to see so many familiar faces, and to see the hustle and bustle of the staff. Harry was doing an amazing job coordinating everything and Emily could tell from his expression that he was loving every moment. She felt so glad to be able to give back, to help others realize their dreams just like she'd realized hers when she'd first opened the inn.

Their starters arrived and Emily tucked in. It was delicious and she was very impressed with the quality of the ingredients. She'd sourced everything she could from Parker's wholesalers, with the rest coming from other local businesses. It was important for Emily to support the local community, to give back to Sunset Harbor when it had given so much to her.

Amy leaned across the table and caught Emily's attention.

"Did you speak to Daniel about our New York City trip?" she asked.

"Yes," Emily replied. "And he's fine with it. I'm not sure about Chantelle, though. She had a terrible day at school so I don't want to drop that bombshell on her."

Amy stuck her bottom lip out in sympathy. "Yeah, she doesn't look too happy. Oh look," she added, becoming distracted by what was happening on the floor below. "Isn't that the guy staying in one of the apartments here?"

Emily looked where she was pointing. "Oh yes, Paul Knowlson, the real estate man." She noticed that he was waiting for a table, but all the waiters and waitresses were busy. Harry, too, was attending to a large table of elderly people who seemed to be celebrating a birthday.

"Excuse me," she said, laying her napkin on the table. "I'd better get him a table."

She hurried down the steps.

"Ah, Mrs. Morey," Paul said, shaking her hand. "This is your opening night?"

Emily nodded. "Are you dining alone?" she asked. It didn't seem right that amongst all the merriment there would be one guest on his own. "If so, we'd be very happy to have you join us. We're up on the mezzanine."

He looked touched. "That would be very kind. I'd like that a lot."

Emily led him upstairs and fetched an extra chair. She introduced Paul to the rest of the group.

"You know, I must say I'm really impressed with this place," he said, taking his seat.

"I'm glad you're enjoying your stay."

"I don't mean from a guest perspective," he said, chuckling. "I mean from a business angle. You know I run a chain of hotels?"

Emily shook her head. "I thought you were a property developer."

"I dabble in a bit of that too," he said with a smile. "But really hotels are my bread and butter. I own twenty across Florida."

Emily almost spat out her alcohol-free champagne. "Twenty?"

He nodded. "Yes, it's my real passion. Every time I think I've got enough, I find another perfect spot and can't help myself. It's a bit of an addiction."

Emily thought of the constant expansion work she'd done at the inn. "I can relate to that. But how do you find the time to manage them all? I have my hands full with just this place!"

Paul smiled. "I don't. There's no way to micromanage everything. You have to let a bit of control go. You become more of an executive rather than a manager."

Emily liked the sound of that.

"Have you ever thought of opening more inns?" he added.

"Well, we've just expanded to the two houses, and now we've added an island to our collection. It's going to be a retreat, with yoga and writing. Daniel's got some fantastic contractors who will be building a three-room cabin out there. But that's all under our control. I've never thought of opening more. Of franchising it."

"You should," he replied. "If you love the industry and have the passion, which you clearly do, not to mention the creativity, you could have your own chain across the state, maybe even a few out of state if you can adapt to the differing markets. It's something worth considering."

Emily felt a tingle of excitement. She'd never considered thinking so big, but she realized that what Paul was proposing was well within the realms of reality for her. In a way she was already doing that, by expanding the inn with different sites, hiring a manager in Harry to oversee the restaurant so she didn't have to micromanage everything. She'd just never thought bigger than that, to a whole chain of Sunset Inns.

"I've definitely got a lot going on at the moment," Emily told him, her hands tapping her belly to iterate her point. "But maybe once the little one has arrived I might spend some time thinking of the future."

Being an executive of a chain of hotels rather than all the hands-on management she had to do just for the one did seem appealing, especially if it gave her more time to devote to motherhood. Though Emily wasn't seriously considering acting on his suggestion, she did realize the idea was percolating in her mind.

She looked over at Chantelle. The girl was looking glum, poking her pizza with her fork. Emily decided she needed to be cheered up. This had gone on long enough.

She stood and went over, then crouched beside Chantelle's chair. "I have an idea," she said.

Chantelle turned her big blue eyes to Emily. "What's that?" she asked without enthusiasm.

"How would you like to be the first person to set foot inside the spa?" Emily asked her.

Chantelle hesitated, then her eyes widened. "The spa is ready?" she asked.

Emily nodded. "It's all done. We were going to open it up tomorrow. But since so many great people are here, I was wondering if it might not be better to do the grand opening now. Would you like to do it, like you did with the speakeasy?"

Chantelle nodded with enthusiasm. "Yes!"

Emily grinned. "Come on then."

She took Chantelle by the hand and led her downstairs. By the looks of things most of the diners had finished their meals and had moved on to evening coffees or extra tipples. The large birthday party had left, leaving just friends inside the restaurant.

Chantelle went up to Owen and whispered something in his ear. Emily watched him nod, then finish up playing his piece. Silence fell.

"Ladies and gentlemen," Chantelle said loudly and clearly. "May I have your attention."

There was a hubbub that died down as people turned to look at her.

"We have an extra special announcement to make. Tonight is not just the opening of the restaurant. We'd also like to reveal to you another very special new extension of the inn. If you would like to follow me."

Emily grinned with pride. She loved it when Chantelle took charge like this. The child was naturally gifted at it, and everyone adored her. They readily followed.

As people streamed out into the warm evening, wine glasses and coffee cups in hand, Emily caught up to Serena.

"Hey," she said, tugging on her friend's elbow. "How are you? It's been ages."

Serena smiled pleasantly. "I know. I've missed you. You're so... pregnant!"

Emily laughed. "Are all your finals done now?"

Serena nodded. Emily noticed a hint of melancholy in her eyes.

"Did they not go as well as you'd hoped?" Emily asked.

To her surprise, tears sparkled in Serena's eyes. "Actually, they went amazingly."

"So those are happy tears?" Emily asked.

Serena shook her head. "Well, yes, on one hand. But on the other, no. My work's been getting a lot of interest. I've been offered a position at an artist's studio. Ang Jin. He's a famous sculptor."

"That's amazing!" Emily cried. "Oh my gosh, congratulations." She hugged her friend. "But why aren't you happy about it?"

Serena shook her head again, looking crestfallen. "It's in Singapore."

"Oh," Emily said, realizing why Serena's news wasn't a complete blessing. "You'd have to move."

Serena nodded. "I don't know whether Owen will come with me. But I can't pass this up. I can't miss this opportunity."

"You haven't told him yet?"

"Not yet. I don't want it to ... you know... break us up."

"It won't. You'll make it work," Emily said. "You two are strong. But you have to tell him. When would you be leaving?"

48

"In the New Year," Serena said. "Just after Christmas."

Emily couldn't help but feel relieved to know Serena would be around for Baby Charlotte's birth. Even though they weren't as close as they once had been, she couldn't bear the thought of Serena not meeting her!

"That gives you a few months to work things out," Emily said. "But tell him sooner rather than later. You can't just spring this on him last minute."

Serena nodded but she didn't look convinced. Emily felt bad for her friend, but at the same time she was thrilled for the Serena she knew before Owen came into the picture. In fact, she was sure Serena was worrying unnecessarily. Owen would follow her to the ends of the earth. Sure, she'd be down a piano player and singing teacher for Chantelle, but Roman could probably recommend a million others to fill the gap.

They reached the spa doors and Chantelle bustled ahead. Emily gave her the key. She held it up above her head theatrically, then placed it in the keyhole. She twisted it until it clicked.

"I now declare the Sunset Spa officially open," she said.

With a flourish, she shoved open the two double doors.

The space was amazing. At the far end, the entire wall was made of glass, giving a wonderful view of the ocean. The infinity swimming pool had one invisible edge so that it was impossible to see from this angle where the pool ended and ocean began. With the dark sky and twinkling stars reflecting on the surface it was like stepping into space.

People began to walk inside, treading delicately, as if they didn't want to disturb the tranquility of the place. Chantelle gasped loudly and looked up at Emily.

"It's even better than I expected," she said.

Emily grinned. She pointed to the mezzanine level. "Up there are the treatment rooms," she said. "The sauna is over there. And of course, there will be a nail bar up and running once we've hired a technician."

"I can have painted nails again?" Chantelle beamed.

Emily nodded. "You bet. But only toes, remember." She was about to say that she didn't want Chantelle to get in trouble at school but thought better of it.

"Am I allowed to swim whenever I want?" Chantelle asked.

"Absolutely," Emily replied. "As long as you're supervised."

"Even at night?" she asked, her eyes widening.

"Even at night," Emily said with a nod.

Chantelle threw her arms around Emily's waist.

"Do you like it?" Emily asked the little girl.

She felt Chantelle's head nod against her stomach. "I love it, Mommy."

Emily felt herself swell with relief. Chantelle was happy again, at last, and that was the most important thing in the world.

CHAPTER SEVEN

Emily felt on tenterhooks over the next couple of days, worrying about whether Chantelle would have another meltdown at school, missing Daniel who was putting in extra hours at work. So it was with great relief when she found herself on Saturday morning sitting in the passenger seat of Amy's car, thrumming along the freeway.

They'd met up at 6 a.m. that morning, knowing that the drive to New York City could take up to eight hours, and were a couple of hours into their journey already. Thanks to the unseasonably hot weather, the windows were open and a warm breeze stirred Emily's hair. The radio buzzed in the background. A song they'd loved from college came on and Amy turned the sound up. They sang along loudly and out of tune, unconcerned about whether any other cars could hear them. Emily felt so free. It felt so much like the old times she'd shared with Amy in their youths.

"Did you tell Harry what the purpose of the trip was?" Emily asked once the song had ended and the volume in the car reduced.

Amy kept her eyes on the road, both her hands on the steering wheel, and shook her head. "I said it was you. That you wanted a layette shower with your New York City friends. I hope you don't mind."

"I don't mind," Emily replied. "But you need to speak to him eventually."

She realized it was the same advice she'd given Serena at the restaurant opening. Communication was essential, something she and Daniel had learned the hard way, after much hurt and many mistakes. She didn't want her friends to go through such unnecessary anguish. But she also knew it was easier said than done.

"The thing is," Amy said, "Harry is basically perfect. A little young, but I have no problems being labeled a cougar." She laughed. "But he's also insanely naïve. Like everything is easy for him. You love each other the rest will work out. I don't want to be the one to shatter that image for him. At the moment he adores me. If I rock the boat, he might realize that I'm fallible. That everyone is. It would be like telling a kid there's no Santa."

Emily laughed. "Ew, Amy, don't compare your partner to a kid!"

"Weird analogy, but you get my point."

Emily's chuckles subsided. "Yes, I get your point. But have you considered yet that Harry might just be right? Maybe the fact that you love each other does make things more simple. Loving Daniel certainly made the decision to stay in Maine easier for me."

Amy gave her a sideways glance. "There was certainly no other explanation for your crazy, flighty behavior," she mocked. "I always thought you were the sensible one."

Emily smiled to herself and shrugged. "It was still the sensible option," she replied. "Just look at what I have now."

Amy looked down at Emily's bump and twisted her lips to the side. "You really think I could have all that with Harry?"

"Definitely."

"Do you think I'd be happy?"

"I am."

Amy sighed. "But we're different, Em. And so are our situations. You were unhappy in New York City when you met Daniel. You had been in a crappy relationship for years. You hated your job and your mom sucked."

"Thanks for reminding me," Emily quipped.

Amy carried on. "It's not like that for me. The context is completely different. I love New York City. I have a business, a group of friends, and my family around. I miss all that stuff when I'm in Sunset Harbor. Hell, I even miss my Pilates instructor!"

"You should get lessons from Tracy," Emily told her.

Amy rolled her eyes. "Not the point."

"Sorry, I know," Emily said.

She mulled over Amy's words. Maybe her friend was right after all. Chucking New York City for love in Maine had been a much simpler decision for Emily to make. She had nothing to lose and everything to gain. The risk for Amy was much greater, the possibility of it all going wrong much more likely.

"Well, I guess this is the time to make the decision," Emily told her friend. "We're heading to New York City. Whether it's for a final blow-out or not is up to you. But use this opportunity to make the decision. Don't drag it out forever. It's not fair to Harry."

Amy looked suddenly very serious. Almost a little pained. Emily recognized her expression as the unique one associated with the thought of letting down the person you loved the most in the world. It was a very telling expression, she thought. Amy had never looked like that for anyone else.

"You're right," she said. "Thanks, Em."

They fell into an easy silence. Then Amy grinned, suddenly brightening.

"Can we stop for sushi the second we reach New York City?" she asked Emily. "There are literally no sushi bars in Sunset Harbor and I'm getting withdrawal."

"Sure," Emily said. "But I'm not allowed to eat raw fish." She patted her stomach.

"Oh, I forgot," Amy said. "Mexican then. Which is also woefully lacking in Sunset Harbor."

Emily laughed. "Mexican is fine. And you know there's one person who can bring the sushi and the Mexican to town. Harry."

Amy's eyes widened. "Oh my God, you're right! I just need to twist his arm and get the menu changed. Rip out that wood-burning oven." She winked.

"I mean for when he opens his *own* restaurant," Emily replied with a laugh. "Not in mine. I'm quite happy with authentic Italian."

"It was really great," Amy agreed. "I'm going to get fat if I eat there all the time."

"Especially without your magic Pilates instructor!" Emily added.

They both dissolved into giggles.

*

They entered New York City and Emily was shocked by the noise of the place. It was amazing how much she had shed her old New York City skin. It was so busy, so loud and polluted. In Sunset Harbor she was used to people strolling down sidewalks, but in New York City people practically ran. It was like the whole place was on fast forward. How on Earth had she ever lived like this?

Amy still had her old apartment, so they went into the underground parking lot.

"When are we meeting Jayne?" Emily asked.

"Not sure," Amy replied. "She said she's got meetings all day."

"On Saturday? That's a shame," Emily replied. She really wanted her other best friend there at the party.

They got out of the car and headed to the elevator.

"I remember these things," Emily laughed, touching the cold metal doors with her fingertips. She hardly ever had cause to use elevators in Sunset Harbor. None of the buildings were tall enough.

Amy laughed. They went inside. The elevator was covered in graffiti and smelled terrible.

"I also remember this," Emily said with a grimace. She covered her nose.

"It's not that bad!" Amy argued.

"Pregnancy hormones," Emily said. "They give me a very honed power to smell."

"That kind of sucks," Amy said.

Emily nodded. "Yup."

They laughed and rode the elevator together to the fifth floor. The doors pinged open and they exited, then walked along the corridor toward Amy's apartment door. Emily felt a wave of nostalgia. Amy had been the first of her friends to own her own home thanks to the success of her fragrance and candle business so they'd spent many carefree days and nights in this apartment as young women. Emily missed those days, even though she wouldn't change anything to go back in time.

Amy rummaged in her purse for her key, then put it in the lock. She turned and pushed the green door open. It creaked and revealed the dark apartment.

Amy reached in and flicked on the light switch. But it wasn't just the bright light that startled Emily. A cacophony of sound and a flurry of movement made her gasp and step back.

"SURPRISE!"

The whole apartment was filled with balloons and streamers, and there were a ton of people inside.

"Oh my God!" Emily exclaimed, covering her gaping mouth with a hand. She turned to Amy, tears glittering in her eyes. "You arranged all this?"

Amy nodded.

"And me," Jayne cried, bustling forward. She hugged Emily tightly.

"I thought you were in meetings all day!" Emily cried.

Jayne shook her head. "Nah, just tricking you."

Emily was taken aback. The shock of it all made her heart race. But she was very touched, and pleased to see so many people had made it out for her.

"Come on," Jayne said, grabbing her hand. "Baby wants some cake."

She dragged Emily over to the table where there was a huge pink frosted cake and cut her a slice. She placed it on a pink polka dot paper plate and handed it to Emily. At the same time, Amy came up from behind and placed a shiny pink cardboard cone hat on her head, affixing it beneath her chin with a pink silky ribbon.

"This is amazing, guys!" Emily exclaimed.

"Better than our last attempt," Amy added.

Emily blushed. She'd been in a bad place psychologically when Amy had tried to treat her to a baby shower. It still made her feel bad to recall how she'd rushed out, leaving all her friends confused.

They sat on the couch and Emily greeted all the old friends and work colleagues who'd come along. It surprised her to see some of them—like Daisy from college, and Zainab from her old marketing firm. She hadn't considered either of them friends at the time, though she'd spent countless evenings out with them. It felt so strange now to compare these old relationships with the ones she had now. Her friendships in Sunset Harbor felt deep and important. These had only ever been superficial.

"Presents!" Amy cried, rushing away and coming back with her arms filled with squishy-looking bundles. She placed them all on the coffee table.

"Guys, you really didn't have to do all this," Emily gushed, excited to see some cute newborn girl's clothes. She herself had only bought the practical things like onesies and sleepers. The thought of pink dresses and floral pinafores made her heart swell with excitement. "I feel completely spoiled."

"Me first," Jayne said, handing her a parcel.

Emily unwrapped it. Inside was a red and black gingham dress, matching tights, and a green cardigan with a Christmas tree on it.

"Oh my god, I love it," Emily gushed, feeling the soft fabric beneath her fingers.

Jayne grinned, clearly pleased with herself. "It's her Christmas outfit. Every girl's got to have one."

Emily moved onto the next gift—this time from Daisy—and was surprised by how lavishly decorated the box was. She opened it up and was surprised by a pair of cute, shiny T-bar shoes. She recognized the brand name as a very exclusive New York City kids clothing company and gasped.

"Daisy, wow," she said. "This is too much."

The shoes were so overblown, especially considering the fact they would only fit the newborn for a matter of weeks, and especially considering the fact that Daisy wasn't even someone Emily spent much time thinking of at all!

Daisy looked smugly across the rest of the people in the room. "Italian leather," she said.

As Emily continued unwrapping the beautiful clothes, she couldn't help but wonder whether the people in attendance were being generous because they liked her or because they were competing to give the best gift. Each parcel she opened seemed to be more lavishly decorated than the last, the clothing inside more overblown. Oscar de la Renta dungarees. A whole outfit from Burberry. A jacket from Armani Junior. Emily was stunned by it all, by the expense and—what she couldn't help but feel—waste. Baby Charlotte would grow out of this stuff before she'd had a chance to wear it twice! Emily didn't want to be ungrateful, but she felt like everything back in New York City was just gloss. Other than Jayne and Amy, her true friends, the rest of these people were here to tick boxes and take photos for their online social media profiles. In fact, half of them were on their phones, lost in their own worlds.

Amy reached over and touched Emily's hand. "Okay, I need to tell you something."

Emily didn't like the sound of that. "What is it?"

"There's someone coming you might not have anticipated."

"Oh?" Emily said, her mind starting to sift through a myriad of absent faces. "Who?"

Amy squinched her eyes. "Your mom."

Emily's eyebrows shot up her forehead. "My mom is coming to the layette shower?"

She'd been anticipating seeing her mom at some point during the weekend to tell her about Roy, but she hadn't known that her mom was going to be here at the party!

Amy nodded. She was gritting her teeth as though in anticipation of Emily losing her cool. But Emily took the news gracefully. In fact, she was kind of glad her mom was going out of her way for her. Usually she demanded that Emily visit her. The only time she made any effort to contact Emily was to give her a piece of her mind. She could drive across states to shout at Emily and berate her, but she wouldn't usually travel across the city to make Emily feel loved.

Just then the bell went. Amy stood. "That will be her. Are you okay about this?"

Emily nodded, surprised to find that she was actually looking forward to seeing her mom. Their last encounter had been more fraught than ever. And with things how they were with Roy, Emily didn't want to leave things so badly with Patricia. What if she died unexpectedly and the last words they'd exchanged had been angry and vitriolic? It may just have been the pregnancy hormones messing with her head, or perhaps the increased sense of responsibility pregnancy had already given her, but Emily discovered that she wanted to make amends with her mom. She wanted to let bygones be bygones. Her maturity startled her.

Amy opened the door and, as predicted, there stood Patricia. She looked like she'd dressed for a meeting with the DA, in a salmon-colored two-piece suit. Her hair was coiffed to perfection, and a row of pearls hung against her neck. Her perfume was floral, in complete contrast to the sharp personality Emily knew she possessed.

She glanced around the room hawk-like, then her gaze rested on Emily. There was no softness there, but Emily hadn't expected there to be. Her mom was incapable of expressing kindness on her face. She wore her confidence like a mask.

She strolled purposely inside Amy's flat and went up to Emily, then handed her a parcel.

"Hi, Mom," Emily said, fighting the urge to wilt under her mom's foreboding presence. "You got me a gift?"

Patricia nodded. "It's customary, isn't it?"

Emily took the gift and chose not to rise to the bait. "Thanks, Mom," she said.

Patricia sat on the couch beside her and folded her hands neatly in her lap. Emily opened the gift wrap and saw a smooth, white box. She opened it up. Inside was a gorgeous gold watch.

"It's for when she grows up," Patricia said. "It's worth something so if she needs to sell it to fund her studies or, god forbid, buy a car, she'll have the option."

"Mom," Emily gasped. She was beyond touched. It was so out of character for her mom to give a thoughtful gift. "I love it," she finished.

Patricia nodded as though she understood.

"Do you want some cake?" Emily asked.

Patricia looked disgusted. "I'd prefer a gin and tonic," she said.

"I'll fetch one," Amy said, leaping up.

Emily could tell she was relieved that things were remaining civil between the two of them.

She became aware then of the sound of cell phones ringing. She looked up and saw both Zainab and Daisy checking theirs. Another woman sitting in the window answered hers.

As Emily surveyed the room, she saw that most people looked thoroughly bored. Some were even making business-sounding calls. She frowned.

"Time for a game?" Amy said as she came back with Patricia's gin and handed it to her.

People reluctantly put their phones away and crowded around the couch. The apartment was small and it felt even more claustrophobic with everyone's knees touching like that. She realized as they sat around in the small apartment that she wouldn't be happy raising a baby here at all. She'd have had to moved out of New York City eventually for the family she'd always wanted to start, so she really had made the right call leaving when she had.

But at the same time it upset her to realize this was not her home anymore. She didn't fit in with these people and it was painfully obvious by their behavior. She'd become a bore to them, falling into line and following a path they all felt they were too superior to follow.

"So, we're going to play baby bingo," Amy began, handing everyone their custom-made board.

Daisy stood then, suddenly, looking at her watch.

"I'm so sorry, I'm going to have to leave," she said. "They need me in the office." She leaned down and air kissed Emily. "Let's catch up some other time," she said, waving.

Then she hurried off before Emily even had the chance to tell her there would probably be no other time.

Amy looked at Emily. "Do you think the baby bingo scared her off?"

Emily laughed.

Amy opened her mouth to begin to explain how the baby bingo game worked, when Zainab leaned in.

"Did you hear?" Zainab said across the table to Emily. "That Christina is sleeping with Franklin?"

Emily wracked her brain, trying to put faces to the old work colleagues she hadn't seen or thought about in years. "Wasn't she married?" Emily asked as she finally formed a vague image of Christina in her mind.

"Still is," Zainab said, flashing excited eyes. "As is Franklin. Martha caught them at it in the printing room. *On* the copy machine. Can you believe it?"

Everyone else gasped and made exclamations, but Emily just couldn't get on board with the scandal. Not only did she not care, she just felt bad for Christina's and Franklin's spouses. The whole anecdote made her feel very uncomfortable.

Amy attempted again to get the attention of the room, but another old work colleague had leaned in to Emily.

"Is it true that you're friends with Roman Westbrook?" she asked eagerly.

Emily felt a squirm in her stomach. How typical that these people would only think to ask about her celebrity contact. None of them had asked after Daniel or Chantelle, or wondered how she was following the death of her friend Trevor, or how her trip to England

58

was. None of them cared about her at all. They just cared about the fact she'd had dinner with a celebrity!

"We've met," Emily said, downplaying the friendship. She didn't want to answer any questions, especially when Roman valued his privacy so much.

"I read in *Sneak* magazine that he played at a wedding in an inn once?" Zainab said. "Was it yours? Is it true?"

"That's just a tabloid rumor," Emily said, shaking her head. She didn't feel like talking about the time Roman had saved a disastrous wedding at the inn by headlining a surprise set.

Zainab looked disappointed. "I should have known," she said. "Nothing that exciting happens in Maine. I mean that's why he moved there, right? To get away from the drama."

Emily couldn't help but be insulted by the comment. Roman had moved to Maine because people there respected his privacy and didn't turn him into a spectacle. He moved there specifically to get away from people like Zainab.

Amy picked up her baby bingo board again, but was interrupted for a third time, this time by Jayne. With a sigh, Amy threw the board on the coffee table, clearly giving up in her attempts to make them play a game.

"Speaking of Maine," Jayne began. "Do you remember Raven Kingsley from college? The one with the white blond hair?"

"What about her?" Emily asked, lackluster.

"She's moved to Sunset Harbor!" Jayne exclaimed.

Emily frowned. The coincidence didn't sit well with her. She felt possessive over the little town. "Why?"

"She read an article about how it was up and coming," Jayne said. "Some guy had written a whole article about this cute inn he'd stayed in."

"It wasn't Colin Magnus, was it?" Emily asked, surprised.

Jayne clicked her fingers. "Oh yeah, I remember now! He was the George Clooney guy who wrote about your inn. That's so weird to think she got the inspiration to start her business from you!"

"Her business?" Emily asked, confused. "What business?"

"She's opening an inn," Jayne said.

Emily gasped. The thought upset her. Not only of someone she knew opening a rival business, but of the fact her lovely town was being tainted by New York City types. She hardly remembered Raven but they'd bumped into each other along the way a few times. She couldn't recall much about her personality but she knew enough to know she was just like everyone else here.

She realized this must have been how people felt when she'd first come to Sunset Harbor. They'd seen her as a snobbish, brash city woman who had no place in their town. Now she was so well integrated she thought the same of others. She knew it wasn't fair but she couldn't help herself.

Just then there was a knock on the door. Amy frowned and stood.

"I wasn't expecting anyone else," she said. "It must be one of the neighbors."

She went over to the door and peered out the spy hole. Then she gasped, turned, and looked at Emily with a worried expression.

"What?" Emily said, immediately worrying. "Who is it?"

Not a neighbor, clearly. Amy wouldn't be wearing such a guilty expression if it was just someone from her apartment block. But she couldn't even think of who else it might be.

"I don't know how he got through the main gate," Amy blathered. "I'd never have let him through otherwise."

"Who?" Emily demanded, feeling anxious now.

Amy chewed her lip. Then she broke the news. "I'm sorry, Em. It's Ben."

CHAPTER EIGHT

"What are you doing here?" Emily said, going over to the door and blocking Ben's entrance.

Behind her, she could hear people whispering under their breath. She realized that this would become the next thing everyone gossiped about, at whatever the next function was they ended up at without really wanting to be.

Ben raised his eyebrows. "Hello to you, too."

Right away, Emily could see that he was tipsy. Memories of tipsy Ben came sharply into focus in her mind. No wonder he'd managed to bypass the intercom system; he must have charmed one of the neighbors into letting him in. It was exactly the sort of thing tipsy Ben would do.

She so wasn't in the mood for this. Ben had managed to infuriate her within seconds of her seeing him. The last time he'd been groveling for her forgiveness. He'd even proposed! That felt so long ago. She was married now. Pregnant. She was a completely different person.

She folded her arms. "I don't want you here."

Ben shook his head, looking hurt. "I'm not trying to stir up any trouble, Em. Can't we be mature adults?" Rather aptly, he hiccupped on the word *adult*. "We were the most important thing in each other's lives for seven years, after all. I don't see why we can't be friends."

"I have enough friends," Emily said. "And it's not like I'm going to be in New York City on a regular basis for coffee dates. There's no point."

"Why are you being so hostile?" Ben challenged, laughing in a sloppy drunken way. He held his hands up. "I come in peace!"

Emily suddenly felt a presence at her side and turned to see her mother hovering at her shoulder.

"Ben," Patricia said, smiling insipidly. "What a pleasant surprise. Are you coming in for some cake?"

Emily shot her a horrified glance. "Are you kidding?"

"Oh, Emily," her mom said in that way that made her blood boil. "A slice of cake never killed anyone."

Amy shot Emily a helpless expression, like she just didn't know what to do. She always played the peacemaker. Being stuck between Emily and her mother was never a pleasant place to be. Adding Ben into the mix was a recipe for disaster.

Emily just sighed and moved away from the door. There was no point arguing with Patricia. The dragon always won, and it wouldn't be fair to make Amy stand up for her and be dragged into a brawl on her behalf. Looking triumphant, Ben entered the room, waving friendly hellos to people Emily wasn't sure he'd even seen since they'd been together. He chose a seat beside her mother, who had just sat down again, and Emily felt her skin crawl. He was always buttering Patricia up. In fact, it was probably their breakup that had made Emily and her mom's relationship break down so dramatically. He'd acted as something of a buffer between them, and Patricia had often sought out his company even though she never seemed to enjoy Emily's.

Frustrated, Emily sunk back down into her seat, folding her arms protectively about her.

"Do you want to be part of the sweepstakes?" Jayne said, handing him a clipboard with paper on it.

Emily shot her a death glare. Jayne pulled a tense expression. She and Ben had remained on friendly terms ever since the breakup, something that frustrated Emily at the best of times. But it didn't usually present itself in such a public way.

"Just date of birth and birth weight," Jayne continued. "Since we know the gender and name."

"Jayne!" Emily exclaimed, exasperated. Ben had no right to know any of this.

Jayne flinched and looked sheepish. She just couldn't help but put her foot in it.

"You know the gender?" Ben asked, taking the clipboard and looking over it at Emily. "What are you having?" Then he noticed all the baby clothes on the table. "Oh, a girl, I guess."

"Charlotte," Patricia added.

Emily snapped her head toward her mom, frustrated. Why was everyone so determined to include Ben in *her* pregnancy all of a sudden?

Ben looked genuinely moved. He hiccupped as he said, "How lovely."

He scribbled something on the paper, his handwriting sloppy and missing the box entirely. Emily sighed heavily, wishing this nightmare would end.

Amy handed Ben some cake and, as he began to eat, Emily at least hoped it would soak up whatever liquor he'd been consuming.

Needing a distraction, she hunkered down and looked over the predictions in the sweepstakes. Someone had put down Christmas as the date of birth, even though Christmas was twelve days after her due date and she'd almost definitely be induced if it went on that long. And the weights ranged from a manageable-sounding seven pounds to a terrifyingly large prediction of ten pounds!

"I hope she's not that big," Emily said, touching her stomach anxiously.

"The weight isn't the issue," Patricia said, swishing her gin and tonic in her glass. "It's the head circumference that's the main thing. You had a very large head, Emily. And didn't I know it!"

Ben roared with laughter and Emily grimaced, her hand fluttering to her forehead. Patricia had already sunk too many gins, her tipsiness reaching similar levels to Ben's. Emily knew how it went from here—a slow descent into her mom putting her down until they ended up having a blazing row. She could almost feel it coming.

"So Emily," Ben said, "I heard that you've been expanding the business. A restaurant, spa, and island! It sounds amazing."

Emily narrowed her eyes at Jayne. "I wonder who told you."

Jayne looked guilty. Amy, clearly sensing that things were getting extremely tense, leaped up to fetch more drinks for everyone.

"I'd love to come and see it some day," Ben added. "Last time it was just a shell."

He chuckled but Emily frowned even harder. Ben was making it sound like the time he'd turned up at the inn had been some kind of planned visit, rather than him barging into her life to shake things up again and force himself back into the spotlight.

"I'd prefer it if you didn't," she said.

Ben laughed, stubbornly pretending that Emily was making a joke. Everyone around looked very uncomfortable.

"How's the kid?" he added. "Danielle, is it?"

Emily couldn't help but think he'd deliberately mixed Daniel's and Chantelle's names up. He knew full well their names. He was just being disrespectful.

She folded her arms, losing the last ounce of patience she'd had for this whole situation.

"What are you doing, Ben?" she demanded. "Pretending like you care about my life? My family? What is your plan here?"

Out the corner of her eye, she caught sight of the worried faces of her so-called friends.

"No plan!" Ben replied with a laugh. He seemed determined to laugh everything off and pay no heed to the fact that Emily was genuinely furious right now. It was typical, Emily thought. He'd been like that when they were together as well, always acting like her emotions didn't matter, always disrespecting her needs. How had she put up with it for so long?

"I want you to go," she said, the anger in her voice rising.

Ben looked like the hurt party, casting appealing eyes around at their witnesses. Emily wondered whether he'd come here expressly to make her look unstable. Or maybe it was just for the gossip, for the drama. He knew she was an easy target, that he could rile her up and make her cause a scene.

"Look, Em, I'm sorry. I didn't come here to upset you. I just miss you and I wanted to see your face again." His voice slurred as he spoke. "I always thought you'd be carrying my child."

Emily heard someone gasp. She herself was rolling her eyes. This was so ridiculous. Ben had never expressed an interest in having kids with her. He always made it seem like it would be disgusting for them to do so. He was just here for the attention, to be in the limelight once again, to score some points in front of their past acquaintances.

"BEN!" Emily shouted, losing her cool entirely. "GET OUT!"

Amy leaped up. She always hated a public outpouring of emotion. She beckoned Ben to stand.

"Maybe you should leave now," she said.

Ben shook his head and put on his best pathetic, hurt expression, playing the wounded party. It suited his face so well, but Emily was impervious to him now.

"Oh, Emily," Patricia said with a sigh. "You're being so unfair."

Emily turned sharply on her mother. "It's got nothing to do with you!" she cried.

In her peripheral vision, she could see people flinching and looking awkward.

Amy, ever the peacemaker, suddenly stood up. "I think perhaps it might be time to wrap things up here," she said to the stunned guests.

They didn't need telling twice. People scurried to collect their belongings and started streaming out.

Emily felt awful as she mumbled goodbye and thank you to each guest. They filed out one by one, giving Emily cautious looks as they passed. Of course, Ben lingered as long as possible.

"GET OUT!" Emily screamed, shoving him to the door.

Once he was out in the hall, she slammed the door in his face and stood there panting. When she turned back, the apartment was empty apart from her mom, Jayne, and Amy. Amy was busying herself collecting paper plates. Jayne, ever the drama queen, was looking entertained by the whole thing, and slightly amused. Patricia, on the other hand, seemed completely unimpressed.

"Emily Jane," she scolded. "What an ungrateful display!"

Emily was furious. "Who told Ben I was coming to New York City? Amy?"

Amy turned from where she was scraping cake into the trash can. "Babe, it was not me. I wanted you to have an amazing party. Why would I invite him?"

Emily turned on Jayne. "You!" she said. "You told him about me moving to Maine. Did you tell him this as well?"

Jayne held her hands up to indicate innocence. "I was not going to make that mistake twice, Em," she said. "I learned my lesson last time!"

Just then Patricia piped up. "Oh, it was me, all right? Goodness, Emily, I didn't think you'd make such a scene about it."

Emily stared at her mom, completely bemused. "Why the hell did you invite Ben? Why are you two even talking?"

Patricia regarded Emily coolly. "I invited him because it's your last chance before the baby comes. There's still time to leave that silly Daniel and his brat of a child and settle down properly with Ben."

Emily's mouth dropped open. She could not believe what she was hearing.

"How DARE you?" Emily screamed. Rage consumed her, turning her vision red. "I should never have thought you could change. I can't believe I wanted to figure things out with you. You don't change. You can't. All you want to do is meddle in my life and make me feel terrible!"

Patricia looked completely nonplussed. "Stop being so dramatic," she sneered.

But Emily wasn't backing down this time. The Mama Bear she'd become had no time to spare on toxic relationships, even if Patricia was her mother. It seemed so clear to her now that things would never be good with her mom. There was no chance for them. Unless she had a brain transplant.

"Mom," Emily said between her teeth. "This is it between us. I can't keep trying to fix things with you. It will never work. So I just have one last thing to tell you."

Patricia rolled her eyes. She clearly didn't think Emily was being serious.

"Dad is dying," Emily said. "Okay? You deserve to know that. But that's it. I don't want to see you ever again. That's the last thing we need to talk about."

Patricia's face changed, finally. The news of Roy's impending death had been able to penetrate her cold exterior in a way Emily's ranting and raging had not.

"What do you mean?" she asked her daughter. "Roy? He's dying?"

"Yes, Mom. He's dying. And I'm leaving. Goodbye."

With that, she stormed out of the apartment. It was only once she was in the safety of the corridor that she let her sobs consume her.

*

"Em! Em, stop!" Amy cried, hurrying out of the apartment.

Emily wiped away tears of fury. "I hate her," she screamed, hearing in her own voice the same anger Chantelle had projected at Laverne.

"I know," Amy said, shaking her head. "I'm sorry. I should have turned Ben away. I didn't realize."

"It's not your fault," Emily said, exhaling. She unclenched her fists.

"What are you doing now?" Amy asked, gently. She rubbed Emily's shoulder. "Will you come back inside?"

Emily shook her head. "Absolutely not. I want to go home, Amy. I don't belong here."

"Hon, you're being melodramatic," Amy said. "Take a minute and come back inside."

"No," Emily said more forcefully. "I mean it. I don't like being here in New York City anymore. All it does is make me sad. From my mom, to Ben, to just everything. I don't want to be here now. I want to go home."

Amy chewed her lip as though deliberating. Finally, she let out a relenting sigh.

"Take my car," she said, reaching into her pocket and handing Emily her keys. "I'll take one of the company cars back on Monday."

Emily shook her head. "You don't have to do that." It was too much of an imposition.

"Em, it's fine," Amy urged her. "I just want you to be all right."

Finally, Emily relented with a nod. She snuffled up her tears and took Amy's keys. "Thanks."

Amy hugged her tightly. "I truly am sorry," she said in her ear. "I didn't mean to rock the boat like that."

"It's not your fault," Emily told her again. "The boat's been about to sink for years. Something was going to be the final straw, you know. I'm just surprised it took as long as it did."

Amy rubbed Emily's arm again. "I should probably get back to your mom," she said. "I think the news about Roy hit her pretty hard."

Emily felt terrible for the way she'd revealed the news to her mother. She was glad that there was a familiar person around to comfort her during this time. She never understood how Amy had any tolerance with Patricia but they'd known each other as long as Emily and Amy had been friends and somehow they just got on. Amy was endlessly more patient, Emily thought, plus she'd grown up in a happy, secure family, so she had more reserves to spare for those in need. It was one of the things Emily admired the most in her.

"Are you going to be okay driving home?" Amy said.

Emily nodded. It had been a while since she'd been behind the wheel of a car and she was a little nervous. But Amy's Chrysler was extremely safe and easy to drive so her anguish wasn't too great.

They parted ways, squeezing one another's hands with support. Emily rode the elevator down to the basement, found Amy's car, and got inside, feeling better inside, like she was encased in a protective bubble. She couldn't begin to understand how she'd ever lived in New York City, how she'd gotten through each day. Life in Sunset Harbor was immeasurably better and she was looking forward to getting home.

She dialed Daniel's number to tell him but it went to his voicemail. He was useless with his phone at the best of times—not to mention almost always occupied with some kind of work activity—so she didn't think much of it.

She looked at the clock and saw that even if she didn't encounter any traffic or stop at a rest stop to pee—something that was unthinkable with Baby Charlotte lying on her bladder—it would be after midnight by the time she got back to Maine. Spending two-thirds of a single day on the freeway was *not* her idea of a good time, but it was better than the alternative, staying at Amy's overnight and mulling over how terrible the party had truly gone.

She started the ignition and the radio blasted out a song, still on high volume from the drive down. She thought sadly of how much happiness she'd felt earlier this morning, how much enthusiasm and excitement she'd had for the trip, and how that had all been dashed.

She reversed out of the parking lot, filled now with a new emotion. It was a sort of melancholy resolve. She'd truly drawn a line under her life in New York City. This was not her home anymore. It never would be again. Sunset Harbor was where she belonged. And she couldn't wait to get back.

CHAPTER NINE

With the women away in New York City, Daniel, George, and Harry had decided it would be a great opportunity to get together and have that long-awaited boys' night out. Chantelle was at a movie night at Toby's house anyway, and Daniel didn't much feel like rattling around the inn alone. So at around 8 p.m. he took a cab into town and headed to the bar. A little while later, George and Harry arrived. Daniel bought them all a beer, and then they sat together at one of the round chestnut wood tables.

They chose a seat with a perfect view of the television. George and Harry were both avid sports fans, and though Daniel was more of a fishing man, he could get behind a good televised sports game.

"Dad-to-be," Harry said to Daniel. "How does it feel? It's not long now, is it?"

Daniel took a swig of his beer. "Three months. And it feels amazing. I'm caught between being excited and absolutely petrified, you know? I missed out on all of this with Chantelle so it's all completely new."

"You're lucky," George said to Daniel. "You both are. I'd love to settle down."

Harry grinned. "I don't know if you can count me and Amy as having settled down," he said. "But I'd marry her in a heartbeat if I thought she wanted to."

Daniel pressed his lips together. Thanks to Emily he had an insight into Amy's state of mind and knew far more about the inner workings of Harry's relationship than he ought to.

"Do they have any single friends?" George pressed. "Clearly this Sunset Harbor man, New York City woman coupling works well."

"There's Jayne," Daniel said. "But I think she's more trouble than she's worth." He laughed. He was fond of Jayne but she did have a remarkable talent of giving him a headache. "Other than those two, all of Emily's friends are in Sunset Harbor now so you know most of them."

George smirked and swigged his beer. "I should've made a move on Serena when I had the chance."

Daniel and Harry laughed.

"I don't know if you're her type," Daniel replied, comparing Owen—shy, gentle, creative—with George—strong, loud, and confident. "But I suppose opposites can attract."

"Like me and Amy," Harry added, chuckling. "Don't ask me how it works. It just does."

Once again, Daniel kept silent.

George was midway through sipping his beer when he paused and his eyes widened. He spluttered on his sip, then put the bottle down on the table.

"Now that is one beautiful lady," he said.

Daniel and Harry craned their heads around to the bar where they could see the back of a woman with long black hair. She had an incredible figure, lean and toned, which she showed off in casual yet elegant sports gear. They turned back, neither making a comment.

George looked from one to the other, waiting for them to make some kind of exclamation about her attractiveness.

"Are you two blind?" he stammered when neither of them did. "Aren't you seeing what I'm seeing?"

Daniel pointed to his wedding ring. "I only have eyes for Emily."

Harry shrugged too. "Yeah, sorry, bro. I've kind of become unable to see women that way now. It's kind of strange to be honest." His face broke into one of his contented grins again. "But awesome at the same time."

"Why don't you speak to her?" Daniel said. "Five minutes ago you were complaining about being alone and bemoaning not having made a move on Serena. Here's your chance."

George looked uncharacteristically shy then, and Daniel realized that for all his bravado, George carried a lot of insecurities. It always surprised him to discover that about people, especially the ones who seemed completely self-assured. It was often his louder, brasher friends who harbored secret anxieties, like Stu and Evan. You'd never guess from their outlandish behavior that they both had deep emotional difficulties that they grappled with every day.

He saw it now in George, a sudden revelation that his friend, who seemed full of confidence, who Daniel had always thought could get any girl he wanted, was actually deeply insecure.

"Why don't I invite her over to join us?" Daniel said. "Take a bit of the pressure off?"

George looked relieved. He shrugged nonchalantly, in a way Daniel instantly recognized was his attempt to hide his true feelings.

"Yeah, sure, why not?" he said.

Daniel stood, taking his beer with him. "Don't worry, I'll make sure my wedding ring is in full view," he added.

He went over toward the bar, where the attractive woman had taken a stool. As he got closer, he realized she was resting both her elbows on the surface of the bar and was resting her face in her hands. Her shoulders were gently shaking. She was crying.

All thoughts of inviting her back to the table left Daniel's mind immediately. Now he saw someone in need, someone in pain. His heart reached out to her, as it always did when he was confronted with someone in distress.

"I'm sorry to interrupt," he said, fueled by compassion. "But is everything okay?"

The woman lifted her head and turned to face Daniel. The second he saw her face—beautiful, despite being tear-stained—he gasped. He knew that face. It was Astrid.

Her eyes widened with shock.

"Daniel?" she stammered. She quickly wiped her tears away with the sleeve of her tight, black top.

"Astrid," he replied, a little breathless from shock. Instantly, words failed him. "What's wrong?"

Astrid looked away, as though embarrassed. "Nothing I should be talking to you about," she said.

Daniel couldn't turn off his compassion just because the woman crying in front of him turned out to be his teenage sweetheart. If anything, it made him want to reach out more. Astrid had been the love of his life once upon a time. She'd been by his side as he'd transitioned from a teenager to a young adult, trying to forge his own path in life in spite of the terrible upbringing he'd experienced. Like Roy Mitchell and his friend Stu, Astrid had always been one of the people he'd counted as saving him from following a darker life path.

"Try me," Daniel said, pulling up a stool. "I've been told I'm a good listener."

Astrid looked hesitant. "I lost my job," she told him.

"I'm sorry," Daniel said. "What were you doing? I'm sure you'll be able to find another."

"I was a fitness instructor," Astrid said. "Pilates mainly. But one of my clients was a mad paranoid bitch who thought I was flirting with her husband. So she destroyed me. She called the police on me, said I'd stolen stuff from her house. The charges were dropped on lack of evidence but now my reputation's been ruined. No one wants to hire me."

71

Daniel listened patiently, feeling awful for Astrid. It wasn't fair. He knew her well. She was the last person in the world who would steal. In terms of a moral compass, Astrid was probably the person he'd known in life who had the strongest. You couldn't meet a more trustworthy person.

"What are you going to do?" he asked, gently.

Astrid wiped away the tears recounting her story had brought back into her eyes. "Honestly, I don't know. I could move but this is my home. I don't think I should be driven out by rumors. I could retrain. But what else could I do? This is the only thing I'm any good at." She turned her dark eyes on him. They were wide and appealing.

Daniel chewed his lip. The cogs in his head had started to turn but he wasn't sure whether he should suggest what he was about to, especially without consulting Emily. But she was a deeply caring person too, and she would surely understand why he'd made the suggestion he was about to.

"I think I might know someone you could work for," he said.

A look of hope glittered in Astrid's eyes. "Who?" she asked.

"Me," Daniel replied. "And Emily," he added quickly.

Astrid frowned. "No offense, Dan, but you and Emily aren't the usual clientele I get. I work with, like, super rich people. I don't know if you'd be able to afford me."

"Not us specifically," Daniel corrected, "I mean the inn." He shuffled in his seat and began to explain. "We've expanded recently. We have an island now, with a ton of work going on ready for the new year. We want it to be like a retreat, for artists or people who are looking to heal. We were going to speak to Tracy, the yoga instructor who works at the inn, about running retreats there. But maybe you could give it a try instead."

Astrid just stared at him, her eyes growing wider. "What about Tracy?"

He shrugged. "Like I said, we haven't even spoken to her about it yet. But maybe you could work together, or share the workload. Our marketing lady is putting together the website at the moment and she says there's been a high amount of demand for it, so I think there might be space for both of you. Besides, she does yoga and you do Pilates, so you're offering different services."

"I do boot camps too," Astrid added, looking excited and animated suddenly.

"I don't know whether boot camps would work on an island advertised for its tranquility," Daniel said with a laugh.

"Not for the island," Astrid agreed. "I mean for the inn. I could be on the staff. Like you said, Tracy offers yoga only. Is there any demand for more vigorous workouts?"

Astrid's enthusiasm was contagious. Daniel found his mind running away with him. "I don't know. I'll speak to Bryony though and find out."

He smiled at Astrid, glad that she had cheered up. But then her face fell.

"Don't you have to check this with your wife first?" she asked, glumly.

"Emily will love the idea," Daniel said. "She's crazily ambitious."

"I don't doubt that," Astrid said. "I mean because of our history." She looked awkward. "She wasn't too happy with my turning up out of the blue that time."

Daniel hadn't spent much time thinking over the night Astrid had appeared on his doorstep. He hated dwelling on things, especially the bad things that had rocked his and Emily's relationship. He hated drama.

"Okay, that's a good point," he said, running his hands through his hair. "We'll need to have a proper conversation about it. She's away this weekend, so why don't you give me your contact info? I'll speak to her and give you a call. I'm sure she'll be fine with it though. She might just need a bit of reassurance. You intimidate her."

Astrid looked bemused. "I do? Why? My life is a mess!"

Daniel laughed. "I'll never understand that about women. When they're drop dead gorgeous but just can't see it. You're stunning, Astrid, that's why people get intimidated. That's why I'm here in the first place, instead of my friend George!" For the first time since he'd sat down, he remembered George and Harry whom he'd abandoned at the table to watch the game.

Astrid looked back. "Which one is George?" she asked, her eyes widening. "The sexy one or the sexier one?"

Daniel let out a large laugh. "Come and sit with us and I can introduce you."

"Sure," Astrid said, sniffing and wiping the residue of wetness from her eyelashes. "Once my eyes aren't blotchy red anymore." She let out a sniffly laugh, and then she reached out and placed her hand on the one Daniel was resting on the bar. "Thank you," she said with deep meaning. "Really, Dan. I don't think anyone would have been able to cheer me up. But you always could."

With his spare hand, Daniel patted hers, the one that lay on top of his on the bar. He was glad that he'd helped her and smiled tenderly. "You're welcome."

CHAPTER TEN

Exhausted after many hours in the car, Emily saw that it was indeed just past midnight by the time she reached the inn and pulled up the drive. She parked up and shimmied out of the car, stretching her legs. She was stiff from the journey.

She headed into the inn and saw Lois on the reception desk covering the night shift. Music came from the speakeasy, which was often thrumming on a Saturday evening.

"Hey, Lois," Emily said wearily.

Lois looked up and frowned. "I thought you were gone all weekend," she said with an air of confusion.

"I had a change of plan." Emily sighed. "Turns out I can't stand to be in New York City anymore. Not even for an hour." She thought of the disastrous party which had gone from fun to catastrophic in a record sixty-minute period.

"You drove all the way here from New York City?" Lois said, shocked.

"I know," Emily replied, shaking her head. "It was a bit crazy. I'm so tired now, as you can imagine. Where are Chantelle and Daniel?"

"Suzanna picked Chantelle up earlier today. Toby's having some kind of superhero movie marathon and Chantelle was the honorary girl. She's sleeping over and insisted on taking her pink pillow, pink cover, and pink pajamas. She said she's representing team pink."

Emily laughed. That sounded just like Chantelle. "And Daniel?"

"Daniel took the opportunity to head to a bar in town," Lois explained. "I think he's watching a game with George and Harry." She looked at the clock behind her. "He actually only left about an hour ago so they'll probably still be there if you want to surprise them."

Emily thought about it. Daniel had been desperate for a night out with just the boys in ages. She didn't want to spoil his fun. But at the same time, she could really do with offloading to him. She could always help him arrange another evening to see Harry and George just the three of them. She'd pull an Amy and make it some

75

kind of super special event to make up for it. Needing Daniel right now after the fallout from the fight with her mom kind of had to come first, she thought. She knew he'd understand.

"I might do that, actually," she said. "I really wish I could have a drink but maybe hanging out with people who have them will give me vicarious happiness."

Lois laughed. "Let's hope so. Have a good time."

Emily waved goodbye and headed back out. She took her car this time, leaving Amy's parked outside the inn, and headed into town to the bar.

As she drove, soaking in the sights of the quiet, manageable Sunset Harbor roads, she felt that sense of home returning to her. Here she felt safe. Here she was loved by people, respected and cared for. It was exactly what she needed to help get over the stress of the day.

She reached the bar and parked in the small lot around the back. Then she got out of the car, filled with relief to know she was just moments away from reuniting with Daniel, and headed into the bar.

It was dark inside and it took a moment for her eyes to adjust to the dimness. She scanned the tables and noticed Harry and George sitting together looking up at the TV screen that showed a game in full swing. But no Daniel.

She glanced around, searching for him. Then she saw something that made her heart drop to her feet. Two figures at the bar—one male, one female. She recognized Daniel instantly. Even from behind she knew every intimate detail about him. The woman she couldn't place from this angle, but she could see her stunningly attractive figure in tight black workout gear.

It wasn't the fact that Daniel was chatting with a woman at the bar that horrified Emily so much. It was the fact that their hands were resting on top of one another's—his, then hers, then his other. It was a strange, overly intimate posture.

Emily stormed over, hard emotion lodged in her throat. The world seemed to swirl around her as she marched up to Daniel. Time slowed down, so that she could make out the joyful expression on his face, the tender look in his eyes. And then she was close enough to see who the woman was. Astrid. ASTRID!

"What the hell is going on?!" Emily screamed.

Her voice ripped out of her chest like the cry of a wild animal. Daniel's happiness faded and his expression turned to something that Emily thought could only be described as terror. He hadn't been expecting to get caught out by her.

"Emily!" he gasped, leaping up, withdrawing his hand from Astrid's.

Astrid's mouth dropped open. Caught red-handed, Emily thought.

"I can't believe this!" Emily screamed. It felt like her entire world was imploding. Her mom letting her down she could cope with; she was used to it after all. But Daniel was supposed to be the one person she could rely on. The one person she could trust with her whole heart. And here he was, breaking that trust, shattering her heart into a million pieces.

She couldn't look anymore. She couldn't bear to. She turned and rushed out of the bar, hot tears stinging her eyes and streaming down her cheeks.

She heard the sound of the bar door screech open behind her then slam shut on its spring hinges.

"Emily!" Daniel yelled.

His footsteps were fast approaching from behind. Emily couldn't run, not with her bump that size. There was no running away from this. She'd have to confront it head on.

She stopped and whirled on the spot. Daniel ran up to her, his hands reaching for hers. She shoved them away. She didn't want him touching her with those hands that had moments before been touching Astrid.

"Whatever you have to say, I don't care," Emily said.

"Just listen," Daniel began.

"Why?" Emily hissed. "There's nothing you can say to make what I just saw okay."

"I know it looked bad, but I promise you it's not what you think. I didn't plan to meet Astrid."

"Oh really?" Emily said, not buying it for a moment. "You didn't take the first opportunity you've had away from your wife in months to meet up with your ex-girlfriend who's still in love with you?"

Daniel looked like he was in physical pain. "I know it looks bad but you have to trust me, Emily. It was a complete coincidence that we bumped into each other tonight."

"And I suppose it was a complete accident that you touched her hand so tenderly?" Emily replied scathingly.

"Please let me explain," Daniel begged her. "Astrid was upset. That's the only reason I was sitting with her. I would have walked away otherwise but she was crying. And we got to talking. That's all. You don't have to worry."

Emily glared at Daniel. "How stupid do you think I am?"

"Not even slightly," Daniel said. "That's why you'll come around and accept the truth I'm telling you. We can get Harry and George to corroborate my story if you still don't believe me. They saw the whole thing."

Emily shook her head, furious. "They'll just say whatever they know you want them to. I know bro code."

Daniel cast his eyes down. He looked desperate but Emily didn't care.

"I'm going home now," she said. "And I don't want you following me."

Daniel's eyes widened. "What? Where am I supposed to go?"

"Not my problem," Emily said. "You can sleep in a ditch for all I care."

She turned and headed back to the car, a cold numbness spreading through her whole body. She thought she belonged to Sunset Harbor, but now she realized she didn't. She didn't belong anywhere. Her life here was over as she knew it.

Just as she reached the car, Daniel was there again. He leaped between her and the driver's seat door, blocking her from being able to get inside.

"I'm not letting you leave like this," he said. "Please."

Emily had no choice. Daniel was in the way of her escape route.

"There is nothing going on between Astrid and I," he said. "I bumped into her completely by accident at the bar. George wanted me to go and ask her over to our table. I didn't even realize it was her until I got there. Before I even saw who it was, I could see she was crying. That's why we started speaking in the first place. I would have walked away otherwise, if I'd realized. But we spoke and, I'm not going to lie, I like Astrid's company. As a friend. That's all. She's a decent person. You'd probably be friends if you gave her a chance."

Emily made a scoffing noise. She couldn't believe what Daniel was saying to her. It was ludicrous.

"But you know that you're the one I love," Daniel said. "You, Emily. I wouldn't do anything to jeopardize what we have. The life we've made together is amazing. I could never have imagined I'd be so happy. You're the love of my life."

His words started to seep into Emily's mind. But the paranoid part her parents had instilled in her throughout years of witnessing their raging fights was strong, telling her not to listen to him. Her dad's philandering ways had taught her not to trust men, and despite all the leaps Daniel's love had helped her make over the past couple of years, that was always at the back of her mind. Trusting men made you a fool. Here was the evidence of that.

"I did make one mistake, though," Daniel admitted. "And I'll tell you now because you can always tell when I'm holding something back."

He attempted a smile, but Emily wasn't ready to return it. She folded her arms tightly against her for protection and braced herself for the truth to finally come out.

But Daniel's admission was not what Emily had been expecting to hear.

"I offered her a job," he said.

It was the last thing Emily had been expecting to hear. In fact, it was so unexpected that she paused, almost stunned and frozen into confusion.

"I'm sorry, what?" she finally managed to say.

Daniel looked sheepish. "She's been fired. One of her Pilates clients trashed her reputation and she can't find work. I thought about the retreat on the island and thought she'd be perfect for it. And she would. I was going to speak to you about it, obviously, but it just seemed like such a good fit I sort of mentioned it to her already."

Emily's mind did a 360 spin. "You did WHAT?" she bellowed.

Of all the stupid things Daniel could have done to upset her, offering a job to his beautiful ex-girlfriend had to top the list! He'd really put her through the emotional wringer over the course of their relationship, with motorbike accidents and a surprise child. But now he was just being plain idiotic.

"What the hell made you think that was a good idea?" Emily yelled.

Daniel looked anguished. "This wasn't how you were supposed to find out," he said. "I was imagining a lovely reunion date together on the island. Picnic, candles, the works. Then I'd tell you the news and you'd be so happy and in love that you'd see you had nothing to worry about at all. Nothing. Astrid isn't a threat to you, or our happiness. Because you're the one I love. You're the one I married, the one who's having my child."

Emily took a deep breath, trying to wrap her head around everything that had happened. She felt stunned. Shaken to the core.

"Can you let me go home now?" she said, coolly. "I need to think."

Daniel shook his head. "Nope. Because when you're away from me you'll think the worst. I know you. I know how you work. You're always expecting people to let you down because they always have. But not me, Emily. I adore you. You're my favorite person in the world. I'll never do anything to hurt you, including whatever it is you think might have happened between me and Astrid tonight. So no, I won't let you get in that car until you've calmed down and accepted what I'm saying."

Emily was beyond infuriated. "You are such a jerk," she muttered.

Daniel just shrugged. "Hurl whatever insults you need to my way. I can take it. As long as it ends with us together, I don't care."

Just then, the door to the bar opened. Emily saw Harry poking his head out, looking around tentatively.

"Come and join the party!" Emily shouted over to him. "Why not!"

"Em," Daniel admonished.

Harry stepped out. "I'm not going to interfere," he said. "I just wondered if everything was okay in New York City. Is Amy okay?"

"Amy, ha!" Emily laughed, bitterly. "She's fine. She's just hanging out with my mother."

Daniel looked shocked. "Your mom? Was that planned?"

"No," Emily said sharply. "And I was really hoping that I could curl up in the comforting arms of my husband tonight after the crappy day I've had. But clearly that's not going to happen."

Harry looked on timidly, like he wanted to speak but wasn't sure if he should get involved. Clearly, he decided to, because he spoke up.

"Emily, Daniel only approached that woman because George was too shy to."

"George, shy?" Emily said with a hard laugh. "I don't believe that for a second."

"It's true," Harry said. "He's a lot less confident than people think. But look, they're getting on famously."

Emily resisted but finally allowed Harry to show her inside the bar. Astrid and George were in deep conversation, looking rather taken with one another.

Finally, it began to sink in that perhaps Daniel really was telling the truth. But that didn't excuse the fact that he'd offered Astrid a job without speaking to her.

"I think I'll say goodbye now," Harry said. "Give Ames a call and make sure she's okay. And give George and Astrid a bit of space, you know."

He said goodbye to Daniel, and Emily saw the look he gave him, a sort of mix between sympathy and concern. He clearly felt bad for Daniel and the wrath that Emily had unleashed upon him. She took some deep breaths as she watched Harry leave.

When she turned back to Daniel, he was looking at her with raised eyebrows. "So where are we at now on the forgiveness scale?" he asked.

Emily folded her arms. "Pretty low," she said. "Although you don't have to sleep somewhere else."

Daniel smiled. He could tell she was cracking.

"Well, that's a start," he said. "Can I get a ride home with you? I took a cab because I was drinking."

"What about Astrid?" Emily said scathingly.

"I think she's being well looked after by George," Daniel said. He took a tentative step toward Emily.

"Fine," she muttered.

She got into the driver's seat and Daniel slid into the passenger seat beside her. She didn't look over.

"Am I sleeping on the couch tonight?" he asked.

"No," she replied. "That room is for the guests. You can stay in one of the empty rooms."

"That's better than the barn," Daniel chuckled. "You can't hate me that much."

"I don't hate you," Emily said, her hands tensing against the steering wheel. "I think you're a stupid idiot moron, but I don't hate you."

Daniel shrugged. "That's progress."

Emily turned her face sharply. "Daniel, this isn't a joke," she snapped. "You can't turn every moment I'm annoyed with you into a game. Seeing you with Astrid really hurt me. It humiliated me. It looked like you were on a date with her! Then your pregnant wife waddles in, looking awful after spending half her day in a car. Do you have any idea how embarrassing that whole thing was for me?"

Daniel's expression was suddenly very serious. "Emily, you don't look awful. You're stunning. I only have eyes for you. I'm sorry it humiliated you. And I'm sorry for offering Astrid a job without consulting you. I got carried away with wanting to fix her problems."

Emily sighed, feeling her body sag from fatigue. The fact that Daniel cared about other people's well-being was one of the reasons she loved him so deeply. Really it was her own paranoia and insecurity over Astrid that had made the situation spiral so quickly out of control. If she'd found out Daniel had offered a job to one of his males friends she wouldn't have had the reaction she did at all.

Overwhelmed with emotion from the day, Emily finally felt her armor break down. She'd been shielding herself behind anger because she didn't want to let herself give in to the pain the day had brought up. But now it was cracking. Tears began to stream down her cheeks.

"Emily," Daniel said quietly, softly. "Let's get home and snuggle up in bed. When we wake up tomorrow things will look different. We'll go somewhere just the two of us, somewhere romantic. We deserve it. You deserve it. Okay?"

She looked over at him, his beautiful features obscured by tears. She loved and trusted Daniel, and knew in her heart he'd never cheat on her or do anything intentionally to hurt her. She was still furious, but moreover she was exhausted. The idea of falling asleep in Daniel's comforting, strong arms was one she couldn't resist.

Finally, she nodded.

"I think I might sleep for a year," she admitted.

It was the first time she'd said anything in a normal tone, without anger or accusations on her tongue. Daniel smiled at her softly, invitingly. She could tell in his eyes that he was relieved, that he was more than ready for this spat to be over. But fatigue and forgiveness were two very different things. Just because she'd invited Daniel into her bed it didn't mean she was over the stupidity of his actions. She just didn't have the energy to deal with it tonight. Tomorrow would be a whole different matter.

CHAPTER ELEVEN

"Hey, Mommy," Chantelle's voice came on the other end of the line.

It was morning and Emily was standing in the kitchen, wrapped in her dressing gown, resting against the work surface, using the vintage house telephone to speak to Chantelle.

"How was the superhero movie marathon?" Emily asked.

"Amazing! Can I stay at Toby's today again? We've still got tons of movies to watch."

Emily paused as she pondered it. "Did you get any sleep last night or were you watching movies all night?"

"We slept," Chantelle said. "A little."

"Have you got any daylight on your skin at all? Or are the curtains drawn?"

"I'm opening them now!" Chantelle said.

"Have you eaten anything other than popcorn?"

"Yes! Suzanna keeps bringing us fruit and vegetable sticks."

Emily smiled to herself. "Okay, put Suzanna on the line. If it's okay with her, it's okay with me."

"Thanks, Mommy!" Chantelle said.

She heard the sound of shuffling, and then Suzanna came over the speaker.

"She's not too much trouble, is she?" Emily asked. She hated taking liberties, but her friends never seemed to mind having Chantelle over.

"She's great," Suzanna said. "I'm just glad Toby is distracted. He's become quite clingy since Robin was born. I had no idea a seven-year-old would be jealous of a baby."

Emily touched her own pregnant stomach. Because of Chantelle's complex needs, it *had* occurred to her that jealousy may soon play a role in their lives.

"We can take Toby another day if you need a break," Emily suggested. "He's always welcome."

She felt bad as she realized then that Toby had often been sidelined by Bailey and Chantelle. They were the best of friends, always sleeping over at each other's houses, and as a result Emily and Yvonne were extremely close. But Suzanna needed just as much support as Yvonne did, and offered it just as readily. Maybe this little hiccup between Chantelle and Bailey would do everyone some good. Emily had certainly never meant to leave Suzanna out; she loved her just as much as she did Yvonne.

"Whenever you need a break, just drop him over," Emily added.

"Thanks, Emily," Suzanna replied, and Emily could hear the gratitude in her voice. That and the exhaustion. Having a two-month-old in the house was clearly hard work. Emily could hardly believe how soon that would be her!

Having arranged for Chantelle to remain at Toby's for another day to finish watching the rest of their superhero movies, Emily prepared some breakfast and took it up on a tray to Daniel. He stirred as she entered.

"I was worried you'd left me," Daniel quipped, only half joking.

"Sorry, you can't get rid of me that easily."

She placed the tray on the bed beside his feet, then climbed back in beside him. The whole Astrid situation hung between them unspoken. Emily was still exhausted from the emotional expenditure of last night's argument. She didn't really want to drag it up again but it wasn't fully resolved and she knew they had to finish hashing it out.

"I wouldn't be comfortable having Astrid on the staff," Emily told him.

"I know," Daniel replied. "And I understand why from a personal perspective. But if you put your business hat on," he said, "Astrid is one of the best in her field."

"Even with my business hat on," Emily refuted, "we're talking about someone whose reputation has been questioned."

"The charges were dropped."

"But her reputation has been tarnished," she insisted.

Daniel sighed. "When did you ever care about that sort of thing, Emily? So a certain rich circle of people in Maine wouldn't want her services, but we don't exactly cater towards them. All our clients are on vacation, visiting from out of state. They won't have heard any of the gossip on the rumor mill. All they'll know is that they've had an amazing retreat on a beautiful island with an awesome Pilates instructor!"

Emily could understand where he was coming from, of course. But she couldn't just forget about who Astrid was, even if it did make good business sense to employ her.

"What about Tracy?" she asked. "She was our first option."

"We'd obviously have to talk to her about sharing the work."

Emily had an idea then. "Look, I know you just want to help Astrid, and that's admirable. But I can't tolerate her being around. Not at the moment, anyway. So why don't we put Astrid in touch with Roman? You know what he's like. He won't care about what the elitists in Maine have said about her, and her whole healthy thing would fit in with his philosophy nicely. Can we just do that instead?"

Daniel twisted his bottom lip in contemplation. "Sure, okay. We'll start there."

Emily held her hand out to shake Daniel's. "I'm glad we found a way to compromise."

He laughed and shook her hand. They settled into bed and ate their breakfast.

"Speaking of the island," Daniel said. "I have an idea for a date for us."

"You do? What is it?"

"A secret."

Emily realized then that Chantelle was going to be away for the day. No sitter required. "Hey, we could go on our date right now!" she said. "Chantelle's staying at Toby's."

Daniel looked surprised. "Really? You want to?"

"Yes!" Emily said. "We have a kid-free day. We ought to make the most of it while we can, because they're going to be much harder to come by in the future."

"Well, okay," Daniel said. He seemed shocked by the sudden turn of events, if not a little relieved. "Come on then. You'll need to wear your leathers."

Emily laughed. But then she realized Daniel wasn't joking. "I can't! Not with this!" She gestured to her stomach. "They won't fit."

Daniel pouted. "But we haven't been out on the bike for months. And it would be the best way to get to where we're going. Why don't you wear everything but the pants? Your maternity jeans will be fine."

Emily mulled it over. She didn't feel like it was safe to ride without full leathers, but there was no way her bump was going to fit inside her suit. Daniel's suggestion would work.

"I promise not to crash," Daniel added, hand on heart.

Emily rolled her eyes. "How about you promise not to ride too fast?" she suggested.

He nodded. Then he flashed Emily one of his wicked, cheeky grins. "We're getting good at this compromising thing, aren't we?"

Emily felt like Daniel's persuasion had indeed been the right thing to do when, a little while later, they were riding along the cliffsides. The temperature had dipped a little but that was actually working to their favor, as the heavy safety gear could sometimes get quite hot. Emily felt a surge of excitement to know she could still ride on the back of the motorcycle in spite of her pregnancy, and she remembered how Doctor Arkwright had told her there was no need to stop doing any of her favorite activities, biking included as long as the roads weren't bumpy.

Emily was glad now that they were on the motorcycle. The sights and sensations of riding through the Maine cliffsides brought back such happy memories for her. It was on the back of Daniel's motorcycle that she'd realized how in love with him she really was. Replicating that moment again was helping her put the Astrid debacle behind her. She and Daniel were too good for petty feuds.

After at least an hour on the motorcycle, Daniel slowed and turned onto a tree-lined roadway. The colors of fall had started to appear, turning the leaves slightly yellow. It was beautiful and Emily gasped as the cool sun dappled her face.

They turned again and the foliage thickened. Ahead was a stone bridge. It was very quaint, the sort of scenery that would appear in a painting, but also surprisingly long, arching over a large body of water.

Once over the bridge, the trees thinned out and Emily saw that they were riding up to a small hotel that wasn't much bigger than her father's cottage in England. Ivy and roses wound all up the facade of the building, and there was a lovely wooden porch painted a mint green color.

"So we're not the only ones with a hotel on an island," Emily said as the motorcycle drew to a halt and the noise of its engine lessened.

"I thought it might be able to give us some ideas," he said.

They dismounted and began to stroll hand in hand around the small island upon which the hotel was built. It had remarkable gardens, landscaped to perfection. The flower beds had been cleared out because of the time of year but Emily could imagine how lovely it would look in full bloom during the height of summer. There were stone pots evenly spaced along the pathways, and benches between them, a raised rock garden, a tennis court, a pergola, and a koi lake.

They stopped in the small cafe—a gorgeous converted barn decorated with vintage chintz and filled with teapots. Daniel ordered them homemade scones with clotted cream and jelly, and a big pot of English breakfast tea.

"What do you think?" Daniel asked, setting his teacup down on the table.

"It's stunning," Emily said. "The tea room especially. It reminds me of being in Falmouth!" She thought of her father, feeling that now common mixture of emotions; melancholy, love, longing, and fear.

"It's quite unique, isn't it?" Daniel said. "Has it given you any ideas for our island?"

"I don't know," Emily confessed. "I can imagine the rock garden looking stunning on our lawns, and converting one of the stone barns into a tearoom or coffee house would be cool. But it's all a bit too cultivated for our taste, isn't it? At least for what we want the island to be like."

Daniel nodded, interested in her ideas. "So your vision is a bit more basic?"

"Not basic," Emily said. "Luxury, definitely. But more in keeping, more rugged. The thing I love about our island is how wild and unkempt it is. I want our structures to blend in with the environment."

"What I do love about this place," Daniel noted, "is the way they've utilized the space. Everything flows really well. They've cleverly made it so that you're directed through the island. It makes it feel much bigger."

"You're right," Emily said. "I hadn't noticed that." As she thought about it now, it occurred to her that the island had sort of been sectioned off by strategically placed trees and shrubbery. There was a route around the whole thing she'd had no idea she was following. She thought of the rabbit warren–style layout of Trevor's house, how unique and amazing it was. "Do you think the Erik brothers would be able to design something similar for our island?" A tingle of excitement went through her at the thought.

"I'm certain they can," Daniel replied with a huge grin. Then he reached across the table and touched Emily's hand. "Em, are things okay with us now?" he asked.

Emily pressed her lips together. She'd been avoiding talking about their fight during the date. Things had more or less been resolved, or at least swept under the rug. Now it was just a matter of spending time together, of rekindling the comfortable feelings between them.

"Yes," she said. "But it will be better once we've spent the entire day on our date."

Daniel grinned. "Good thing I have another thing planned."

"What's that?" Emily asked, feeling a little tug at the side of her lips.

"There's a rooftop cinema nearby. They show old black-and-white movies, serve homemade ice cream and lemonade. It's usually closed this time of year but they kept it open a little longer because of the mild weather. What do you say?"

Emily couldn't suppress her smile any longer. She grinned back. "That sounds great."

They stood and Daniel wrapped his arm around her as they left the tea room. For the first time since she'd left for New York City, Emily felt like things between them were back on track. She was ready to move on from the horrible fight and look forward, once again, to their future together.

CHAPTER TWELVE

Emily's high spirits remained all through the day and back when they were home at the inn. Suzanna dropped Chantelle back, and the little girl looked exhausted, but happy and flushed-cheeked.

"You need to brush your hair!" Emily commented, looking at the nest of knots the child's blond hair had become.

They congregated in the dining room for dinner that night, sitting together around the small corner table reserved for the family. Paella was on tonight's menu.

"Are you looking forward to going back to school tomorrow?" Daniel asked Chantelle as they ate.

She looked sad then, and shrugged. "Maybe. I don't know. Miss Butler is way more grumpy than Miss Glass was. And I still don't like being in the same class as Laverne."

Emily's heart went out to the girl. It seemed so unfair that her school days should be ruined by a bully, especially when school was a place Chantelle loved and in which she thrived.

"But she hasn't said anything else mean to you, has she?" Daniel asked. "After that first day on Wednesday?"

"No, not me," Chantelle said. "But other than Bailey, she's mean to *everyone*. She made fun of Toby's Superman backpack, and then she said Ryan had a disease because he couldn't eat wheat."

Emily raised an eyebrow and looked at Daniel. He seemed just as unimpressed by Laverne's behavior as she was.

"Did Miss Butler do anything about it?" Emily asked.

Chantelle just shrugged. "Not really. She just tells her to stop talking and do her work. But if she says mean things at recess no one does anything."

Emily decided then and there that if the school wasn't going to do anything about Laverne, she would, starting with speaking to the girl's mother. They would have to make sure they were first at the school gates tomorrow in order not to miss her but Emily didn't care. The sacrifice was worth it for Chantelle.

After dinner, they retired to the lounge for a lazy Sunday evening. Chantelle colored pictures at the window table and Emily kicked back with a book on the couch. Mogsy and Rain lay curled up beside her, both snoring lazily. Daniel sat in the armchair across from them, busy texting someone. Emily tried not to get suspicious but Daniel was hardly ever on his phone, and whoever was on the other end was making him chuckle under his breath.

Finally, she couldn't stand it anymore. "Daniel, who are you typing away to?" she asked, trying to sound amused rather than paranoid that it may be Astrid.

"I'm in a group message with Stu, Evan, and Clyde," Daniel replied. "We're trying to organize another weekend together. They're threatening to come to the inn."

Emily wasn't so sure about that. She'd grown fond of the three of them when they'd stayed for the wedding, but they were still a bit on the brash side. And they loved to tease, which Emily wasn't always in the mood for. Plus, they were friends with Astrid. She was the missing member of their gang. How likely would they be to try to encourage this friendship Daniel was on the verge of forging with her? Would they try and persuade Emily to let Astrid into their lives?

But what could she do? They were Daniel's best friends. She couldn't ban them from the inn just on a paranoid worry.

Just then, Emily's phone began to buzz. She looked down and saw an incoming video call coming from her father.

"It's Papa Roy!" she exclaimed.

Within seconds, Chantelle had leaped up from the table, scattering her pencils in her haste to get to the couch, and appeared at Emily's side. Daniel, too, stood from the armchair and came and sat with them.

Excited, Emily answered the call and held her phone out at arm's length so everyone was in view. Roy usually only ever telephoned, saying that video calls were far too futuristic for his old mind to handle. But today he'd made the exception, and Emily wondered why.

"Dad!" she exclaimed. "How nice to see you!"

"Hello, everyone," he said, smiling.

Emily could tell he was thinner but she wasn't going to focus on it or draw attention to it. Her father had assured her he would handle his demise with grace and dignity and it wasn't her place to act distressed when he himself was not.

"How's the weather in England, Papa Roy?" Chantelle asked. "It's really sunny here!"

Roy chuckled. "It's raining, my dear. Has been for three days in a row!"

Chantelle laughed.

"So to what do we owe the pleasure?" Emily asked.

"I was calling to invite you somewhere," Roy said.

Chantelle started bouncing with excitement.

"Oh?" Daniel asked, looking intrigued.

Roy continued. "I've had just about all of the drizzle I can handle," he said. "I'm going to head over to my house in Greece. And I was wondering whether you might all like to join me?"

Emily gasped. She hadn't been certain she'd see her father again.

"When?" she asked, excited but also wary that Baby Charlotte was growing every day and soon traveling would be inadvisable, if not prohibited.

"When is Chantelle's next vacation from school?" Roy asked.

Emily mulled it over. "They're not off for Columbus Day in October this year for some reason, although there's still going to be a parade. There's the long Thanksgiving weekend. Other than that, it's Christmas when she gets a real break, and Charlotte will be born then!"

Roy looked crestfallen. "She has no proper vacation? No weeks off? Over here the children have a whole week vacation in October!"

Emily shrugged. "I'm sorry, Dad. I don't know what to say."

Chantelle clutched Emily's hand. "Mommy, please, I really want to see Papa Roy. Can't we ask the school for time off?"

Emily thought of mean Mrs. Doyle, the principal, and of how unhelpful the school had been during the whole Laverne situation. She couldn't help thinking that it was very unlikely they'd let her have time off. Maybe if she explained about the situation with Roy's ailing health she may be more sympathetic, but the idea of speaking to them filled her with dread.

"Even if the school agreed," Emily explained, feeling heavy-hearted, "I just don't know where we'd find the time. We have a lot going on here, with doing up the island, not to mention Daniel's promotion."

Roy looked crushed.

"But why don't you come here?" Emily suggested. "If it's the British weather that's the problem, we're in the middle of an unseasonable heat wave!"

Roy shook his head. "I've already bought my plane tickets and made the arrangements. I can't change plans now."

Emily could sense the disappointment coming from Chantelle. She wished her father had mentioned this to her in advance, or at least before he'd made all the arrangements to go to Greece.

Perhaps then she'd have been able to organize something. Instead, she felt like she'd let everyone down.

The call hadn't gone as anyone wanted. As Emily ended it sadly, feeling blue, the doorbell rang. She frowned and looked at Daniel.

"Are we expecting anyone?" she asked.

He shook his head and went to answer it. She heard a swell of noise come from the corridor, hooting and hollering, cheers and laughter. Right away, Emily knew what the noise was. Stu. Evan. Clyde.

She stood from the couch. The timing couldn't have been worse.

Out in the corridor, the four men were in one of their strange wrestling embraces, which was half affection, half fight. She shook her head, unamused.

"What are you guys doing here?" she asked, hands on hip.

Realizing she was there, Stu, Clyde, and Evan released Daniel. They rushed at Emily, sweeping her up into a similar strange hug, though this one a lot more gentle than the one they'd subjected Daniel to. Her cheeks were kissed, her back patted. In spite of herself, Emily couldn't stop the smile tweaking up the corners of her lips.

"I said what are you doing here?" she asked again once she was finally released. "A minute ago you four were in a group text chat!"

"That was Stu's idea," Clyde said. "Thought it would be funny to pretend we were talking about visiting when we were actually on our way to surprise Danny Boy."

Emily shook her head, amused but also exasperated. With everything that was going on in their lives, having these three drop in out of nowhere was a bit of an imposition.

"We knew there'd be some free rooms for us now the summer rush is over," Evan added.

Just then, Chantelle appeared at the doorway. Now it was her turn for an exuberant greeting from Daniel's friends. They cheered, swept the little girl in the air, and paraded around with her. Emily's heart flew into her mouth at the sight of her held at least six feet in the air, but Chantelle was overjoyed. She laughed merrily and Emily was grateful that something had distracted her from her sad mood at returning to school tomorrow and the unlikelihood of a trip to see Papa Roy in Greece.

A horrifying reality dawned on Emily then. The three of them had drifted here not for a vacation but for work! Like Daniel, they were all handyman types. Stu was a mechanic and had the most stable employment situation of the three, but Clyde and Evan made ends meet through plastering and painting, putting shelves up for old ladies, and cutting grass. They weren't just here for a fun weekend or a couple of nights camping, they were here to stay!

She floundered, not knowing what to say or do. Though they'd grown closer during the wedding, Emily still found their behavior to be a bit on the infuriating side. With her pregnancy would it be too stressful having them around?

It was Chantelle who made Emily's internal thoughts known.

"How long are you staying?" she asked, as she was placed gently on her feet, unscathed.

"That's up to your mom," Evan said, sheepishly.

"For as long as we're useful," Clyde added with a cheeky shrug.

"I know how you can help!" Chantelle exclaimed. "You can work on the island!"

By the look on Daniel's face, Emily could see the suggestion delighted him. So far the two young college guys were on board to do the island renovation, but they hadn't yet employed any handymen. In fact, assembling a team was next on Daniel's to-do list, to be completed first thing Monday morning. So really, Chantelle's idea could kill two birds with one stone.

"Would you want to?" Daniel asked them. "You're not too busy with other work?"

The three of them looked thrilled at the suggestion, like they hadn't already had it at the backs of their minds before they got here.

"Definitely!" Stu exclaimed. Evan and Clyde also nodded exuberantly.

"Amazing," Daniel said. "We have work all through the winter and into next year. It's casual so there's no commitment to stick around for all of it. And you can stay at the inn if you need to. Emily? Are you okay with that?"

"Is it okay for us to stay?" Stu asked. He was always the slightly more considerate of the three, Emily thought.

Everyone looked at her hopefully. Emily didn't feel like she had much of a choice. She tried to look at the positives; any way of reducing Daniel's stress levels and the amount he had to work was a good thing, and anything that made him happy, and made Chantelle happy, was also worth it in her mind. The downside, Emily thought, was that by allowing the three of them to work for them, her resolution against Astrid lost even more of its power.

With her hands tied, Emily finally relented. "Fine. You guys can stay here and work on the island. But you have to behave yourselves. Chantelle is back at school and I will not having you sitting on the porch drinking and chatting all hours. Understood?"

Everyone cheered. Clyde swept Emily into a bear hug. With her face pressed against his broad chest, his musty sweat smell in her nostrils, Emily's sense of trepidation seemed only to grow.

CHAPTER THIRTEEN

The next morning, Emily woke early, fully prepared to enact her plan to catch Laverne's mom at the school gates. She showered and dressed for the day and then went into Chantelle's room to wake her up. The girl murmured unhappily.

"It's too early," she complained, trying to pull her covers back over her head.

Emily peeled them off. "I know. But we have to get in early today."

"Why?" Chantelle complained.

Emily didn't want to reveal her plan to Chantelle. She knew the girl would resist.

"Toby," she blurted. It was the first thing that popped into her head. "He wants to play a superhero game with you before school starts."

Chantelle looked suspicious, but she dragged herself out of bed nonetheless.

As they headed downstairs for breakfast, Emily texted Suzanna.

Can I pick Toby up for the school run today?

Suzanna's reply came shortly after.

That would be amazing! But why are you awake this early? I've been breastfeeding for the last hour. What's your excuse?

Emily laughed and rubbed her tired eyes.

It's a long story. I'll explain another time.

Then, on second thought, she added: *Can Toby wear his superman cape?*

Suzanna replied quickly. *Lol. Of course. This is all very mysterious.*

With everything planned, Emily and Chantelle sat together and quickly had a bowl of cereal.

"Come on, let's go pick up Toby," Emily said as soon as their dishes were empty.

"You're rushing," Chantelle said grumpily.

"Don't you want to play with Toby?" Emily said.

"Of course," Chantelle replied, dragging her feet as she followed Emily along the corridor. "I just don't want to see Laverne and Bailey. That's all."

Emily let out a sad sigh. She was right not to mention the real plan to Chantelle. It could easily have caused her to melt down.

They headed out to Emily's car and piled in. Chantelle practically fell asleep in the backseat.

When Emily pulled up outside Suzanna's, she saw her friend already sitting on her porch in the rocking chair with baby Robin.

"Do you feed him on the porch?" Emily asked, laughing as she greeted her friend.

"The fresh air stops me falling asleep," Suzanna told her. The bags under her eyes were dark. "I swear it wasn't this hard with Toby. But I suppose that's the difference between having babies in your twenties and babies in your thirties. And going from one child to two. You'd think the workload would double but somehow it increases tenfold!" She shook her head and cast her gaze at Emily's bump. "Sorry, you probably don't need to hear this."

"It's good to prepare," Emily replied.

Suzanna stood and went to fetch Toby. As requested, he was wearing his Spiderman cape. He offered Chantelle the Batman one. Then they said goodbye to Suzanna and got back into Emily's car.

Emily pulled up in the school parking lot and was pleased to see that she was the first car there.

"Right, kids, off you go," she said, ushering them into the playground. To her delight, they instantly began playing a superhero game. Her plan was coming together.

She kept one eye on the children and the other on the entrance to the parking lot. A car arrived but it wasn't Laverne and her mom; instead, it was Holly dropping Levi off, her little one, Minnie, in her booster seat in the back.

"You're never here this early," Holly said.

"Neither are you," Emily replied with a laugh. Levi ran off to play with Toby and Chantelle, and Emily revealed her secret to Holly. "I'm actually on a mission to meet Laverne's mom."

Holly raised an eyebrow. "Why? I'm hearing bad stuff about that family."

"Really?" Emily asked, intrigued. "Like what?"

Holly folded her arms. "They're real estate developers who just move where the money is. They have a pretty bad track record as well, of buying up old properties and leveling them to build new, modern apartments that are totally out of keeping with the area. I heard the children have already lived in seven different states, bearing in mind Laverne is the eldest. That's a new house every year. No wonder she's so mean. All her friendships must be so temporary."

Emily felt bad for the child, suffering because of the actions of her parents.

"They don't usually send them to public school, either," Holly continued. "The others are at Mallory's, you know the private school on the cliffs. The only reason Laverne is here is because her grade was full so they couldn't accommodate her. That's why she's dropped off so early. The others start at seven a.m. so the mom drops Laverne here straight after."

Emily's eyes widened. She didn't usually like to gossip but this was all quite fascinating. It certainly went some way in explaining why Laverne was so prickly.

Just then, a car turned into the parking lot, shiny black with tinted windows.

"Speak of the Devil," Holly said under her breath.

The car was driving far too fast. It swung into a parking space and the back door opened. Out hopped Laverne. So her mom couldn't even be bothered to get out of the car and socialize with them? She was just going to shove her kid out and drive off?

"Excuse me a moment," Emily said to Holly.

Holly gave her a curious expression as she headed in the direction of Laverne's car. When she reached it, she rapped on the driver's window with her knuckles. The windows buzzed down and Emily was confronted with a pair of huge, gold-rimmed sunglasses sitting on top of a small, surgically redesigned nose. Pursed pink lips that looked like they'd been injected with fillers opened and said, "Yes? What? I'm in a hurry?"

Emily held her tongue. "I'm Emily Morey. Chantelle's mom. Our kids are in the same class."

"Right. And?"

The woman had an abrupt way of speaking and an accent Emily knew all too well. New York City.

"And... I think they've gotten off to a bad start. Laverne's made friends with Chantelle's best friend so there's a bit of jealousy. And dare I say bullying? Laverne thinks my daughter has a stupid accent."

The woman sighed roughly. "This always happens," she muttered. She leaned out the window. "LAVERNE!"

The little girl stopped and hurried back to her mom, clearly well trained to be obedient. Emily spotted Chantelle looking

97

curiously in their direction. She beckoned to her but Chantelle shook her head resolutely.

"I hear you're being mean," Laverne's mom said when the girl was beside the door.

Laverne dropped her head but not out of shame, she was hiding a smirk. Emily felt rage take hold of her.

"No," Laverne said. "I just pointed out that Chantelle has a Texan accent. That's all. It wasn't an insult. It's just true."

Emily took an instant disliking to Laverne. She had a haughty attitude and a smug expression. But she remembered what Holly had told her and tried to be sympathetic. It was Laverne's circumstances that made her unpleasant, not the child herself. And with such an awful mother it was to be expected.

"We spoke about this," Laverne's mom said. "Sometimes it's not what you say but how you say it. Did your tone imply that Chantelle was stupid because of her accent?"

Laverne just shrugged.

"LAVERNE," her mom snapped. "I do not have time for this. I have a meeting with the bank today. I don't want to be late. So just cut the crap, okay?"

Emily's eyebrows rose. Laverne's mom was quite fierce.

"Fine," Laverne said to Emily. "I'm sorry I was mean. I don't think Chantelle is stupid."

Emily nodded, though she didn't think the child really meant it. "I think maybe Chantelle might want to hear that from you directly," she said.

Laverne huffed. She stomped across the playground and stopped underneath the climbing frame where Toby and Chantelle were pretending to rescue Levi. She watched as Laverne looked up at them and spoke. Then she saw Chantelle turn her gaze toward Emily. Emily braced herself, wondering whether Laverne really had apologized or whether she'd just said something equally mean. But then Chantelle grinned at Emily and Emily knew that it had worked.

She turned back to Laverne's mom, satisfied. "Thank you," she said. "It's always best to nip these things in the bud."

"Sure," the mom replied, sounding bored. "I have to go now, though. A meeting in town."

"Is this about your real estate work?" Emily asked.

The woman glanced over the top of her sunglasses suspiciously. "News travels fast in small towns," she said in a dry voice. "Yes. I'm buying that old oceanfront inn. You know, the one that's falling apart."

Emily knew it. It was a magnificent old place. It hadn't been used as an inn for dozens of years, although she vaguely remembered it being in business when she'd visited Sunset Harbor as a child. It was a huge place, a magnificent old Victorian manor house, with a substantial amount of land around it.

"You're moving in?" Emily asked. This woman would need to be rich to turn it into a family home, but she was very familiar with the sort of wealth that could come out of New York City.

"God no," the woman said, laughing. "We're tearing it down."

Emily was horrified. "But why?" she cried, shocked.

"I prefer modern architecture."

"So you're turning the space into apartments or something?" Emily asked.

She was still reeling with the news that the gorgeous old piece of history was going to be destroyed. She remembered how Trevor had wanted it to be turned into a museum but had been consistently voted down by the other members of the zoning board. There'd even been discussion about it since his death, of making it a historical museum in his honor. But there just wasn't the money right now. Clearly Mayor Hansen had now given up on the possibility of the money ever being there, and had given the go-ahead to have it sold into private hands.

"No, I'm going to start an inn. I read this article about how Sunset Harbor is up and coming. And Roman Westbrook lives here now so I figured I would capitalize on that while I could. You never know when the next financial crash is coming, know what I mean?"

Emily found the woman's attitude disgusting. At the same time she was terrified about what a new inn in town would do to her business. The sight was prime real estate, far better located for the harbor and town amenities than Emily's inn. Plus, it was in the same part of town where Roman lived, so if people were only coming to Sunset Harbor hoping to spot him then that was a better place to do it than the inn was.

As these thoughts raced through Emily's mind, she suddenly realized that she already knew what Laverne's mom was planning on doing in Sunset Harbor. She'd heard this story before; a New York City lady reading Colin's article and coming to Sunset Harbor to open an inn. It was Jayne who'd told her.

"Raven?" Emily asked, as it dawned on her. "Raven Kingsley?"

The woman snapped off her sunglasses. "Yes. Do I know you?"

"Emily Jane Mitchell. From college. I'm friends with Jayne."

"Oh jeez, I see it now!" Raven exclaimed. "I didn't recognize you with the, you know…" She pointed at Emily's protruding stomach. "And your name is different. You're married?"

Emily nodded. "Yes, six months now."

"Still in the honeymoon phase," Raven said, drily. "Enjoy it while it lasts. 'Cause it gets bad. It gets so, so bad."

Emily was shocked by the turn of events. As she said goodbye to Raven Kingsley and headed home, her mind was spinning.

To make matters worse, as she pulled into the parking lot at the inn, her phone began to ring and she saw, with horror, that it was Patricia calling her.

Her instinct was to ignore the call. She'd made it quite clear during the party on Saturday that she'd had enough of her mother. Did her mom really think she'd change her mind within two days about that?

As she deliberated over accepting the call, the flashing screen suddenly blinked to darkness. Voicemail had picked it up. Emily watched, looking at her cell to see whether her mom would leave a message. She didn't usually. But sure enough, a minute later, she received a notice saying she had a message.

Feeling a bit shaky with anxiety, Emily dialed her voicemail and listened to the robotic voice telling her she had one new message.

"Emily, it's Mom. I know you said that you didn't want to speak to me again, but listen. What you said about Roy has really shaken me. I'm getting old, as much as I hate to admit it. And I dread dying with us fighting and hating each other. So, I'm sorry. I was wrong. Can I try again? I want to be a good mom. I want to be a grandma. Take your time to think about it, but let's not leave it as we did."

There was a long pause then, the call still connected but Patricia saying nothing. Then she spoke again, words that Emily rarely heard from her mom, words that she'd always so desperately craved.

"I love you."

Then the message cut out. Emily slumped forward, her head on the steering wheel, and wept.

CHAPTER FOURTEEN

By the time Columbus Day arrived, the nursery was complete. Amy had been a great support, helping Emily prepare everything. She put the final load of folded towels into the bottom drawer of the dresser and straightened up.

"That's it." She beamed at Emily. "Everything's set now. Just the baby to come."

Emily could hardly believe that Charlotte was due to meet them in just two months. She already felt like she'd reached full term. It was impossible for her to grow any bigger, surely!

She rested in the nursing chair, putting her feet up on the stool.

"Thanks for all your help," she told Amy. "With Daniel busy running Jack Cooper's and overseeing Stu, Clyde, and Evan for the island construction, I don't think I could have done it without you."

She buttoned her lips once she'd finished speaking, realizing that she was putting a lot of pressure on Amy with the statement. Amy hadn't been sure whether she was going to stick around in Sunset Harbor and Emily didn't want her pregnancy to be a factor in Amy's decision making.

But Amy smiled as she perched on the stool by her feet. "Anything." She smiled. "You're my best friend."

They hadn't spoken much about Harry for a while. After Emily had left Amy behind in New York City, there'd been something of a lull to that particular conversation. Amy had avoided talking about it and Emily assumed she was just trying to sort her own thoughts out without the constant opinions of everyone else clouding her judgment.

As though reading her mind, Amy said, "Things are good between me and Harry now."

Emily let out a breath she hadn't realized she'd been holding. "It is? Oh good. That's a relief."

Amy nodded. "I'm going to be basing myself here. For the time being, anyway. We're going to review things after Thanksgiving."

Emily thought it all sounded a bit formal, but that was Amy's style after all.

They heard the sound of footsteps thudding up the stairs and in rushed Chantelle. She beamed at them excitedly.

"It's time for the parade," she said. "Come on!"

Amy helped Emily to her feet.

"Where's Daddy?" Emily asked.

Chantelle shrugged. "He didn't pick me up from school, so Laverne's mom dropped me off."

Emily exchanged a glance with Amy. It wasn't like Daniel to forget about his responsibilities. And it certainly wasn't like Raven Kingsley to do someone else a favor!

"I'd better give him a call," Emily said.

They went downstairs, Emily having to take it much more slowly now. She used the inn's phone to call Jack Cooper's. Daniel answered the call.

"Sorry, babe, I'm running late," he said.

"I can tell that," Emily replied. "You forgot to pick up Chantelle."

There was stunned silence on the other end. Then the sound of Daniel panicking.

"It's okay!" Emily assured him. "Raven Kingsley gave her a ride home."

"Raven Kingsley?" Daniel said, sounding surprised. "You mean she did someone a favor?"

"I know, it's hard to believe," Emily chuckled. "Anyway, there's no harm done. So will you meet us at the parade?"

"I'm leaving now," Daniel confirmed.

*

The town center was decorated in lots of Italian flags for Columbus Day, and there was a parade. Everyone gathered to watch and cheer them on. As she looked around, Emily realized the crowds were now mainly just locals. The part-time, summer-only residents had entirely cleared out now, leaving just the Sunset Harbor core. It always made Emily feel a little melancholy when the town population shrunk so dramatically. There was a homeliness to it, but also a nostalgia for the summer that had now departed.

Along the harbor front, there were barely any boats. Most people had put them away for fall, especially the residents who had returned to their main homes in other states and other cities. Again, it was only the local folk whose boats remained in the water, and even they were starting to be put away.

Emily spotted Birk from the gas station collecting the waste oils to recycle, as people drained their boats for the winter. Workers from the marina's boat yard were also there, ready to haul boats away for storage. Others were in the process of being shrink-wrapped.

"Are you putting your boat away, Daddy?" Chantelle asked Daniel.

He shook his head. "Not yet. I need it for the renovation work on the island. It's like Stu, Clyde, and Evan's taxi at the moment."

Chantelle giggled. "But won't it break the boat if it stays in the water? What about the ice?"

"It will definitely increase the wear and tear," Daniel told her. "But I'm putting in a great heater system to help."

"Won't it be dangerous?" Chantelle pressed. "Sailing in winter, I mean."

Emily picked up on the anxiety in the girl's voice. Daniel crouched down so he was eye level with Chantelle.

"I will only use it when the weather is good, trust me," Daniel said. "I'll take extra special care of the boat so it doesn't get any cracks or damage from the cold weather, and I won't go out on the water unless the weather is good. Is that a deal?"

Chantelle seemed to relax. She nodded. "Okay." Then, with curiosity, she added, "Can we go to the island today? I haven't seen it all month!"

"Of course," Daniel replied. "The weather's nice today so we may as well use the opportunity."

"Can we have a picnic?" Chantelle added.

"Great idea!" Emily said. She enjoyed any activity that involved eating these days.

They headed to the food stools and stocked up on cornbread and hummus, scampi, sausage patties, olives, and little tubs of pesto pasta. Then they got pumpkin biscuits and a selection of cheeses. Sadly, Emily had to walk right past the cocktail stand. Even only water to wash it all down with, the food smelled delicious and Emily's taste buds watered.

They loaded everything onto the boat and set sail.

*

The boat ride across to the island was pleasant, thanks to the calm waves and the beautiful fall sunshine. Emily loved this weather—crisp days, a cool temperature, clear skies, and rays of sun—especially now she was pregnant. It was the most comfortable she'd been during her pregnancy.

The changes to the island were visible even before they'd made land. The old dock had been replaced with a new one which was sturdier and much more appropriate for the amount of traffic they'd soon be getting. As they got out of the boat and looked around, Emily could see that the frame was already up for the three bedroom cottage. There was a well for water, and solar-powered lights everywhere. There was also a propane generator to provide the emergency power backup.

Emily was in awe. It was really shaping up.

Chantelle was too. She looked thoroughly impressed.

"I didn't know Stu, Clyde, and Evan would be this good," Chantelle said.

Daniel laughed. It was a fair assessment, Emily thought. The view they presented the world of themselves was skewed. They weren't really lazy drifters like they acted. They were as hardworking as Daniel, just still down on their luck as he'd once been. If Emily hadn't arrived and turned the old house into a B&B, Daniel would still be its unofficial groundskeeper, living in the small carriage house earning the occasional buck from growing produce and flowers, living hand to mouth. Like him, his three friends just needed a break, and Emily was glad to have been there to give it to them, like she had been for Daniel.

Once they'd looked around at the progress that had been made on the island, they settled down with their picnic foods and began sampling all the amazing Columbus Day foods.

"I wonder if Harry's had an increase in bookings for this evening," Emily said aloud. The restaurant served authentic Italian food, and Columbus Day was an Italian celebration, after all. "Or maybe it's the opposite. Ninety percent of his staff are Italian so he probably gave them all the day off."

She chuckled. But her musings were met with silence, and when she glanced over at Daniel she saw that he seemed completely lost in his thoughts.

"Did you hear what I said?" she asked him.

He snapped to attention. "No, sorry. What?"

"I was wondering about the restaurant," she said. "About whether Harry's busier because of Columbus Day or whether he's given his staff the night off."

Daniel just shrugged. "I guess we'd have to ask…" he muttered, absentmindedly.

"Honey, you're miles away," Emily said, a little nervous. She hated it when Daniel's mind was in another place. It always made her anxious.

"It's just work," Daniel admitted. A perfectly timed yawn iterated his point. "I'm stressed, you know. And thinking whether it might not be better to run my own woodshop rather than running Jack's after all. I mean, if I'm going to work this hard, I may as well make the money of the owner."

Emily was surprised to hear him say that. Daniel hadn't said anything on the topic since she'd first suggested it, and since he'd been so stressed at the time she hadn't brought it up again. It pleased her to know he'd been mulling it over all this time.

"Well, you know I'll support you whatever you choose to do," she told him.

He nodded and picked at the stones on the ground, flicking them away. "Stu, Clyde, and Evan think I should," he added. "They've seen firsthand how I'm managing this place and think it would be a great idea. They even said they'd work for me full time."

"That's amazing!" Emily exclaimed. It was important that Daniel had friends around him and she was glad the group had reconciled after years of estrangement. Then on second thought she added, "As long as they don't think they can move into the inn or anything."

They'd been pretty respectful guests over the last weeks, quietly rising at dawn and leaving for the island, only to return for the dinner shift before slipping away again for an evening at one of the bars in town. Emily wondered if they were secretly trying to give her space and not make themselves too much of a nuisance. Whatever their reasons, she wasn't prepared to indefinitely give them food and board in exchange for labor.

Daniel went back to his quiet brooding as they finished eating the last of the yummy Columbus Day foods. Above them, the sky was beginning to turn slate gray. Daniel peered up at it.

"I think we should head home," he said. "I did promise to be extra careful about the weather, didn't I, and it looks as though it might be turning."

Chantelle nodded. "Yes, let's go."

"Also," Emily added, "we have an extra special surprise waiting for you at home."

"For me?" Chantelle asked, her eyes brightening with excitement. "But why?"

Emily pressed a finger to her lips. "You'll have to wait and see."

CHAPTER FIFTEEN

Daniel and Emily grinned at each other all the way back to the inn, much to Chantelle's chagrin.

"You have to tell me what the surprise is!" the little girl kept exclaiming from the back seat of the truck. "Please!"

"It makes it more fun this way," Emily kept telling her.

Eventually they pulled in at the inn, and Chantelle saw that the parking lot was filled with cars.

"What's going on?" she asked, sounding more and more excited.

They parked and Chantelle hopped out, rushing up the porch steps and into the inn. Emily and Daniel quickly followed her.

Chantelle made a beeline for the lounge and flung the door open. A chorus of voices erupted from inside.

"Happy birthday!"

Emily caught up with her on the threshold of the room. Inside were all of Chantelle's school friends. The room was filled with rainbow-colored balloons.

Chantelle turned and looked at her parents, her expression one of complete surprise. "But it's not my birthday yet," she stammered.

Daniel spoke. "We know. But we wanted it to be a proper surprise. And we wanted to throw it early this year to make up for what happened last year."

He didn't mention the other reason; Papa Roy's demise. Even though her father had been given a year to live, Emily knew that fate had a habit of intervening. She wanted to play things cautiously, especially when it came to special events like birthdays and Christmas. Whenever a special event approached, she couldn't help agonizing over whether her father would make it, and the closer the date came the worse the feeling was. What if he passed away a week in advance? What about a day? How especially awful would it feel if he passed on one of these days? Such thoughts would circle around and around Emily's mind, driving her crazy with worry. If she had it her way, every single special occasion would be brought forward just to alleviate the possibility of Roy dying on one of them. But she accepted that this wasn't always practical. It had been quite a hard sell to get Daniel to agree to moving Chantelle's birthday a few weeks early, but he'd put his foot down at celebrating Thanksgiving in October.

Luckily, Chantelle didn't seem to think the change of date was strange in the slightest. Emily watched on as she threw her arms around Daniel's waist and hugged him tightly.

"Thank you, Daddy," she said. Then she hugged Emily in turn.

"Come outside and have a look at the lawn," Daniel said to the child.

Emily hadn't thought it possible, but somehow Chantelle's face lit up even more eagerly. She thundered down the corridor—her friends in tow, racing to keep up—and emerged out into the back lawn.

The whole space had been taken over for Chantelle's birthday. Several gazebos had been erected, one with a face-painting booth inside and professional makeup artists hired for the day, another filled with all the finger foods and the enormous carnival-themed cake. There was a mini carnival, a set of fairground rides, a bouncy castle, and a petting zoo filled with rabbits. Even with the weather turning and threatening to shower, Chantelle looked utterly thrilled at the sight, and her mouth dropped open in disbelief.

Her friends seemed just as excited. Everyone screamed and ran around, jostling to be the first to get their faces painted, or to pet the cutest giant rabbit, or to win at the coconut game. Levi and Ryan went straight for the "duck" pond to fish for bright yellow plastic ducks, while Toby had his face turned into Superman. Emily was delighted to see them all enjoying the carnival that she and Daniel had arranged for them. But she still felt a sense of anguish, like an itch that needed to be scratched. Until the prearranged phone call with Papa Roy had taken place she wouldn't get any relief from the constant sense of anticipation.

"We have some very special presents for you," Daniel said, gesturing to the large red picnic tent filled with bales of hay for seating.

He led Chantelle inside the tent to where all her gifts had been piled up. It was a mountain of sparkles and stripes, polka dots and patterns. But Chantelle's attention was immediately caught by something else: the laptop set up on one of the picnic tables.

"Papa Roy?" Chantelle exclaimed, excited.

Emily nodded, finally able to relieve her itch of anguish. "He's on standby to wish you a happy birthday! You just have to dial him."

Chantelle hurried over, more excited to speak to her beloved Papa Roy than she was by the enormous pile of pretty, sparkly wrapped gifts. She hit the green button to dial and bounced up and down with nervous excitement as she waited for Papa Roy to answer. A moment later, his face filled the screen and Emily felt herself able to truly let out her tense breath.

"Happy birthday, Chantelle!" he exclaimed, holding up a handmade banner.

Chantelle dissolved into giggles. "But it's *not* my actual birthday!"

"Oh," he said, feigning disappointment. "Maybe I should get your mom to put your present away until it is then?"

"No!" Chantelle cried, laughing. "I want my present, please, Papa Roy."

Emily went over to the stack of gifts. She'd prepared it this morning so knew which one had come from her father. She fished it out of the pile and brought it to Chantelle. It was a rather heavy, large box. Emily could smell the familiar scent of grease and iron that always accompanied her father.

Chantelle opened it eagerly, ripping off the paper and opening the flaps of the box quickly. Then she gasped.

"What is it, honey?" Daniel asked.

Chantelle reached inside and heaved up a golden object in her arms. Emily could see that it was a clock, an ornate one made of gold. It had Roy's signature design on it, of carved roses.

"I made it," Roy said. "Do you like it?"

Chantelle burst into tears. "I love it, Papa Roy! It's my favorite thing ever!"

She ran over and hugged the laptop. Everyone laughed, touched by the sweet scene.

"I wish I could hug you for real," Chantelle added as she sat back down.

Emily bit her lip guiltily. She'd been dragging her feet over the whole Greece issue. Her father wasn't well enough to travel to them, but she was anxious about speaking to the school about authorizing leave for Chantelle considering how unhelpful they'd been over the Laverne issue, and how embarrassed she felt about blowing up at them all. Plus there was the pregnancy to think about. Emily didn't want to jeopardize her health or Baby Charlotte's health.

"You can come to Greece soon," Papa Roy told her. "Maybe in the new year."

"That's too long!" Chantelle wailed.

Emily felt a tug of anguish in her chest. Too long, and possibly too late.

CHAPTER SIXTEEN

The next big event to come their way was Halloween, Chantelle's actual birthday. Daniel had persuaded Emily that it had to remain on the actual date, because the whole point of Halloween was to enjoy it with other people. Chantelle couldn't exactly run around the neighborhood dressed as a zombie demanding candy any old day of the year! Reluctantly, Emily had agreed that she'd have to wait until October 31 before she could send a ton of cute pictures of Chantelle to Roy.

They devoted the morning to Chantelle's birthday, freeing up the evening for Halloween.

Emily dressed herself in her bedroom, sliding into the jack-o'-lantern outfit that worked perfectly thanks to her round belly. Instead of cutting the black felt into the shape of a grinning ghoul, she instead made it into the shape of a baby, in honor of Charlotte who was sleeping soundly in her stomach, then stuck it on her stomach.

Once she was dressed, she painted her entire face bright orange, then hurried out of her bedroom to see how Chantelle was getting on with her costume. The little girl had decided to dress as Storm from the X-Men this year, with Toby, Levi, and Ryan all agreeing to the theme—as Wolverine, Beast, and Gambit respectively.

Emily and Chantelle bumped into each other on the landing.

"You look amazing!" Emily exclaimed, seeing Chantelle in her silver wig, long silver gloves, and black cape for the first time.

Chantelle giggled. "Your costume is perfect." She beamed. She patted the image of Baby Charlotte.

They went downstairs and threw themselves into decorating the inn. Since it was quiet at the moment with the only guests booked in staying at Trevor's, they didn't hold back. Not that the guests ever seemed to mind when Chantelle allowed her creativity to flow during the public holidays, Emily thought, but this year Daniel was extra busy with work and Emily wanted to make sure Chantelle's mind was occupied. So they turned the whole place into a nightmare grotto with black paper on the walls, papier maché rocks (homemade) dotted all over the place, and fake spider webs in every corner. It was a tremendous—and terrifying—achievement.

They'd decided to invite all the kids to the inn for a party. Most of the other parents didn't have as much space in their homes to host so many kids, and they certainly didn't allow their children to turn their entire homes into nightmare grottos, so it made sense to host it at the inn. Besides, Emily loved it when the place was full of joy, and anything that made Chantelle happy was worth the effort.

She and Chantelle were just putting candy into a bowl shaped like a skull when the doorbell rang. Emily looked up and grinned at Chantelle.

"Our first guests have arrived," she said.

They stopped what they were doing, discarding the bags of candy on the counter, and hurried to the front door. Emily flung it open. To her surprise, their first guest was none other than Raven Kingsley and Laverne. The skinny, blond child had dressed up as a Victorian-era ghost. With her solemn expression she genuinely looked like one, and Emily felt a chill run up her spine.

She looked at Chantelle and frowned. "Laverne's here," she said, surprised.

Chantelle nodded. "I invited everyone in my class," she explained.

Emily shouldn't have been surprised to learn that her daughter had been nice enough to invite her bully; it was quite typical of her sweet-hearted nature. She just wished that she'd been forewarned. Raven Kingsley was a stickler for time and would obviously be the first to arrive, and Emily would have appreciated a chance to mentally prepare herself for that eventuality. Making small talk with Raven would be a challenge.

"Come in," Emily said, turning on her polite hostess persona.

Mother and daughter stepped inside, looking around them at the ghoulish decorations. Neither looked particularly impressed with what they saw, and Emily had to stifle a giggle at their matching snooty expressions.

"Chantelle, let's fix our guests some drinks," she said. "Worm juice for Laverne and a glass of blood for Raven."

They giggled together as they led the two down the corridor to the punch bowl of neon green Gatorade. Chantelle scooped out a ladle full and filled a plastic cup with it, handing it to Laverne while Emily poured a glass of red wine for Raven. She wasn't sure, but she thought she saw a hint of an amused smile on Raven's lips as she passed her the fresh "blood."

"Are you excited about your first Sunset Harbor trick-or-treat?" Emily asked Laverne.

The child remained mute and just shrugged.

"Here, let's start you off," Emily added. She scooped up one of the candy bars that had fallen on the counter and popped it into Laverne's sack.

"Thanks," the child mumbled.

"Laverne's not allowed candy," Raven explained. "We're donating anything that isn't sugar free to charity."

"How lovely," Emily said, feeling bad for the poor kid. "I have some fruit if you'd like that."

Raven shot Emily a deadpan expression. "Fruit has sugar in it, Emily. As much as any candy bar. We only have blueberries in our house, and only on special occasions."

"Oh," Emily said, feeling put in her place. She hurriedly put the banana she'd picked up back in the fruit bowl. "I suppose you won't be drinking the worm juice either," she added, noting how Laverne had discarded the cup on the counter without even attempting to take a sneaky sip when her mom wasn't looking. She was well trained, clearly.

"I may as well admit I had an ulterior motive for coming here," Raven said in her overly loud, brash voice. "I wanted to check out the competition."

Emily squirmed uncomfortably. It was hard enough for her to dredge up any compassion for Raven, and thinking of her as her competitor certainly didn't help matters.

"And?" Emily asked. "What do you think?"

"I think there's space in the market for what we're both offering. You've gone the whole... shabby chic route. I'm more modernism. You can do the weddings and funerals and whatnot, and I'll hold all the corporate events."

"Great," Emily muttered through her fake grin, seeing straight through the back-handed compliments.

"Except there's going to be a town meeting before I can get permission to do any work," Raven said, rolling her eyes, clearly thinking she was above such a thing. "I assume it's held in a barn or some kind of shack made of wood." She cackled.

Emily thought of their charming town hall. "Bricks and mortar, actually," she said through gritted teeth.

Just then, the doorbell rang. At last, Emily thought. Saved by the bell. She hurried to answer it, Chantelle following right behind her.

"Why did you invite Laverne?" she whispered out the side of her mouth as they went, unable to hide the air of exasperation. "I thought you hated her."

"I realized that she was just scared," Chantelle whispered back. "I figured it would be mean not to ask her to come just because she's too scared to talk to people."

Emily felt humbled by Chantelle. She decided to take a leaf out of her book and be kinder to Raven. Maybe her spiky persona was a defense mechanism.

They answered the door to the rest of Chantelle's friends, all dressed as various superheroes. They all looked fantastic.

"Come in, come in," Emily exclaimed. "Help yourselves to worm juice!"

Everyone piled inside, talking animatedly and enthusiastically to one another. They grabbed drinks and stuffed handfuls of chips and carrot sticks into their mouths.

Emily walked up to Logan and Suzanna, who were chatting at the kitchen counter. Suzanna was wearing a black cat suit and matching ears, her slim frame looking amazing in the costume. Emily didn't expect herself to bounce back into shape quite as remarkably as Suzanna had. She must have amazing genes.

She hugged them both.

"How are you?" she asked Logan excitedly. It was the first time she'd seen him since Holly's announcement. He was holding Minnie on his hip and the toddler was wearing a beautiful fairy costume. Logan himself was dressed as a pirate.

"Good, thanks," he said, his attention half on Emily and half on Levi, who was charging around like a bull in a china shop. "Excellent decorations as usual," he added.

"Thanks," Emily laughed. "Daniel's working tonight so I wanted to make it extra special for Chantelle. No Holly?"

"Oh, uh no," Logan said. "She's sick."

Emily wasn't sure but she thought she picked something up in her friend's voice. "I'm sorry to hear that. I hope she gets better soon."

"Thanks," Logan muttered. Then he headed away to catch Levi before he tripped over his own feet.

"Are you ready to trick-or-treat?" Emily asked Suzanna, turning her attention to her.

"I certainly am." Suzanna grinned. She rocked her stroller back and forth. Inside, Robin was sleeping, dressed in a cute caterpillar onesie.

"You have to tell me where you got that," Emily gushed. "It's adorable."

"You can have it," Suzanna said. "He'll have grown out of it in a week. They grow so fast."

Emily felt a tingle of excitement. She couldn't wait to meet her own little one.

She herded everyone together and then they headed out onto the streets. Emily saw Yvonne up ahead walking with Raven. It had been a while since they'd last spoken. Emily hadn't been able to call Yvonne after the bullying incident. It had hurt her, too, to know that Bailey could cast Chantelle aside like that, even if the whole thing had been Laverne's fault. But she thought that Yvonne could have had the good grace to call and discuss everything rather than sweeping it under the carpet and avoiding Emily altogether.

Swallowing her nerves, she went up to them now, feeling very much like she herself was the school kid.

"Nice costume," she said to Yvonne. "Is it a Mexican sugar skull?"

"Yup," Yvonne replied. "Orange suits you."

"Thanks," Emily said. She was feeling a little stilted. "What did Bailey come as? I haven't seen her yet."

"Medusa," Yvonne laughed. "Her fairy phase is well and truly over!"

"Laverne never had one of those, thank God," Raven added wryly.

Just then, someone started wailing loudly. They looked ahead and saw that Bailey had fallen. Yvonne hurried off to tend to her daughter, who was rubbing a grazed knee, wearing an expression of distress that the world could be so unjust.

So much for catching up with Yvonne, Emily thought. Now it was just her and Raven. Again.

Emily looked over at Raven, a little awkward. But she remembered Chantelle's words of wisdom and tried to remain cordial. They had stuff in common after all, both having left big city life for the intimacy of a small town.

"How are you finding it living here?" Emily asked Raven. "Bit of a shock to the system, huh?"

"Honestly," Raven began, "I'd be enjoying it a whole lot more if my ex-husband wasn't being such an ass."

"Oh, I'm sorry," Emily said. "Do you want to talk about it?"

Raven let out a bitter laugh. "Not much to talk about. He swapped me for a younger version, a plucky Spanish girl over here to learn English. She's nineteen. *Nineteen*. It's disgusting. And now he wants half of our money. No doubt to buy her clothes and take her on vacation. Meanwhile, it's like he's forgotten the kids even exist. I shouldn't be surprised. He did the same thing with his first wife. She warned me that he'd do the same to me but I was an idiot and thought I was special." She sighed heavily.

Emily could hardly believe it. Her heart swelled with compassion for Raven.

"I came here after a breakup, too" she revealed. "Not to the same extent, but I was in pain. This town is a great place to heal. Everyone is kind and loving. They'll bend over backwards to help you, if you just ask."

Raven pursed her lips. "I'm not one to ask for help."

"I get it," Emily replied. "I was the same. It takes some getting used to. But you could always offer something first. There's a reason I host these things," she added with a chuckle. "The amount of playdates we've had for Chantelle. It's a Godsend, really, when you need a break there's always someone to help."

Raven Kingsley frowned like the concept was alien to her. "I don't need playdates. If I need someone to look after the kids I just leave them with the nanny."

Okay, so they didn't have *that* much in common, Emily thought. But she realized that even if she and Raven were rivals, she could still feel compassion for her. She couldn't envisage them being friends, exactly, but they could certainly be friendly acquaintances.

They wandered on through the neighborhood, laughing with delight at all the terrifying decorations. Soon, the kids' bags began to bulge with sugary treats.

Just then, Emily noticed Logan hurrying over. Minnie was bawling and Levi looked extremely unhappy as he hop-skipped to keep up with his father.

"We have to head home now," Logan said. He looked extremely stressed.

"Don't go," Emily said, concerned. "We can cheer these two grumpy pants up if that's the problem."

"It's not that," Logan said with a harried voice. He lowered his tone and said in Emily's ear, "It's Holly. She's … she lost the baby."

Emily drew back and gasped. "No! I'm so sorry."

"I shouldn't have come," Logan said. "She insisted. But I can't deal with these two on my own right now."

"Why don't you go back and be with her? I can keep an eye on them."

"Thanks," Logan said, "but it's okay. I might not have the patience for their tantrums right now, but I want them close, you know?"

Emily nodded, fully understanding what Logan was saying. She watched as he disappeared into the blackness, utterly stunned by the news. She felt terrible for Holly. Life was so unfair. It could be so cruel. They didn't deserve to go through this.

Something about the news made Emily feel very fragile. What if something went wrong with Charlotte? There really were no guarantees in life. Just like she and Daniel had been doing for weeks, Holly and Logan must have made preparations. At the very least they'd have discussed names. And now that child was never going to get to exist.

She yearned, suddenly, for her mother. It wasn't often that Emily wanted Patricia's attention, mainly because it was always unpleasant. When she needed affection, her mom often just made her feel terrible about herself. But the voicemail she'd left the other day had been different. It really sounded as if something might have changed in her mind.

Would it be a terrible idea to call her? Had she really changed like her voicemail suggested? The draw for her mom was like a magnet. They were bonded through blood and DNA. Nothing could break that, not even Emily screaming at Patricia that she never wanted to see her again.

She mulled it over the whole rest of the evening, feeling stunned by the news of Holly's miscarriage. When they got back to the inn and the kids started counting their steals, Emily retreated to the porch with her cell phone. She dialed her mom's number.

"I didn't think you'd call again," Patricia said in her clipped tone.

"Mom," Emily said, and to her surprise, she started to cry.

Even more surprising was Patricia's response. "What's wrong, darling?" she said, softly.

"My friend had a miscarriage," Emily said. "And now I'm worried about Charlotte. And then there's Dad. Why do people have to die?"

"I know," her mom replied. "It's not fair. Especially when it's innocent babies. Or good men, like your father."

Emily paused. She'd never heard her mom call Roy a good man before. Usually he was a useless man, or an evil man, or an irresponsible man. Never a good one.

She didn't know what to say. But then she heard the sound of her mom sobbing softly.

"Mom?" she said. "Are you okay?"

"Yes," came the sad reply. "I just can't believe it about Roy. You must be devastated."

"I am," Emily replied.

Her mom didn't usually think of how things would affect Emily. She seemed unable to realize that anyone other than herself could be affected by life events. The fact that she'd been able to this time made Emily feel able to open up even more.

"I keep thinking about how each event will be the last one," she continued. "Like this is his last Halloween. Next it's Thanksgiving and that will be his last one of those, too. He wants us to visit him but Chantelle doesn't have a vacation until Christmas and Charlotte will be too small to take on a plane."

"But you must, darling," Patricia said. "It's far more important that Chantelle see her grandfather than learn about fractions. Honestly, she's so bright you'll be able to teach her everything she missed in an afternoon anyway. I doubt her public school is giving her much of an education."

Emily couldn't help but laugh. Patricia may have surprised her with her soft side, but she was the same snooty woman underneath!

"You really think we should go?" Emily asked her. But then she sighed, thinking with anguish about asking the school for time off. "I don't know how to approach the topic with the school."

"What's the worst that can happen?" Patricia said. "Just tell them what's going on with your father. They ought to authorize an absence for that. And if they don't, just call in and say she's got norovirus. They wouldn't dare challenge that and risk all the students and staff catching it."

In her own way, Patricia was offering support and comfort. Emily felt like her mom had wrapped warm arms around her for the first time. And though she wasn't prepared to lie to the school and say Chantelle had a vomiting bug, she should be brave and tell them about the circumstances and ask for the time off. The worst thing that could happen would be a no. Then perhaps she could revert to Patricia's slightly more wacky plan.

"Maybe you're right," Emily said.

"Darling, I'm your mother," came Patricia's reply. "Of course I'm right."

CHAPTER SEVENTEEN

Emily woke the next morning with her mind in a fog. She couldn't stop thinking about Holly and her devastating miscarriage. But it was also the conversation with Patricia last night that was playing on her mind.

"What's up?" Daniel asked tenderly as he rolled over in bed.

Emily saw the furrow in his brows. "I'm just thinking about life," she said.

Daniel chuckled. "At seven in the morning? Before coffee?"

Emily smiled wanly.

"Want to share your worries?" Daniel added, touching her arm lightly.

Emily sighed. "Would it be crazy to go to Greece?" she asked him.

Daniel rubbed his chin. "From a pregnancy point of view? Not really. Doctor Arkwright said it was safe. But it's taking Chantelle out of school for it that's the issue."

"Right," Emily said with a nod. "So you think it would be crazy?"

"Personally, no. I just don't think the school would approve. At least not without knowing everything." He touched his fingertips to her back. Daniel knew full well that Emily was reticent to reveal her business to the school. "Why are you asking?" he added.

Emily turned to fully face him. "Because I think it's more important for Chantelle to make memories with Roy than be at school."

Daniel pulled an expression that Emily struggled to read. It seemed approving on the surface, but there was something like reticence beneath.

"Then you should go," he said. "I'll support you whatever you choose. Chantelle's a smart cookie. She'll catch up what she's missed in no time."

Emily was surprised to hear this from Daniel. Considering how busy he was at work, not putting a fight up over taking time off seemed a little out of character. She wondered whether that was what she'd seen in his eyes, if that's what the reticence was. He didn't want to let Jack down but was putting his family first anyway. She smiled as it dawned on her that that must be the truth.

"I really don't want to speak to Mrs. Doyle," she said with a sigh. "I don't want such a sour-faced shrew knowing about my dad's illness."

Daniel laughed heartily. "Sour-faced shrew? That's original." Then he stroked her shoulders tenderly. "I'm sure she'll be understanding. Just take a deep breath and speak from the heart."

Emily felt bolstered by Daniel's support. She really hadn't been expecting it. At the very least she thought he'd try to defer the trip. But he seemed completely on board.

With a sudden tingle of determination, she got out of bed and wrapped her dressing gown about her. She took her cell phone downstairs and went out onto the porch—her favorite place to make difficult telephone calls—then dialed the school's number. When the receptionist answered the call, she remembered her earlier resolve to be kinder to the girl who had gone out of her way to remember Emily by name.

"Hey, Tilly, it's Chantelle Morey's mom."

"Emily, hey," Tilly replied brightly. "Is everything okay? Chantelle hasn't picked up the norovirus, has she? I've already taken five calls for sick kids this morning!"

Emily recalled Patricia's scheme, briefly considering taking the easy way out, then quickly changed her mind. She didn't want to take the coward's approach. She wanted to face this like an adult. It was ludicrous for her to be nervous of Mrs. Doyle.

"Actually, I was hoping to speak with Mrs. Doyle," she said confidently. "It's about some family circumstances."

"Can I pass on a message to her?" Tilly asked. "She's very busy, as you know, and doesn't usually take parent calls before school unless they're urgent. I could probably get her to call you once the school day is over if it can wait."

Emily chewed her lip as she deliberated. It would be so easy to hang up now and use Patricia's deceitful—yet, ultimately, *easy*—approach, and avoid the whole unpleasantness of sharing her life experiences with a stranger. But she'd geared herself up for this moment. It was now or never. Chantelle and Papa Roy deserved to see each other. She, too, deserved to see her father. It was time to bite the bullet.

"Tilly, if I explain to you what the situation is, will you be very careful to keep it confidential? Because Chantelle doesn't even know this yet."

"Of course," Tilly replied whole-heartedly. "I'll write the memo and take it straight to Mrs. Doyle's in-tray. I can seal it in an envelope if you'd like."

Emily felt relieved to know Tilly would take the issue seriously. She took a deep breath, steadying her heart rate.

"My father…" she began, and immediately her voice cracked from the strain she felt. She tried again, swallowing the hard lump in her throat. "Chantelle's grandfather has been diagnosed with a terminal illness. Cancer."

There was a pause on the other end of the line, then a small gasp.

"Gosh, I'm so sorry," Tilly said. Her voice sounded small.

"Thank you," Emily replied, her own voice quivering from the effort of holding back her emotions. "The thing is he lives abroad so we see him very rarely. There's no vacation until Christmas and …" Her voice cracked again. "I'm worried that it will be too late if we leave it until then."

Emily wasn't sure but she thought she heard Tilly sniffle on the end of the line. Was she crying?

"I know we don't know each other that well, Emily, but can I tell you something?" Tilly asked.

Emily frowned, confused. This wasn't how she'd expected this telephone call to go at all.

"Um...okay," she said, uncertain.

"I just found out my mother has cancer," Tilly said.

"Oh," Emily said with a shocked hiccup. Immediately she felt her throat thicken with unhappiness. She felt terrible for Tilly, and a deep empathy that seemed to stretch across the distance between them from her heart to Tilly's. They didn't know each other and yet they were suddenly bonded by one of the cruelest blows fate could give. "I'm so sorry, I truly am."

"Thank you," Tilly said with an intake of breath. "That's the first time I've said it out loud. Sorry for offloading."

"Not at all," Emily said genuinely. "It's important to share, to get things out."

"I only found out last night."

"Have you told Mrs. Doyle yet?"

"I was going to ask for some leave once the day was over," Tilly replied. "I know she hates to be disturbed in the morning with anything that's not urgent."

Emily could hear the strain in her voice. But, suddenly, it grew bolder.

"You know what?" Tilly said. "I am going to do it right now. I'm going to tell her about my mom and your dad."

"Oh," Emily said, taken aback. "I don't want you to get in any trouble on my account."

"I'm not going to sit here all day stewing on it," Tilly replied. "I'm doing it right now."

Hold music began to play, a piercing tune that made Emily wince and move the phone inches away from her ear. She felt a surge of shame for how long she herself had stewed on this without taking action. She should have spoken to Mrs. Doyle right away. She should have introduced herself to Miss Butler on that very first morning and told her everything about their current circumstances. Instead, she'd missed her chance and then made a dreadful first impression, and her own anxiety about facing that embarrassment head on had caused uncertainty for everyone in her family.

As she was berating herself in her mind, the hold music suddenly cut out.

"Tilly?" Emily asked. "How did it go?"

"This is Mrs. Doyle speaking," the stern voice replied.

Emily instinctively straightened her back. "Mrs. Doyle, good morning. I didn't mean to interrupt you. Did Tilly pass on my message?"

"She did," Mrs. Doyle replied. "Of course you can take Chantelle on leave. Family always comes first. I lost my own father to cancer many years ago so I fully understand what you're going through."

Emily was stunned. Though Mrs. Doyle was being supportive, and giving her exactly what she wanted, she said it with the sort of forcefulness of a drill sergeant. Emily realized then that her barky mannerisms were just how she spoke. She wasn't a sour shrew after all. She was just, well, a school principal!

"We can really take her out of school?" Emily asked, a little too shocked to believe it. "Right away?"

"Yes, if that's what you need. I'll put it in writing and send a copy of the letter home for your own records if you want. The other will be filed here."

"That's..." Emily faltered, not knowing what to say. "Very kind of you. Chantelle will be thrilled when I tell her."

In her ever-efficient manner, Mrs. Doyle replied, "I'm sure she will. Good day to you, Emily."

The line didn't cut out but instead went back to the same shrill hold music as before. But this time it didn't make Emily wince.

This time she hardly heard it at all. She was too busy floating on cloud nine to care.

"Emily?" came Tilly's breathless voice. "What did she say?"

"She said yes," Emily told her. "What about you?"

"I'm being given compassionate leave for a week," Tilly replied.

It felt like a victory, but Emily reminded herself it was a hollow one. Nothing would save their parents' lives. But at least they'd been gifted some more precious time to spend with them.

"Tilly, you and your mom should come to the spa here," Emily said. "Have a pamper session on me. As a thanks for your help today."

Tilly let out a cough of emotion. "You'd do that for us? That would be lovely. I can never usually afford those kinds of treats!"

Emily grinned to herself, feeling very satisfied. "I think you deserve it."

"Thank you!" Tilly cried.

They ended the call and Emily felt more confident than ever. She'd faced her fear and got what she'd wanted. She'd even made a new friend in the process. It couldn't have gone better really.

Excited to break the news to the family, she hurried inside, following the sound of their voices to the kitchen. They were seated at the kitchen table, absorbed in breakfast eating (Daniel) and clock making (Chantelle).

"I have an announcement," she said from the threshold of the door, clasping her hands together with excitement.

Daniel looked up from his plate. "You're pregnant!" he quipped.

Chantelle dissolved into giggles.

"Ha. Ha," Emily said, deadpan. "Nope. We're going to Greece!"

Chantelle clapped a hand over her mouth in surprise. "All of us? You, me, and Daddy?"

Emily nodded, grinning from ear to ear, glad to be the bearer of good news for once.

"All of us?" Daniel repeated, his eyebrows immediately drawing together.

Emily was confused to see his expression. He looked panic-stricken. But hadn't they discussed it just this morning? She couldn't understand his reaction. Maybe he'd only supported her in calling the school because he'd never expected her to succeed in getting time off for Chantelle.

"Can we call Papa Roy and tell him?" Chantelle asked, bouncing up and down.

"Of course," Emily said. "Why don't you go and fetch the laptop?"

Chantelle didn't need telling twice. She leapt up from the table, scattering cogs and springs in her haste, then thundered out the room.

The second she was gone, Emily turned to Daniel.

"What's wrong?" she asked. "You look as if you've seen a ghost."

Daniel muttered something Emily couldn't hear, as though he were struggling to find the right words. Finally he overcame his tied tongue. "I thought it would be you and Chantelle going. I didn't realize you meant me as well."

Now it was Emily's turn to frown. "What do you mean? We literally just spoke about this. Why would I just mean me and Chantelle?"

Daniel rubbed a hand through his hair. "I just assumed because of my work and everything…"

Emily couldn't help but react with frustration. She'd known that something wasn't right by how readily Daniel had agreed to the vacation in the first place. Now she understood why. Once again, he'd failed to realize that his husbandly duties meant putting his family before his work. He'd probably been looking forward to a week alone, for beer with the boys, maybe even some flirting with Astrid.

"Well then don't come," Emily said, folding her arms. "If your job matters more."

Daniel opened his mouth to protest, but there was no chance to continue the conversation because Chantelle bounded back into the room, the laptop tucked under her arm. She set it up on the table.

"Let me do it," Daniel murmured, busying himself in the task, typically seeking any distraction he could find.

The call connected and began ringing. Emily felt a bitter taste in the back of her mouth. Daniel had ruined her moment. The high she'd been on after her victory call had been replaced with weariness.

When Papa Roy answered, his sallow-cheeked face filling the screen, Chantelle couldn't contain herself.

"We're coming to Greece!" she yelled.

Papa Roy's expression transformed into one of utter surprise. "You are? When?" he asked.

Chantelle frowned. "I don't know." She looked over at her parents. "When?"

Daniel's face was turned down to his cell phone. Emily saw he was searching for flights. For two seats or three? she wondered.

"There's some for tomorrow," he said, looking up.

Chantelle's eyes bulged. Papa Roy couldn't stop from grinning. "That sounds perfect," he said.

Emily raised an eyebrow at Daniel; a not-so-subtle gesture.

"So?" she said, directing her words at him like an arrow. "What's the plan? Are we *all* flying out tomorrow?"

She left no doubt in her tone what she wanted him to do. No, what she *expected* him to do, for her, for Chantelle, for the family.

"Yeah," he said, sounding less than thrilled. "Tomorrow."

Emily turned to her father on the screen and nodded with satisfied determination.

"Tomorrow."

CHAPTER EIGHTEEN

The flight to Greece was going to take over eight hours. Emily wasn't particularly looking forward to it, especially since their last flight abroad—to Cornwall, in England—had made her extremely sick. Chantelle, too, had been something of a handful last time around. Occupying an eight-year-old, especially an extremely energetic one like Chantelle, was no easy task. And then there was the issue of *Daniel.*

She hadn't spoken to him about the misunderstanding yesterday. Partially because she'd been too busy arranging everything at the inn for their week-long absence, and he, in turn, was arranging the same with his work. But it was always because she just didn't want to have that same fight with him over again. They'd been through this before, with Daniel failing to see where his priorities lay, forgetting that his presence in their family's life was worth more to them than whatever money he earned. It didn't seem fair that it would always fall to her to tell him, either. He needed to realize on his own accord to put them first. Otherwise she'd become a nagging fish wife, like her mom had been. That was the last thing she wanted to be.

The family waited at the boarding gate, each one of their carry-on bags filled with activities for Chantelle. Coloring books, electronic games, stories, reams of paper for drawing and writing, puzzle books filled with sudoku and word searches, a magnetic mini-chess set, snacks, drinks, earplugs (in the rare event she decided to nap), paper dolls, fuzzy felt, the list was endless. Emily and Daniel only had space in their carry-on luggage for one book each, but of course one book each was all they needed to distract themselves from each other.

The gate opened then and the family had their boarding passes checked. Then they headed onto the aircraft. It was an Airbus, and Emily had never flown on anything so large. It was quite exciting, and looked very modern which set her slight nerves at ease.

Luckily they had window seats and they slid into them, putting Chantelle in the middle, partly so they could take it in turns to entertain her, Emily reasoned in her mind, but also so the little girl could act as a buffer between them.

Once seated, Emily realized that soon their little family would no longer fit in the usual three-seat row of an airplane. Once Baby Charlotte arrived, they'd need to split into a new configuration, with one adult beside each child. She smiled to herself at the million tiny ways their new child would change their lives, at all the things she'd not yet considered.

Emily took the window seat in the hope that seeing the outside world would help with her motion sickness.

The plane soon filled up, and it was extremely noisy and busy. There seemed to be a larger than usual number of children on board, and Emily realized with a little burst of despair that they were on a flight with a school class.

"I never got to go to Greece when I was at school!" Emily said to Daniel, breaking the silence that had been following them for hours. "We thought a trip to Central Park was a luxury. Besides, I would have been terrified to go abroad without my parents. Those kids look too young to be going on vacation without mom and dad to supervise."

Daniel looked a little confused, probably because Emily had decided to break her silent spell with inane chatter, but he took it nonetheless.

"Just think of the poor teachers," Daniel replied. "We need two adults and three bags of games just to entertain one child!"

The sound of the airplane engines increased, whirring in that way that made Emily feel equal parts exhilarated and nervous. The flight attendants took to the aisles and began their safety demonstration. Emily always watched it intently; it usually calmed her and made her feel at least a semblance of control over the situation.

As the demonstration continued, they began to taxi to the runway. The group of school kids yelled and made a ruckus. Emily wished the teachers could quiet them down. It always made her more nervous to hear others' nerves!

The flight attendants finished their announcements and walked down the aisles, checking that everyone's belts were buckled. Chantelle grinned at the young man who checked hers.

"I did it myself," she told him proudly. "I remembered how from the last time I went to see Papa Roy. But that was in England and this time it's Greece."

Emily caught the flight attendant's eye and smiled. Chantelle seemed compelled to make friends with everyone she ever came into contact with, to speak proudly about her grandfather. But he was clearly used to it. He gave her a thumbs-up and then moved on to the next row.

The plane bumped along and then slowed. Emily realized that meant they'd reached the runway. She instinctively held onto the armrests.

The flight attendants sat down and buckled themselves in. Quiet descended over the aircraft in anticipation of the terrifying yet miraculous experience of flight.

She felt Chantelle's hand on top of hers.

"Don't worry, Mommy," she said, confidently. "It might feel a bit strange but it's perfectly safe."

Emily couldn't help but smile. She saw Daniel looking over with pride. She allowed her iciness to thaw somewhat. Being angry with Daniel was exhausting, especially when she knew deep down that she'd hit gold with him. She just wished he didn't keep testing her patience.

The engines roared and they accelerated forward, juddering along the runway, picking up speed. Then Emily felt the almost impossible sensation of the plane lifting, of the friction beneath its wheels disappearing as they took to the sky.

She looked out the window, at the airport as it shrunk before her very eyes, disorientingly, almost unfathomably. It was true that it felt very strange to fly, but the fact was these miraculous vehicles had given her another chance to see her father again, and that was worth all the discomfort in the world.

*

They touched down at Kalamata International Airport eight hours later, tired but excited for the vacation ahead.

Just like their last meeting, Roy was to collect them from the airport. As they staggered from the plane, stiff after hours being cooped up onboard, Chantelle immediately began scanning the vicinity.

"We have to get through passport control first!" Daniel told her, laughing. "Then baggage reclaim!"

But Chantelle could barely contain herself. She tugged on his hand, trying to pull him through the crowds. She was like Mogsy straining against her leash to chase a squirrel.

As they passed a large window, Chantelle began to point and leap up and down. "I see Papa Roy!"

Emily peered across and realized Chantelle was right. The arrivals area of the airport could be seen far below them through the glass window, though how she'd picked Roy out of the crowds was beyond Emily. From here, he looked like just another stick figure.

Chantelle began banging on the glass.

"Stop that," Daniel told her sternly. "He won't be able to hear you."

Chantelle did as she was told, but the fleeting glimpse of her adored Papa Roy seemed to make her even more eager to get through the crowds. She couldn't stand still, constantly craning her head to see how long the queues were moving, complaining that they'd chosen the slowest one. Just listening to her was exasperating. Ten minutes in the queue was more tiring than eight hours on the plane, Emily thought.

Finally they made it through the gates and out to the luggage claim area. Here, Chantelle became more like a stick of dynamite waiting to explode. Finally, Daniel had had enough.

"Okay, you take Chantelle out to find Papa Roy," he said to Emily in a huffy tone. "I'll wait for the luggage."

Emily knew it wasn't fair to expect Daniel to carry all three of their cases but at the same time she could tell that a respite from Chantelle, even of five minutes, was needed. She took the child's hand and nodded.

They went together out into the arrivals lounge. Once again, Chantelle seemed to possess X-ray vision, because she blurted out, "It's-Papa-Roy," in one hurried, slurred breath, let go of Emily's hand, and disappeared.

Emily floundered momentarily, feeling a horrible sensation in her chest of having lost her daughter. But it abated within a second when the crowds shifted and revealed Chantelle ahead, running at full force into Papa Roy's open arms.

Emily sighed, relieved to know Chantelle was safe, relieved also to be in the presence of her father one more time. But as she walked toward them, she noted how much sicker he looked now. He was even more frail looking than he had been in England, his knees and elbows looking big and knobby in his now baggy clothes. It hurt Emily to see her father withering away before her very eyes.

But his manner was jovial, she could tell as she approached. He was smiling broadly at Chantelle, speaking to her in a bright tone. His illness may be robbing him of his physical strength, but mentally he was sharper than ever.

Emily reached his side, a huge swell of emotion taking hold of her. She hadn't realized how much she'd been bottling up Roy's illness until she was confronting it in the flesh. Even during their video calls and numerous correspondences she hadn't allowed herself to reach those raw places, those deeply buried pains. But with Roy standing in front of her, literally half the man he'd been before, she had no choice but to confront the reality of his impending death.

"Daddy," she whispered, throwing her arms around his neck.

In her mind she felt as vulnerable as a child, but it was her father who felt fragile in her arms, small and kidlike. She knew she'd have to be strong for him, to take on the role of parent again just as she'd promised to do last time she'd seen him. She would not go to pieces, because it was so clear to her how much her father needed her right now.

"Where's Daniel?" Roy asked as he released his arms from around Emily.

"Waiting for the luggage," she told him. Then she ruffled Chantelle's hair. "Someone was a bit too eager to see her Papa Roy to wait patiently."

Roy smiled, pleased. He looped Chantelle's arm through his and together they paraded across the concourse. Roy pointed out all the signs, explaining the Greek alphabet to Chantelle as he went. She listened eagerly, far more entertained by Roy's knowledge than she had been by any of the toys, movies, or games that Emily and Daniel had bombarded her with on the flight.

Finally, Daniel joined them, dragging their wheeled cases along with his strong arms. When he reached Roy, they shook hands first, but it quickly turned into an embrace. Emily always loved to see the two of them together, knowing that without her father Daniel would have become a completely different man, perhaps a man she would never have chosen to marry and make a life with. Once again, she felt another crack in the stony facade she'd been wearing since yesterday's misunderstanding. It really was amazing how much time was a healer.

"Is everyone ready for some sunshine?" Roy asked the family.

"We've been having an Indian summer," Emily told him, "so we're not in fall mode quite yet."

"Indian summer or not," Roy replied, "the Greek heat is like no other!"

Chantelle seemed enthused at the thought. They followed Roy out of the airport and into the blistering sunshine.

"Okay, I see what you mean," Emily said, instantly shielding her face with her hand.

As they strolled through the parking lot, Roy reached into the satchel slung around his shoulder.

"Good thing I bought everyone one of these," he said, producing a baseball cap.

He handed it to Emily, then pulled out another for Daniel. Daniel turned it over in his hands, a little dubious, before finally getting into the spirit of things and placing it on his head. Chantelle took her cap eagerly and plopped it on at a wonky angle. Finally, Roy put his own cap on. They looked like a baseball team, and Emily couldn't help but find the whole thing thoroughly amusing.

They climbed into Roy's car and began the hour-long drive to Proastio, the cliffside village where Roy resided. The city of Kalamata seemed very beautiful itself, but it was when they drove out onto the main freeway that Emily really got a sense for why her father had fallen in love with this part of the world.

In an instant they'd gone from a bustling city with cars and cafes, shops and honking buses, to bumpy, single-track roads with no markings, lined with trees, and barely another soul in sight. There wasn't much grass, and what was there was a scorched, faded color as though parched. The sight made her instantly thirsty.

They passed a property, a humble-looking stone cottage surrounded by a chain-link fence, then carried along the road another five minutes before they reached the next house. It seemed that the farther they traveled from the city, the farther apart the houses were. Five minutes from your closest neighbor, six minutes, seven, until the houses were few and far between.

There were many churches on the route, too, nestled into the cliffsides, made of the same kind of dusty stone as the old properties. The place was craggy and rustic, with overgrown bushes growing either side of the potholed roads. Emily noticed that there were no roads signs, street lamps, or road markings.

They climbed further and further up the cliffsides, zigzagging at strange angles, until the view of the ocean was breathtaking and magical. Finally, Papa Roy turned into the driveway of a stone cottage with a balcony.

"Is this your house, Papa Roy?" Chantelle asked excitedly.

"It is," Roy said, parking.

There were baobab trees in the garden, which was also filled with flowers and lemon trees, with a brick-bordered pond to the side. As for the cottage, it had a beautiful arch over the front door, a balcony, a turreted roof, and wooden shutters over the windows. Just like his Cornwall house, his Greek one was completely suited to Roy's personality.

"Shall I show everyone around?" Roy said.

They all went inside. The interior of the house was very much in keeping with the Greek style. It was small and cozy, the walls unplastered so that the same stone on the outside of the cottage was visible on the inside. They were painted crisp white and the long windows let in huge amounts of bright light. The whole living room sparkled with light, accentuated by the white armchairs, the white-cushioned window bench, and the white wooden floorboards. The only splash of color came from the light shade and lamp, which were as blue as the ocean that could be seen through the windows.

"It's gorgeous, Dad," Emily said, breathing in the fresh, warm Greek air, picking up the scent of the lemons and ocean on the breeze.

He led them next into the kitchen, which was as cute, quaint, and rustic as the living room had been. It had the same white stone walls and white floorboards, though there was only one window so it wasn't as bright. The appliances were old, in keeping with the property as well as Roy's personal taste of retro kitchenware. Emily thought of the huge 1950s-style fridge she'd inherited with the house in Sunset Harbor, and the amazing oven. Neither would fit in such a small kitchen but Roy had found equally antique-looking items to deck this place out with as well.

On the small kitchen table there were bits of clocks and cogs and Chantelle exclaimed aloud at them, delighted.

Roy next showed them up the rickety stairs, where there were two small rooms. The family would all be sleeping in one room this time, as Roy wasn't well enough to give up his bed for the couch.

"Let me make us some dinner," he said. "The weather will remain clear so we can eat in the garden under the stars."

Chantelle was incredibly excited by the prospect of eating under the stars. Despite the warm weather at home, it was still cold at night so their days of porch picnics were now behind them for another year.

"What are we having?" Chantelle asked.

"Greek tapas," Roy said. "Ever had it before?"

Chantelle shook her head.

"Grilled aubergine," Roy told her, "Fried halloumi. Chickpeas in lemon. Homemade red pepper hummus. Olives. Pita. Goat cheese. Fresh fish."

Emily's mouth watered as Roy reeled off all the delightful-sounding dishes.

"Do you want some help with it all, Dad?" she asked.

"Yes, but not from my very pregnant daughter," he said. "Daniel can help me in the kitchen."

Emily wasn't about to argue with that! She settled in the living room with Chantelle, recuperating from the flight while the house filled with the smells of food and the sizzling sounds of a frying pan. When it was all ready they carried all the little dishes out to the table on the lawns. Chantelle's eyes bulged with excitement.

"Tuck in," Roy said.

"This looks amazing," Emily told him. "Daniel, I hope you know that you'll be cooking this regularly once we get home."

Everyone laughed. The looked of relief in Daniel's face was not lost on Emily. He could probably sense that she was getting over their spat in her own time.

They settled down into the meal. Emily managed to keep her spirits up, not focusing on the skinniness of her father, the slow way he was eating, or the smallness of his appetite, but instead listening to the words he spoke, reveling in the aliveness and presence of him in this exact moment. It was one of those picture postcard moments that Emily wished would never end, with the sky turning blood orange behind them, sinking down beneath the horizon of the ocean.

Chantelle yawned deeply.

"Maybe we should put this little one to bed," Emily suggested.

"I want to stay up with Papa Roy," Chantelle said.

But her eyes were rimmed with darkness. She was clearly exhausted.

"Better to get some rest and be ready for a full day tomorrow rather than fight it and end up grouchy for the rest of the trip," Emily told her.

Chantelle frowned, but even she knew that Emily was speaking wise words. Finally, she relented, standing from her seat. She hugged Papa Roy tightly, then headed inside and up the stairs to bed.

"She takes herself to bed now?" Roy asked.

"Sometimes," Emily told him. "She wants to be mature for when Charlotte comes."

Roy chuckled. "How sweet."

"Has she changed much since you last saw her?" Emily asked.

Roy nodded and Emily noticed the sparkle of tears in his eyes.

"She's growing fast," he said, choking back emotion.

Emily reached for her father, gripping his arm. "Dad?"

He shook his head. "I'm sorry. I'm not doing well," he finally admitted. He looked at Daniel, his expression somewhat panic-stricken.

"I know, Roy," Daniel said softly. "Emily told me."

Roy seemed to crumple forward then, as if the fact that Daniel knew meant he no longer had to keep up any kind of charade. Emily felt her throat tighten with emotion. Daniel stood from his chair and went over to Roy's, practically scooping the frail man to his feet. He embraced him for a long time, and Emily watched on as they both wept. Then she stood and joined them. They all held each other for a long time, letting the fears and anguish they'd all been harboring for the last few months go in one cathartic moment of shared grief, while the bright stars twinkled above them.

CHAPTER NINETEEN

When she woke the next morning, in a dazzling burst of sunshine, Emily felt dazed. She could still feel the echo of tears on her cheeks from last night. It was only through sheer exhaustion that she'd even been able to sleep—grief like the type she'd felt that night had in the past induced a state of insomnia in her that could last for days.

She turned to see Chantelle beside her, sleeping as though in a coma. Jet lag always knocked the child out, but she recovered from its effects much more quickly than Emily was ever able.

Beside Chantelle, Daniel was sleeping with a frown on his face. It made Emily's heart ache to see that his worry for Roy had carried through into his sleep. Sleep was supposed to be a time for peace, but it looked as though Daniel hadn't found any at all. Although of course it could be a work-induced frown, in which case her sympathy only stretched so far!

The clock read 5 a.m. and Emily knew she was only awake because of her body clock being messed up from the flight. But she also knew her father would most likely already be up. There was a garden to tend to, after all, flowers that needed watering, koi that needed to be fed.

She got out of bed, careful not to wake Daniel or Chantelle, and strode to the window. Sure enough, there was Roy, hose in hand watering the grass. Emily watched him silently, sorrow growing in her breast. He was thin, frail looking. He looked closer to ninety years old than seventy.

"What are you doing, Mommy?" Chantelle's sleepy voice came from behind.

Emily rearranged her features into a smile before turning around and taking in the beautiful sight of Chantelle. "Looking at the ocean," she said. "It looks very pretty today."

"Does Papa Roy have a boat in Greece as well as England?" Chantelle asked.

"I don't know," Emily said. "We'll have to ask him. Why? Would you like to go sailing?"

Chantelle nodded eagerly. Like father like daughter, Emily thought, and she smiled in spite of herself. She'd have to accept it soon enough; her heart had forgiven Daniel even if her mind *thought* she should still be mad. But how could she stay mad at a husband who wept in the arms of her father? She couldn't. It was time to bury the hatchet.

She came back to the bed and sat beside the girl, stroking her sunshine-warmed hair.

"We'll have to ask Papa Roy if we can go out boating," she said. "If not, perhaps he can take us to a beach for swimming."

Chantelle seemed satisfied by the suggestions. She rested her head against Emily's bump—a habit she'd developed over the last month.

Just then, Daniel stirred, clearly disturbed by their talking. He looked extremely tired, worn out from emotion and from working so hard for so many months.

"How are my girls?" he asked, reaching for them both.

"Sleepy," Chantelle said. "And excited for the day."

"Sleepy *and* excited," Daniel said with a laugh. "Only you."

He caught Emily's eyes and a silent communication passed between them; an acknowledgment of the emotional evening they'd shared, of the weight of their fight still pressing on their shoulders.

"Does anyone think they're going to get back to sleep?" Emily asked. "Or shall we just get up and have breakfast now? If we want to go boating, we ought to get an early start anyway."

She needn't have asked. Chantelle was up like a rocket, and Daniel wasn't far behind. The mention of boating was probably the only thing that could help clear his mind of worry, after all.

Emily slung her legs out of bed and used the post to help herself to her feet.

"What do they have for breakfast in Greece?" Chantelle asked as they left the room as a group.

"Let's find out," Emily said, ruffling her hair.

They headed down the stairs and entered the kitchen just as Roy was coming in through the back door.

"Good morning, everyone!" he said jovially, placing a watering can on the side.

Emily knew better now though. His happiness was put on, faked for Chantelle's benefit. All those months she'd forced herself not to get sad about his illness because he himself was not had been an embellishment of the truth. Roy had been sad and hurting that whole time and she'd been none the wiser. She felt like a fool now for not having seen through it.

Chantelle hurried over and hugged Roy tightly. "We're here for our breakfast," she said in a jokey tone, looking up at him with adoring eyes.

Roy clapped his hands. "Well, I have a wonderful selection for you to choose from. Here in Greece we like to start the day with a pastry, so I bought some freshly baked spinach ones from the store this morning." He opened the fridge and peered inside. "There's also buffalo milk yogurt, mountain cheese, bread with either tahini and honey or sliced salami. Then of course there's vine-picked tomatoes for the side, and freshly squeeze lemon juice. And how could I forget." He opened the kitchen cupboard to reveal a row of jars. "Homemade jam!"

"Dad!" Emily exclaimed. "You didn't have to go to all this trouble."

"It's no trouble," Roy replied. "It gives me great joy to treat you all. So please, let's sit and eat."

They took all of the food outside onto the patio. Since it was so early the heat of the sun hadn't reached its full force, and they were quite comfortable. They tucked into the copious amounts of food on offer. Emily found herself suddenly ravenous.

"Do you have a boat in Greece, Papa Roy?" Chantelle asked.

"I don't actually," he replied. "I'm not here often enough to warrant the cost. But I do go boating quite frequently with a good friend of mine, Vladi. Why? Did you want to go sailing today?"

Chantelle grinned and nodded. "Yes please!"

"Then we must," Roy said. "I'll give Vladi a call after breakfast. He'll come and pick us up."

Sure enough, once breakfast was over and everyone was dressed and ready for the day, the family had only to stroll five minutes down the cliff path to the shoreline before they were picked up by Vladi—a golden-skinned, weather-beaten, mustached man in a flat cap—and his gorgeous yacht. Daniel seemed enamored by the boat from the get-go.

"Where are we heading?" Vladi asked as he helped them climb aboard.

"Somewhere Chantelle can swim," Roy said. "Then we'll stop at a *taverna* for lunch. See some beaches and explore some caves. And we should also check out the fort from the ocean."

"Sounds fantastic," Emily gushed. She couldn't think of a better way to relax and unwind.

Vladi set sail through the crystal clear water. The boat was clean and comfortably fit all of them aboard. They had a great view of the beautiful coastline from here, which gave them access to hidden beaches that would be unseen from the roads.

"There is a protected cove up here," Vladi explained. "Perhaps Chantelle would like to swim there?"

Chantelle nodded with excitement.

Vladi took them to the completely empty beach and cove.

"Anyone want a dip?" Daniel asked.

"I think I'll stay dry today," Emily said. She handed Daniel sunscreen from her purse. "It's going to be super hot soon so make sure she's covered."

Chantelle changed into her swimsuit, then Daniel helped her climb down the ladder of the yacht into the ocean. Emily watched them, her heart swelling with love as they splashed about in the clear water.

Roy and Vladi took out a chess set and began to play, and Emily smiled contentedly to herself, glad that her father wasn't alone in Greece, that he had friends around him. She hated the idea of something happening to him and no one being there to help him. Relaxed by the gentle motion of the boat, and full from her huge breakfast, Emily found herself growing sleepy. She pulled her sun hat over her face and fell into a doze.

After an hour or so napping, she was awoken by the sound of Chantelle and Daniel climbing back on board.

"How was your swim?" she asked, stretching and yawning.

"Amazing," Chantelle said. "You could see all the way down. There were fishes and corals and everything. I'm hungry now though."

"I'm not surprised," Emily said. "You've been up since five a.m. and swimming for at least an hour straight!"

She herself wasn't even anywhere close to digesting her breakfast, but the food she'd eaten thus far was so amazingly tasty she could certainly force herself to have another meal.

Vladi sailed them to the waterfront *taverna*, a wooden structure with its own jetty. He tied the yacht up and gestured them all inside.

Clearly, Roy and Vladi were friends with the owners of the restaurant. Vladi spoke to them in Greek, his voice loud and jovial. Roy, who didn't speak the language as far as Emily was aware, still seemed on good terms with the owner, and they embraced. Then he introduced his family in simple, broken English. "Daughter, son-in-law, granddaughter." He patted Emily's stomach. "Another granddaughter!"

Everyone laughed.

They were shown to a table, which seemed to be made of the same wood as the jetty. It was covered in a bright tablecloth and was positioned right up beside the ocean, so close that waves occasionally lapped up over the side. It was a beautiful little place, and the view was stunning.

They didn't need to order, because the *taverna* owner brought out plate after plate of traditional Mediterranean home-cooked food—Greek salad, feta, chicken, cheese, pasta, bread, and watermelon. It was all very healthy and super fresh.

Chantelle seemed to have the biggest appetite of them all. She devoured everything that was put in front of her.

"Remember when we were in England and you couldn't eat anything?" she asked Emily.

Emily smiled at the memory. "It was only white food for months at the beginning."

But her smile faded quickly at the sight of her father picking at his food. Her nausea had been temporary, and a minor inconvenience really in the grand scheme of things. For Roy, it was affecting his quality of life. The chances of it being temporary were very slim. She felt terrible for him, losing one of his great passions. No wonder there was so much jam in his kitchen. He must have lost the taste for it.

As the last treat at the *taverna*, Roy surprised them with a prearranged birthday cake for Chantelle. The owner began to sing "Happy Birthday" and everyone joined in.

Chantelle blushed, but she was also secretly loving being the center of attention.

"I had three birthdays this year," she joked. "One early, one on time, and one late."

They all tucked into the traditional Greek honey cake.

"This is amazing," Chantelle mumbled through her mouthful.

Everyone laughed.

Once lunch was over, they all climbed back on board the yacht. Emily marveled at the way she never grew tired of being out in the ocean. It was the most relaxing place to her in the world. To think they'd be spending much more time at sea in their own town now they had the island pleased her immensely.

"I know a very good place to watch the sunset," Vladi said. "Shall we head there? Then I will drop you home and you can have your dinner together without me interrupting."

"Oh, please," Emily admonished him, "you've been delightful company. Hardly an intruder."

Vladi seemed shyly pleased with the comment. He sailed them out further into the ocean, so far that the coastline was no longer visible. It meant that every which way they looked, all they could see was water and the cliff tops poking up through it. Emily held her breath with excited anticipation for what she knew would be a truly remarkable moment.

She felt Chantelle's arm around her waist and held the child tightly. Beside Chantelle, she had her hand slipped into Papa Roy's. Emily reached out for Daniel, guiding him toward her so that their family circle was complete. Vladi stood a respectful distance behind, giving the family this moment together.

As the sun began to dip in the sky ahead of them, Emily felt so blessed to have had the chance to create these memories with her father. Though their time was finite and running out fast, they'd still been able to experience beauty together. This burning orange sky, the warm Mediterranean breeze stirring the hairs on her neck; this was what she would remember when she thought of her father.

Just then, Chantelle let out an exclamation, and Emily felt a tug on her side. She turned, startled, and saw that Roy had fallen to his knees, dragging Chantelle after him, who had in turn yanked Emily across the boat.

"Dad?" Emily cried, disengaging herself from Chantelle and Daniel.

Chantelle began to cry at the sight of her Papa Roy struggling. He crouched forward, seemingly unable to draw in enough breath.

"Vladi, we need to get him to a hospital," Emily said hurriedly.

Vladi was on it immediately. He leapt into position and turned the boat around, cutting through the waves at full speed, heading toward the shore. Emily suddenly wished they hadn't decided to travel so far out.

Chantelle wept bitterly, clutching Papa Roy's hand as the boat bobbed them up and down uncomfortably. Daniel was fiddling with his cell phone.

"I can't get any damn reception!" he said, the stress audible in his voice. But finally he must have been able to connect, because Emily heard him talking to someone, asking for an ambulance to meet them on the shore.

An ambulance. The thought was alarming, and the moment felt surreal and dreamlike to Emily. She watched her father in disbelief. Despite the knowledge she'd had for months that his life would soon end, it still took her completely by surprise to see him so vulnerable. It was one thing to know the end was coming, and quite another to watch it unfold in front of her eyes.

"Hang on, Dad," she said, holding his hand tightly. "I'm not ready to say goodbye yet. Hold on."

CHAPTER TWENTY

The bright yellow ambulance was waiting for them on the coastline. Emily could see its flashing lights as they cut through the waves at speed. But every second felt like a minute. Every gasp of breath her father took sounded like it could be the last.

Emily was still crouched on her knees beside Roy. The erratic motion of the yacht had caused ocean spray to come overboard, and her knees were drenched as she knelt in it. Daniel had Chantelle in his arms. The little girl wept, peeking through his arms at the sight of her beloved grandfather struggling for breath.

Finally they were in spitting distance of the shore. Two paramedics stood waiting, wearing navy-colored jumpsuits and blue gloves; a woman with dark hair in a high ponytail and a man with a shaven head and large sunglasses. The sight was surreal to Emily, so different from what she was used to. She felt like she was in a strange dream land.

Vladi took over the communication duties immediately, speaking in Greek to the two paramedics who, instead of taking Roy off the boat as Emily had anticipated, actually jumped on board with their gear to tend to him there.

"*Karkinos*" was the only word Emily could pick out from what Vladi saying to them. Then another, "*Termatiko*."

Was he telling them about Roy's terminal cancer? She hoped Chantelle wouldn't be able to figure it out. Now was not the time for such terrible news to be broken to her.

The paramedics checked Roy's vitals, then slipped an oxygen mask over his face. They brought their bright red stretcher board down into the boat and spent some time maneuvering Roy onto it. Daniel attempted to help but because of Roy's light body weight the two paramedics were perfectly able to handle it between them.

Emily watched, her hand on her mouth, as he was removed from the boat and loaded into the back of the ambulance.

"You go with them," Vladi said to Emily, gripping the tops of her arm.

"But I can't speak to them," she said, beginning to panic, feeling utterly useless and out of her depth. "What if they need to know something?"

"He needs you," Vladi assured her. "He needs his little girl at his side. I will drive your family to the hospital."

"Hospital," Emily repeated, as if the thought that a hospital would be their final destination hadn't yet dawned on her. "Okay. Yes. Of course."

Vladi gave her arms a little squeeze, then gently gave her a shove toward the open ambulance.

"Chantelle," Emily called as she put her foot on the steps at the back. The girl looked up from Daniel's arms. Her face was red and tear-stained. She looked closer to five than eight all of a sudden.

"Honey, I'm going with Papa Roy to the hospital," Emily called. "I'll see you there, okay? Be a good girl for Daddy."

She launched herself up the steep steps into the back of the ambulance. The paramedics were busy tending to Roy. The smell of antiseptic made Emily's stomach swill with nausea.

She watched them work, her hand gripping Roy's. They spoke to one another in Greek, leaving Emily floundering, lost. It was the worst imaginable situation for her. They could be saying literally anything and she had no idea. Finally the female paramedic jumped out the back doors and slammed them behind them. A moment later, she climbed into the driver's seat and started the engine. In an instant, the siren sounded out and they surged forward.

Emily's head spun as she sat in the jolting, rickety ambulance, speedy through the tiny streets. She had no idea where the nearest hospital was, nor how long it would take them to reach it. She had no idea what kind of a state Roy was in, whether he was close to death or whether he was stable now. She had no idea where her daughter was. Though she knew she was safe with Daniel it still felt wrong to not have her in sight while in a foreign country. Her mind was a mess of confusion.

Her ability to keep track of the time was completely impeded by the state she was in. After what could have been anywhere between five minutes to an hour of driving down the bumpy streets, she felt the ambulance slow to a stop. Then the female paramedic was back at the open ambulance doors, a silhouette against bright floodlights.

Roy was removed from the ambulance and Emily climbed out, following the paramedics as they wheeled him in through the main doors to a team of waiting doctors. A cacophony of rapid speaking followed, and Emily felt completely out of her depth, as though she'd been submerged in water.

A doctor approached and took her arm. She was young, far too young to be a doctor, Emily thought.

"You speak English?" the woman said in a soft accent.

"Yes," Emily said, nodding. It was the first time she'd been able to understand someone for what felt like hours. "Is he okay?"

"Your father is having trouble breathing," she explained gently. "It is a symptom of the advanced stage of cancer he is at."

It was the first time Emily had heard someone refer to his cancer as advanced, but of course it was painfully clear to her now that it was. His lack of appetite, his fatigue, these were all signs that he was getting closer to the end.

"It may just be that we need to fit an oxygen tube, which is completely painless and just rests in his nose," the doctor continued. "Or there could be some fluid that we'll need to check for. We can prescribe medicine for that. Are you here with anyone else?"

"My family was following behind the ambulance."

"Good," the doctor said, giving Emily's arm a gentle squeeze. "Why don't you take a seat in the waiting room? I'll let you know as soon as we're ready for you to see him."

Emily nodded, feeling completely dazed. She wasn't even sure how much of the doctor's words she'd absorbed. Her mind had stopped functioning properly as soon as she'd said advanced stage of cancer. It didn't matter how reassuring her tone had sounded after, or how simple she'd made it sound to fix her father's symptoms, all she could think of was that term. Advanced stage.

Somehow she found herself in the waiting room. It was a strange peach color with brown furniture. A claustrophobic combination in Emily's mind.

She'd just sat down when the door flew open. It was Daniel, Chantelle, and Vladi. The little girl flew into her arms.

"How is he?" Daniel asked, his voice strained.

Emily clutched hold of Chantelle so tightly she felt like she might break the child. "He's struggling to breathe. They made it sound very... I don't know, solvable? A breathing tube or medicine for fluid. I can't remember now. It's all a blur."

Daniel held her in his arms, his warm body offering her reassurance. She looked over and saw Vladi wipe a tear from his eye.

"Thank you, Vladi, for everything you've done. My father needs good friends like you."

Vladi gave her a pained, but grateful smile.

Finally, the door opened again and the doctor walked in. It was the same one who had spoken to Emily earlier.

"Your father is waking up now," she said. "We will be moving him onto the ward and then you can come and see him. He is asking for Charlotte." She looked down at Chantelle. "Is that you?"

Emily felt her whole body tense. Chantelle looked perturbed at the mix-up.

"He's just confused, sweetie," Emily explained. "He got his names muddled."

But Chantelle looked skeptical. Emily wasn't sure but she got the distinct impression that the little girl was more aware of the situation than she'd realized. Perhaps she'd failed entirely to protect Chantelle from the reality of Roy's illness. Had she figured it out? The thought terrified her.

A short while later they were shown out of the waiting room and down a corridor, into a ward with lots of elderly patients all wearing breathing apparatus. Emily knew instinctively that this was a cancer ward, and that the men upon it were at the advanced stages of their illness as well. But they were all older than Roy. None was as young as he was. It seemed so unfair.

They were led up to a bed in the corner, and there was Roy. He was sitting up, propped by several white fluffy pillows. There was a mask on his face, and a pulse monitor attached to his index finger, feeding information into a large, bleeping machine.

"Hello, everyone," Roy said, in his usual chipper way.

Chantelle ran forward and hugged him tightly.

"I'm sorry, darling, did I give you a fright?" he said gently, stroking her hair.

Emily choked back her tears. "You gave us all a fright."

"Thankfully Vladi was there to help," Daniel added.

Roy reached for his friend and the two men shook hands affectionately.

Chantelle sat up then, looking at Roy with a frown on her face.

"Are you going to tell me what's wrong with you?" she asked. "Or are you going to keep pretending everything is okay?"

Roy's expression fell. He looked pained.

"Chantelle," Emily said under her breath, her tone warning her to back off.

But the girl turned on her sharply. "No. It's not fair. You're always whispering and giving each other looks. I know something's going on. And Papa Roy is half the size he used to be and he's never eating anything." She turned her stricken face back to her granddad. "So what is it? I want to know!"

Emily reached for Daniel, desperate for his comfort in the fraught moment. Had they been wrong to hide the truth from their astute daughter? Or was this for the best? To hear it from his own lips rather than as secondhand information.

Roy took a deep breath, his chest rattling as he did. He stroked Chantelle's hair tenderly, then tipped her chin up with his wizened finger.

"I have an illness," Roy said. "You might have heard the word before. It's called cancer."

Emily choked out a sob. Daniel drew her closer into him, his arms tightening around her protectively.

"Are you going to die?" Chantelle asked. She seemed to be holding her own, but Emily could see the tremble in her bottom lip.

"Yes, darling," Roy said, his voice drenched in sorrow. "I'm afraid so."

"When?" Chantelle asked. Her eyes were huge and pleading.

"I don't know."

"Before Christmas?" she demanded. Her voice was pitching higher as emotion crept into it.

"I don't think so," Roy replied.

"Before my next birthday?"

Emily could take it no more. She turned and buried her head in Daniel's shoulder as sobs racked through her body. Through the sound of her own tears she heard her father's voice.

"Yes, Chantelle. I'll be dead before your next birthday."

Then the next sound pierced Emily through the heart. It was the sound of her daughter's heart breaking at the news her favorite person wouldn't be there to celebrate with her when she turned nine. That he wouldn't hold a sign up for her over a video message. That he wouldn't give her honey cake in a Greek *taverna*. That all those millions of things they did together would abruptly stop before her next milestone was reached.

Chantelle's wail of grief echoed through the corridors of the hospital and there was nothing Emily could do to take her pain away. All she could do was hold on. Be close. Be there. All she could do was cry alongside her.

CHAPTER TWENTY ONE

Everyone sat in silence in Vladi's truck as he drove them through the pitch-black streets. Roy had been admitted for an overnight stay at the hospital and so the family had no choice but to return to his home without him.

Once they reached the cottage, Vladi's truck idling in the driveway as they climbed out, Emily turned back to him.

"Thank you for everything you've done," she said. "Not just with the emergency but for the whole day on the yacht. It was really magical." She reached in through the window and patted his hand. "I'm so relieved my dad has a friend like you."

Vladi nodded, struggling to hold back his emotion. "Roy is a good man."

Emily smiled sadly. Then she rummaged in her purse for a business card and handed it to him. "This is our number," she said. "Once we're back home, will you call us if anything..." She struggled to get the words out. "...If anything else happens to him?"

Vladi looked at the small slip of card. "I will keep a good eye on him, Emily. Don't you worry. I will check on him every day." He pressed his hand to his chest. "That is a promise."

"Thank you," Emily said, meaningfully. It eased her worries somewhat to know her father would not be alone when they left here, that he had people to look out for him. And after everything they'd been through today, she trusted Vladi fully with that very important task.

Sensing he wasn't one for overblown goodbyes, Emily decided to leave it there.

Daniel emerged from the backseat with Chantelle in his arms, dangling like a dead weight. She'd wailed herself into exhaustion and had fallen asleep before they left the hospital. Emily hadn't been sure that it was a good idea to move her from the hospital while sleeping, fearing the disorientation on waking up would upset her further. But she'd been impossible to wake.

They waved goodbye to Vladi and watched as his truck disappeared into the inky night. With a heavy sigh, Daniel turned and headed along the path, walking slowly. Emily followed, feeling weariness seep into every one of her bones.

"I had no idea it had gotten so bad," she said to Daniel.

He looked at her with a strained expression. "I know. I feel terrible. He kept saying he was all right. Were we fools for believing him?"

Emily thought of the man her father had been in her youth—a man who had let her down, who had lied and kept secrets.

"No," she said, finally. "We weren't fools. It's what he does."

She didn't want to think bad thoughts about Roy, especially not now, while he was lying alone in a hospital bed. She pushed the memories away.

They entered the cottage. It was completely dark and devoid of life. Without her father inside, it was like the spirit of the place was completely gone. Now it wasn't a charming house in a beautiful town, but simply a series of stone bricks arranged in a square. It was Roy who gave the home a heart.

"Can we just go straight to bed?" Emily asked Daniel.

They'd not had dinner but their lunch had been enormous and Emily didn't much feel like eating anything else. She knew Doctor Arkwright would be disappointed if she found out Emily had skipped a meal—keeping her blood sugar levels stable was very important, especially since she'd had blood pressure issues at the beginning of her pregnancy—but her fatigue was too great to fight. The emotion of the day was like a burden weighing on her and all she wanted now was to give in to her exhaustion.

"Of course," Daniel said.

They climbed the stairs together and went into the room they'd been sharing. It was dark except for a ray of moonlight streaming in through the open curtains. Emily drew them, plunging them into complete blackness.

She reached forward, searching for the bed, and found it. She climbed in beside Chantelle. The girl was snoring. She hadn't moved a muscle, so deep was the sleep that had consumed her. Emily slung an arm around her, drawing comfort from the girl. She didn't even notice herself drifting off. The second her head hit the pillow, sleep took her.

*

Emily was awoken the next morning by the sound of an unfamiliar telephone ringing. Disoriented, it took her several moments to realize where she was. Then she remembered her father was not here, that he was in the hospital, and that answering the ringing telephone was now her responsibility.

She hurried downstairs and began searching for the phone. She hadn't even known her father had a landline in his home. He probably didn't know himself.

She followed the noises and found a dusty, beige plastic phone down the back of an armchair. She plucked it out and answered the call. It was the hospital.

"Is he okay?" Emily asked, her heart flying into her mouth.

"Yes, he is ready to come home."

Emily felt a wave of relief rush over her. "Oh thank God," she said breathlessly. "We'll come and pick him up right away."

She ended the call and went upstairs as fast as her bulging stomach would allow her. Daniel and Chantelle were sprawled out on the bed, sheets and pillows kicked up around them suggesting a fitful night's sleep.

"Guys, wake up," Emily said loudly. "We can go and get Papa Roy from the hospital. He's feeling better."

Chantelle shot up to a sitting position. Daniel stirred, a little more slow to come back to consciousness. But Chantelle turned and shook his shoulders to hurry him along.

"Daddy, come on," she said. "We have to go get Papa Roy!"

Daniel finally sprung into action. As he dressed and helped Chantelle into her outfit, Emily called for a taxi. She didn't want to keep relying on Vladi. It didn't seem fair. He was elderly, too, and Emily didn't want to compound his stress.

The taxi arrived ten minutes later. It was bright yellow, reminding Emily immediately of New York City. They hurried inside.

"Where are you going?" the driver asked.

"Hospital," Emily told him.

He nodded respectfully, and asked no further questions.

The drive didn't take long, and it was only then that Emily realized just how short the distance she'd traveled in the ambulance had really been. It had felt like an eternity, but in reality it couldn't have taken much longer than fifteen minutes.

They pulled up outside the hospital and the taxi waited for them outside.

They hurried in, greeting the staff at the reception desk.

"We're here for my Papa Roy," Chantelle told them, acting very much like the organizer she was. She seemed very grown up all of a sudden.

"Roy Mitchell," Emily added.

"Of course," the receptionist said. "He's waiting for you."

A doctor came along to collect them, and led them through the corridors to the ward where they'd left Roy last night. He was sitting in a wheelchair beside his bed, chatting jovially with an orderly. There was a tube in his nose and an oxygen pack sat next to him.

"There they are." Roy beamed as his family approached.

He was using his carefree voice, trying to put them all at ease. But the truth was out now and he wasn't kidding anyone.

Chantelle hurried to Roy and climbed onto his lap, throwing her arms around his neck.

"Careful," Daniel warned her. She did have a tendency to squeeze quite hard.

The orderly stood. "I will push him to the car. The wheelchair stays with us though, if that's okay."

"Of course," Emily said. "He doesn't need it?"

The doctor shook her head. "No, he will be okay after a bit of rest to move around on his own. We just want him to be safe and healthy as we escort him from the hospital."

Chantelle stayed on Roy's lap as the orderly wheeled them through the corridors. Roy waved to the doctors and nurses as he went. He was always so friendly it didn't surprise Emily that he'd made friends while being here.

They reached the taxi and Daniel helped Roy to his feet, then into the back of the taxi. He handed the oxygen canister in after him.

Chantelle wanted to sit next to Roy, of course, so she went around to the other side and got into the middle seat. Daniel took the one beside her so that Emily could have the comfort of traveling in the front passenger seat.

"Did you have any breakfast yet?" Chantelle asked Roy.

"No, and I'm ravenous," he told her.

Chantelle giggled. "We'll have to stop to get things for breakfast," she told the taxi driver.

He looked over to Emily for confirmation. She just laughed and shrugged. "Yeah, okay. If you know of a market on the way that would be great."

He seemed happy to oblige and drove the family to a cute market in the back streets of the town. The sun had risen now, drenching everything in warmth and light.

"We won't be long, Papa Roy," Chantelle said.

Daniel decided to stay in the taxi with Roy, and so Emily and Chantelle went out to purchase food for breakfast.

The market was truly beautiful, a busy, bustling place filled with stalls and amazing fresh produce. Emily and Chantelle buzzed around, selecting olives and artichokes, fresh fruit, cheese, and yogurt.

Chantelle found a stall selling amazing-smelling fresh bread.

"We'll take a loaf, thanks," Emily said to the stall owner.

Beside it was a stall selling whole watermelons the size of Chantelle's head.

"We'll take one of those, too!" she added.

Once their arms were laden with fresh produce, they scurried back to the taxi and finished the rest of the drive back to Roy's cottage. Emily paid the taxi driver and everyone went inside. The house felt completely different this time, now that Roy was back to inject some life and soul into the place.

Daniel helped him upstairs to his bed as Emily and Chantelle prepared the breakfast, making up a tray of goodies for him.

"I have an idea," Chantelle said, suddenly.

Emily watched her curiously as she disappeared out of the room. She heard her footsteps thudding up the staircase, and then, after a short moment, the sound of them hurrying back down.

"Ta-da!" Chantelle exclaimed as she skidded into the kitchen.

Emily frowned when she saw that there was something in Chantelle's arms. "What is that?" she asked.

"It's my clock," Chantelle said.

"The one you were building at home?" Emily asked, shocked. "But what's it doing here? In Greece? Did you take that on the plane?"

Chantelle looked bemused at Emily's shocked tone. "Yes. I put it in one of my toy bags."

"But why?" Emily asked, laughing now. "What kind of eight-year-old carries a big heavy clock halfway across the world?"

"It's a present for Papa Roy," Chantelle said simply. "I was going to give it to him on the last day but I figure he'll want it now."

"Sure," Emily said, still laughing.

Chantelle placed the clock on one side of the tray.

"Do you think he'll like it?" she asked, stepping back to admire her handiwork.

"It's beautiful," Emily told her. "He'll love it."

They went upstairs to Roy's room. He was propped up in bed, the oxygen tube still in place. Daniel was sitting in a chair by the window. He looked tired, more tired than Roy did. This whole ordeal had really hit him hard, Emily thought.

"What's this?" Roy said as he saw the tray. "Breakfast for me?"

Chantelle nodded brightly. She hopped onto the foot of the bed as Emily positioned the tray over Roy's lap.

"Wait…" he said, noticing the clock. "This doesn't look edible."

Chantelle giggled. "It's not!" she exclaimed. "It's a clock. I made it for you."

Roy looked stunned. He picked it up lightly, turning it over in his hands. "You made it?"

Chantelle nodded. "All by myself."

Roy looked up at Emily. Tears were sparkling in his eyes.

"Chantelle, it's wonderful," he uttered, sounding completely overwhelmed. "I don't understand how you did this all on your own."

"I just remembered everything you showed me when we were in England," she said. "Do you like it?"

Roy looked up at her, his eyes deep pools of emotion. "I love it, Chantelle. It's amazing. Thank you. Thank you so much."

Chantelle threw her arms around his neck and hugged him tightly. As she watched on, Emily dabbed tears away from her eyes.

CHAPTER TWENTY TWO

"I think we should make a Thanksgiving meal," Chantelle announced later that day, while Roy was taking a nap.

The family was sitting in the garden, soaking up some sunshine and trying to release all the tension the events of the evening had caused.

"While we're all together," Chantelle added, squinting against the sun.

Since Papa Roy was confined to his bed, there wasn't much in the way of sightseeing for the family to do. Staying in and cooking a big meal would be a good way to spend their time together.

"We could go back to that market," Chantelle said. "Do you think Papa Roy would like that?"

Emily looked at Daniel. He'd been the one who was reticent to move dates forward. She wondered if he'd be more willing after what had happened. And more willing since it was Chantelle's suggestion.

"Sure. I think that's a great idea, honey," he said.

This time, Daniel went to the market with Chantelle. Emily needed to rest. All the stress was starting to make her tired. So she went into Roy's bedroom and napped in the bed beside him.

She was roused by the sound of clattering coming from downstairs, the unmistakable noises of her family. Emily was feeling much more energetic after her nap and went downstairs to help out as much as possible in the kitchen.

She entered to a scene of chaos.

"How much did you buy?" she exclaimed.

Daniel looked up from the bags he was emptying. "We might have gotten a little carried away."

Chantelle gave Emily a very serious look. "This will be our last Thanksgiving with Papa Roy," she said maturely. "We want it to be the best ever."

Roy's kitchen was very small, nothing like the space they were accustomed to in the inn. They all had to dance around each other but the chaos just added to the fun.

They made potato gratin, green bean casserole, mac and cheese, cornbread, glazed carrots, roasted beets, creamed kale, wild rice stuffed butternut squash, and cinnamon and honey roasted sweet potatoes. Chantelle enjoyed cooking with them.

Then they placed all the food out in the garden, on the patio table so they could eat overlooking the sea. Daniel went upstairs to help Roy come down.

When he saw the Thanksgiving dinner, he let out an exclamation of joy.

"Did you do all this?" he asked.

"It was Chantelle's idea," Emily told him.

"You helped surprise me with an early birthday," she said. "So I thought we should surprise you with an early Thanksgiving."

Roy looked touched. "This is so wonderful."

He walked slowly to the table and sat. Everyone joined him. The ocean sparkled in the distance. And for the rest of the evening, Emily forgot about her worries.

CHAPTER TWENTY THREE

The next day, however, Emily awoke with a heavy heart. It was departure day, and it had arrived like an unwanted storm cloud, bringing a sense of foreboding with its gloom.

She looked over at Daniel and Chantelle sleeping in bed. Though she felt blessed for them, she knew half her heart belonged here with her father, that leaving him would feel like tearing it in two. The urge to remain was overwhelming, though she knew she couldn't heed it.

Daniel woke then, his eyelids fluttering open. Emily could tell by the look on his face that he was feeling the same as she was.

"I wish we could take Dad with us," Emily said to him softly, projecting her voice over Chantelle's sleeping form.

"I know," he replied. "Or that at least we could stay longer. Leaving him like this doesn't seem right."

Despite their whispers, Chantelle was awoken by their voices. She looked up at her parents, rubbing her sleepy eyes.

"We're leaving today," she said, glumly, her shoulders sagging.

Emily ruffled her hair. "I'm afraid so."

Chantelle nodded as though she understood, acting once again older than her eight years. "Will we ever see Papa Roy again?"

Emily chewed her lip, deliberating what to tell the child. Her father's advanced stage of cancer coinciding with her late stage of pregnancy meant it was very unlikely either would be able to travel in the future. There was a very real possibility that this would be it.

"We'll have video calls," she told Chantelle, searching for a diplomatic response.

Chantelle turned her sorrowful eyes to Emily. "You know what I mean. This will be the last time we're with him. The last time we get to hug him."

Her words repeated in Emily's mind. An echo, each repetition causing a stab of pain in her heart.

"Yes," she said finally, her voice resigned.

Daniel reached for her, squeezing her arm for comfort. But Emily felt numb, like she was in shock over the whole thing. This simply couldn't be the last time she saw her father. It wasn't fair.

"We'd better make the most of our time with him, then," Chantelle said, heaving back the covers. "Come on. Everyone up."

Emily was relieved that the child was taking charge. She herself felt paralyzed.

They washed and dressed, then quickly packed their belongs. Then Chantelle herded them out of the room, allowing Emily no time to poignantly gaze at it one last time.

When they made it down to the kitchen they discovered, with surprise, that Roy was up and out of bed. He turned as they entered.

"Good morning, family." He beamed. "I've made fresh coffee. Decaf for the ladies."

Emily looked at her family, surprised. Had it not been for the oxygen tube in his nose, there'd be nothing to suggest Roy was sick. His eyes were bright, his face flushed with color for the first time in days. Even his movements were no longer hampered by fatigue.

"Dad, are you okay?" Emily asked him. She strolled over and touched his arm lightly, as though checking to make sure he was real and not a ghost.

"Never better," he said. "Those pills they gave me at the hospital are really taking effect now. And two days in bed, having all my chores done for me, errands run for me, and meals cooked for me have been extremely recuperating!"

Emily was relieved to see her father so animated. She was slightly suspicious it was an act for their benefit, but even the best actor in the world couldn't make color return to their cheeks. That had to be real, and a sign that he was starting to feel better.

But on the other hand she was also bitten by guilt. Once they left her father would have no one other than Vladi to care for him. If having help at home had made such a difference, how could she really leave him now?

It was then that she struck on an idea.

"Dad, have you thought of having some home help?" she said.

With everyone now holding a steaming mug of coffee, they sauntered over to the kitchen table and sat down amongst the pieces of strewn clocks.

"What do you mean?" Roy said. "I don't need help."

"But you just said that having people look after you had been recuperating. Why not get someone in permanently? You have a spare room after all. I'm sure there'd be plenty of people who'd love the chance to be abroad in a lovely sunny country in exchange for doing some washing and cooking."

Roy looked at her kindly but shook her head. "I'm too stuck in my ways now," he said. "I'd be too much of an imposition."

"You're not an imposition, Papa Roy," Chantelle refuted. "If I was allowed to stay and be your maid I would."

He patted her hand tenderly. "You're very sweet, my dear."

"I mean it though, Dad," Emily continued. "There might be someone in Sunset Harbor even who'd like to come out. I could fly one of the inn's maids over on a sabbatical."

Roy shook his head. "You're being silly now, Emily."

Daniel spoke next. "I think that would be too much to ask. Why don't we hire a local nurse to come in once or twice a week?"

Emily's face snapped up to meet Daniel's. She'd really wanted someone there who she trusted, one of her housemaids for instance. She thought Lois or Marnie would love the opportunity. The idea of hiring someone random filled her with dread. She'd heard horror stories of home helpers exploiting vulnerable elderly people, stealing from their wallets when they weren't looking, stealing their expensive items. She wouldn't be happy with just any person doing the job.

"Let's think about it," she said, leaving the suggestion lingering in the air between them like a bad smell.

"What shall we do with your last morning?" Roy said then. "I feel like you haven't had much of a chance for sightseeing since you arrived here."

"I have an idea," Chantelle said. She grinned. "Breakfast on the patio overlooking the ocean."

Roy smiled. "But you've been doing that for three days straight now!"

Chantelle nodded. "I know. And it's been the best."

Roy looked touched.

"I think that's a good idea," Daniel said. "I'll help with the cooking."

"So will I," Emily said.

"Me too," Roy added, firmly.

Emily looked at her father. He didn't want to be treated like an invalid, like he was incapable. Maybe she should respect that rather than trying to tell him how he should live his life.

They got to work in the kitchen, cooking up all the fresh Mediterranean dishes that they'd learned since being here. Chantelle was an old hand at it now.

"We should cook this at the inn," she said.

"Maybe in the summer," Emily told her. "By the time we get home it will be all about pies and turkey."

Everyone laughed.

"Chantelle, I was meaning to ask you," Roy said, as he stirred up his freshly made hummus. "Did you ever find the hidey hole in your bedroom at the inn?"

Chantelle looked at him and frowned. "What's a hidey hole?"

"Ah," Roy said. "I'll take that as a no, then!" He chuckled. "There is a loose brick in your bedroom wall. I won't tell you where, you'll have to find it. And I won't tell you what's hiding in the gap behind it either." He tapped his nose.

Chantelle looked delighted at the new information. She loved a riddle, and loved even more the experience of unearthing the house's secrets.

"Really, Papa Roy?" she asked, wide-eyed. "There's a secret brick in my bedroom?"

"Oh yes," Roy said, nodding. "Honestly, I'd have thought you would have found it by now. You've answered most of my riddles."

Chantelle squealed with excitement. Emily wondered whether Roy was just giving her something to look forward to, a reason to want to go home, and something to focus on when she was there other than his impending death.

They finished cooking and sat down in the sunshine to eat their final breakfast. Despite knowing it may be their last time together as a family, the mood was happy. Emily felt like everyone was doing their best to make the most of their last moments together.

They were so absorbed in their time together, it was only when the bright yellow taxi pulled up at the drive that Emily even remembered they had to leave, that they had a flight to catch. The emotion caught her off guard.

"That's our taxi," she said.

Everyone's faces paled. Chantelle, who had been up until that moment full of spirit and joy, burst immediately into tears. She clung to Roy.

"I don't want to go," she wailed.

Roy cupped her face in his hands. "Now listen, buttercup," he said. "We've had a grand time together. Let's not end it with tears."

She snuffled, somehow managing to stop the flow.

"There's a good girl," Roy said.

He pulled her into an embrace. As Daniel loaded the luggage into the back of the taxi, Emily joined her father and Chantelle in the embrace, fighting her own tears. A moment later, she felt Daniel's arms around her, strong and protective, joining in the family huddle.

"I love you all," Roy said from the middle of the bundle.

"I love you," Emily said.

"I love you," Daniel repeated.

"I love you," Chantelle concluded.

Then they all released one another. No one was going to say goodbye, because no one wanted it to be the last words spoken. Better to leave their last face-to-face communication as an expression of enduring love.

And so with nothing left to say, Daniel, Emily, and Chantelle got into the taxi. As its engine thrummed to life, they all gazed at Papa Roy through the window, waving, their eyes welling with fresh tears as the distance between them grew, his figure shrinking before their very eyes until he was gone.

CHAPTER TWENTY FOUR

The flight home was uneventful, passing Emily by in a numb haze.

Landing back in Maine was a shock to the system; the weather had become much colder, not to mention Emily had never quite gotten over her jet lag from when they left and her body clock felt like it had gone haywire.

They took a cab home, everyone stunned into an exhausted silence. When the inn loomed into sight—twelve hours after they'd left Roy's home—Emily finally felt a sense of peace overcome her.

They got out the taxi, paying the driver and collecting their luggage, then headed up the porch steps to the inn. Marnie was on duty.

"Welcome home," she said. "Did you have a good trip?"

But she must have seen by the looks on their faces that something had happened because she trailed off.

"How's it been here?" Emily asked. The inn had been the last thing on her mind.

"Fine," Marnie said. "There's been some mail for Chantelle." She grinned happily and rummaged through the stack of letters for a large, pink, sparkly envelope.

Emily immediately felt a sensation of ice sweep through her. There was only one person who'd write to Chantelle, and that was Sheila.

Chantelle must have sensed it too. She hurried to Marnie and grabbed the letter before Emily even had a chance to stop her.

"Chantelle…" Daniel said, as she scurried away. He looked at Emily, his expression one of exasperation. "You know who that will be from."

Emily nodded sadly.

Marnie looked distraught. "I'm sorry. What did I do wrong?"

"Nothing," Emily said with a sigh. Lois would have known not to give personal mail straight to Chantelle but Marnie wasn't as experienced. "We just prefer to vet Chantelle's mail first. There are some unsavory people in her life we try to protect her from."

"I'm so sorry," Marnie gasped. She looked devastated.

"Marnie, it's fine," Daniel told her firmly but kindly. "You couldn't have known." He turned to Emily. "Come on, let's see what the fallout is."

They went upstairs toward Chantelle's bedroom, knowing that had been where the child was heading. Emily knocked on her door and listened. There was no answer.

"Chantelle?" she said. "Can we come in?"

Still no answer.

"Honey, I'm opening the door," Daniel said.

When Chantelle still did not reply, Daniel opened the door.

She was seated on her bed, the sparkly envelope, opened hastily, lying discarded on the floor. Across her bedspread were a myriad of photographs.

"What are these?" Emily said, reaching for one that showed a beautiful, smiling, blond baby girl. "Baby photos?"

Then it dawned on her. They weren't pictures of Chantelle as a child. This was Sheila's new daughter.

"Her name is Darla," Chantelle said, not looking up from her lap. "Darla Elizabeth."

"Oh," Emily said, her hand fluttering to her mouth in shock.

Daniel reacted to the news with anger rather than shock. He grabbed the photographs, all showing Darla at different ages from newborn up to a chubby, grinning infant, some also depicting Sheila, who looked transformed into a happy, healthy woman.

"How dare she?" he muttered. "Doesn't this violate the court order?"

Emily touched his arm lightly, trying to urge him to relax. Now was not the time to think about legalities. Now they had to support Chantelle.

Her eyes fell to the other items lying on the bed. A birthday card with a big silver number eight on the front, and a pink letter written in Sheila's distinctive cursive writing. She didn't want to violate Chantelle's privacy but she couldn't help but see from this distance some of the words Sheila had written.

I hope one day you can come and move home with us. Darla wants to meet you so bad. We've been decorating your room. I've included a picture.

Emily turned to Daniel and took the photos from his hands. As she flicked through, she found the one that must be Chantelle's room. It was pink and flowery, with a big four-poster bed surrounded by lace, like a princess's. Emily knew it wouldn't suit Chantelle's personality—her bedroom at the inn was currently a shrine to every female superhero who'd ever existed—but that didn't mean it wouldn't affect Chantelle to see it, to know it was there waiting for her, empty without her to occupy it.

"I want to be alone now," Chantelle said quietly.

Daniel and Emily exchanged a look. Neither was sure if it was a good idea to leave Chantelle in this state.

But she looked up at them, her voice stern. "Please."

Emily could see the thunderstorm brewing inside the girl. On one hand she wanted to be there when she exploded, to help her through it, but she could tell from the pleading tone in Chantelle's voice that she didn't want any witnesses to this meltdown.

Emily backed away, drawing Daniel back with her. Chantelle shut the bedroom door after them. From the other side of the closed door came the sounds of her erupting.

CHAPTER TWENTY FIVE

Emily's nerves felt frayed from all the events of the last few days. As she sat at the kitchen table on Monday morning, she could see the toll it had taken on everyone else's faces.

Chantelle was barely eating, just prodding her cereal with her spoon. Daniel was busy on his phone. He seemed to be neck deep in work since coming back home. His toast lay uneaten on the plate in front of him.

Emily sighed deeply, sadly. Her phone pinged with a message from Amy. She felt herself smile for what felt like the first time in twenty-four hours.

"Amy wants to know if she can come by later with a birthing book she picked up," Emily said aloud, skim-reading the message.

Daniel looked at her from his cell phone with a frown. "Why? I thought everything was arranged. You wanted a water birth."

Emily shrugged. "I know, but things can change, you know. Suzanna was going to have a water birth with Robin but couldn't at the last minute because of how he was lying. If I end up needing to have a normal delivery it might be cool to see what other options are available."

Daniel's expression remained a mixture of angry and confused. "I don't understand," he muttered. "How many different ways can there be?"

Emily sensed the hostility in his voice. "Amy doesn't have to drop by if you don't want her to."

Chantelle looked up then, clearly noting the tension in the air.

"It's not Amy," Daniel replied, a little gruffly. "It's just that we went through all that planning and now you seem to want to be changing things last minute. I thought the whole point of planning in advance was so we could stop worrying about it, not so that we had enough time to replan it all over again."

"We're just looking at a book," Emily snapped. "Jeez."

Daniel folded his arms. "I doubt that. You know what Amy's like. She'll bring up something else we haven't thought of yet. She'll add a new thing into the mix for us to get anxious about."

Emily stared at him coolly. "I can't tell if you're pissed at me or pissed at Amy."

"I'm not pissed at anyone," Daniel shot back. "It's just that Amy moves in a different circle of wealth than us and I don't want her twisting your arm about things you don't need and can't afford. It's been hard enough getting her to drop the idea of a baby nurse. And what about all that stuff about special child-led nurseries. What was it called? Free Range Kids?" He tutted and shook his head.

"That was just a joke," Emily said. "I know we can't afford to send her to a silly hippy-dippy nursery school. I wouldn't want to anyway."

"No, but you've let Amy talk you into thinking about Mallory's, haven't you?"

"It's not like I've let her," Emily replied. "It's a good school, that's all. We never had a chance to think about where Chantelle should go because it all happened so quickly but we have time to plan now for Charlotte. And once one kid is in it's easier to get the other."

"See!" Daniel exclaimed. "This is what I mean. In what world would we be able to afford to send two kids to Mallory's?"

Emily couldn't understand where his attitude was coming from. "Well, last time I checked we'd bought an island and were turning it into a writer's retreat and health resort. Our financial situation will change as time goes on."

Daniel looked even more unimpressed. "Why did you have to bring up the island?" he muttered.

"Am I not allowed to?" Emily scoffed. "That's news to me."

Chantelle looked from Emily to Daniel, seeming to shrink under the weight of their hostility. Emily didn't want to argue in front of her. In fact, she had no idea how this spat had even begun.

"Can we talk about this another time?" she said, lowering her eyes.

"Oh, because now that I've reminded you how much hard work has to go into these flights of fantasy of yours you don't want to think about it?" Daniel replied.

Emily couldn't believe what she was hearing. Where had this come from? And since when did Daniel think that he was the only one who worked hard? They'd built the inn together from the ground up. They'd worked side by side the whole time. Just because her pregnancy had forced her to take a bit of a back seat recently didn't mean she didn't work hard!

"No, because the last thing Chantelle needs right now is to hear us bickering," Emily replied.

Daniel let out an exasperated sigh. "You're using my daughter to silence me," he said. Then with spiteful sarcasm, added, "How pleasant." He turned to Chantelle. "Come on, kid. It's time for school."

Chantelle obeyed her father immediately. Before Emily even had a chance to blink, the two of them were gone, leaving her sitting at the kitchen table alone, stunned.

CHAPTER TWENTY SIX

Daniel wasn't quite sure what had come over him. He gripped the steering wheel of his truck tightly as he tried to focus on the road, but he was seething. He hated the way he reacted with anger when deep down he was actually desperately sad. He hated the look in Emily's eyes when he snapped at her, when he threw his unhappiness in her face and blamed her for it. It was a terrible way to behave, an awful habit he'd learned from his own parents.

"Daddy?" Chantelle's voice said from beside him, snapping him back to the moment.

"What?"

"If you're angry because of my tantrum yesterday, then I want you to know I'm very sorry," she said.

Daniel looked at her sadly. "That's not it, honey."

"But I *am* sorry," she implored. "I don't mean to get so angry."

He sighed, saddened that his daughter thought she might in any way be responsible for his foul mood. "Thanks, sweetie. But I promise you I'm not mad about it."

"Are you worried then?" Chantelle asked. "You know I don't want to move back to Tennessee. Sheila has Darla to play with so it's not like she's lonely. I want to stay here and live with my new sister when she arrives."

Daniel felt a heaviness in his chest. It was all so cruel. An eight-year-old shouldn't be burdened with such things.

"I know," he told her. "And I'm not worried about that. Honestly. My mood has nothing to do with you."

She nodded and went back to peering out the window. Silence fell. A moment later, Daniel heard Chantelle's voice again.

"Daddy?"

"Yes, honey?"

"You missed the turning for the school."

Daniel realized she was right. He slammed on the brakes and did a three-point turn in the middle of the road. He headed back to the school and turned in.

Up ahead he saw a group of Emily's friends. Suzanna was there looking fresh and happy with her baby. Yvonne, too, but he could vaguely recall some falling out between her and Emily. And then there was Raven Kingsley, actually deigning them worthy of her attention. The last thing he wanted was to speak to them.

"Have a good day, honey," he said to Chantelle.

She peered at him, surprised. "Aren't you getting out?"

"Not today," he mumbled. "I'm late for work. Sorry, sweetie. I'll see you tonight."

Looking perturbed, Chantelle opened the back seat and slid out of the pickup truck. He watched her trundle, dejected, across the parking lot to the playground. Emily's friends were peering at him, confused by his antisocial behavior.

Daniel thrummed the pickup truck to life and accelerated away. He couldn't deal with speaking to them. They'd ask about Greece and then he'd be forced to think of Roy, the man he thought of as a father figure. It was too painful. He didn't want to think about it.

He headed to the carpentry shop and went to unlock the big garage door. To his surprise he found that it had already been opened. Jack, who'd been covering the store while Daniel was in Greece, must have come in today as well. Maybe he'd misunderstood the dates of Daniel's vacation. Or maybe Daniel had told him the wrong ones. That was more likely, he thought, since he'd had next to no time to organize it and was in a highly stressed state at the time.

Daniel heaved the garage door up and the sounds from the woodshop swarmed him; the radio, the whirring saws. He spotted Jack bent over one of the tool benches using the sanding machine or a large bit of beech wood.

"What are you doing in?" Daniel said, walking up to the older man.

Jack removed his protective goggles and clapped Daniel on the back in a gesture of welcoming.

"This early retirement thing isn't what it's cracked up to be," he said out the corner of his mouth. "My wife's driving me crazy. She seems to think that it was only ever tiredness from working in this place that made me not want to tend the garden or bake cakes! I'd much prefer to be here, even if I do ruin my back in the process."

Daniel smiled automatically, but deep down he felt on edge. Was Jack planning on returning? If he did, what would that mean for the promotion, for the extra money? He was relying on that to pay for Charlotte. Emily had a million and one things she wanted for the kids and without that income, how was he supposed to provide it for them? Not to mention all this talk of sending a home help over to Greece to help with Roy. He had no idea how he was supposed to afford it all.

"Jack, if you're in for the day, do you mind if I take an extra leave day?" Daniel asked.

Jack looked at him, concerned. He knew the bare basics of what was going on with Roy; that he was ill and Daniel had taken the news hard.

"Sure. Is everything okay?" he asked. "Did something happen in Greece?"

Daniel felt a wave of grief come over him. He blocked it out, forcing it not to take hold. "Yeah, but I don't want to talk about it right now if that's all right."

"Sure, sure," Jack said, kindly, respectfully. "Just take as much time as you need, son."

Daniel felt extremely grateful, but at a risk of cracking his carefully constructed exterior, he gave a lackluster response of, "Thanks, buddy. I'll see you soon."

He left the store, not even sure of where he was going to go, knowing only that he didn't want to be around people.

He got in his truck and took some deep breaths. His bike would have been a better choice. He could always numb his emotions by driving too fast through the cliffsides. Something about the danger, about taking his life in his hands, made him feel calm and in control. But he didn't want Emily to know he'd shirked a day off work and if he headed back to the inn for the bike he'd be busted.

Then he had a better idea.

His boat was still down at the harbor—no one was working on the island today, he recalled; instead, they were off on a errand to source marble for the fireplace. He could take a trip there, get a bit of peace and quiet, get his thoughts in order. It seemed like the best option, so he turned the key in the ignition and accelerated away from Jack's.

The drive to the harbor was short, but for the first time Daniel paid attention to the weather. Emily had been right when she'd predicted that the fall weather would be upon them on their return from Greece. It may have arrived late but it was certainly making up for lost time. The sky was almost black. Just as he peered up at the clouds, speckles of rain appeared on his windshield.

He reached the harbor and through the windshield of his truck, he saw that his boat was the only one still on the water. The waves were forcing it up and down again in a nausea-inducing rhythm. But Daniel knew he was a proficient sailor. He could handle a bit of seasickness no problem.

He shut off the engine and hopped out of the truck. The rain was little more than a drizzle, closer to wet air than rain, and absolutely nothing to worry about. Still, Daniel pulled his hood up over his head as he trudged toward the boat.

He got to work preparing his boat for a short voyage. Already he felt calmer, his mind relaxing as it focused on the single task ahead of him. The weather was unfortunate but this had definitely been the right call. After a day on the water and the solitude of his lonely island, he'd be able to return back to his family a better man, the man he wanted to be, not the grumpy, short-tempered one he became when his emotions got too heavy to handle.

With the boat ready, he set sail, wrapping his jacket more closely about him as protection from the rain. It was getting heavier, he realized, and he wanted to get across the water as quickly as possible.

As he went, there was an almighty crack from above. Daniel looked up, surprised. A thunderstorm had appeared out of nowhere. Sailing in a storm was inadvisable, but it wasn't like he hadn't done it before. He plowed on.

The boat rocked more violently beneath him. The waves were getting bigger. Now, Daniel felt the first hints of panic. Rain was one thing, storms another, but rough seas were never fun to be out in. Nor safe. He considered turning back.

Looking behind him, he realized that he was equidistant between the harbor and the island. It didn't matter now whether he kept going or turned back, the outcome would be much the same. He decided to head onward as planned.

It was just as he'd made his decision that it happened. A swell, bigger than any he could ever have anticipated, made the boat lurch dangerously to one side. As it rode the wave it catapulted him across to the other side. Daniel slipped, the water on the deck eliminating the friction he needed to stay grounded. In the blink of an eye he was over the side, and plunging into the dark, raging ocean.

CHAPTER TWENTY SEVEN

Emily was still reeling from her fight with Daniel as she went about her day. She found herself in Charlotte's nursery, tidying it for what felt like the millionth time, while rain lashed against the windowpane. The weather seemed to perfectly match her mood—both growing darker and stormier with every passing moment. She was so upset and stunned by Daniel's behavior, she soon collapsed into the nursing chair.

How dare he say such horrible things to her? She felt like he'd been harboring resentment for ages. They'd made a pact to communicate better but now it seemed like Daniel had been keeping his true feelings from her. All that had needed to happen was a frank and open conversation about money and what they could afford for Charlotte, where they could reasonably expect to be financially speaking when the time came to enroll her at school. Instead she'd gotten barbed insults and veiled anger.

She grabbed her phone, feeling miserable and needing to offload to Amy. But before she had a chance to call, it started ringing in her hand.

The number was one she didn't recognize. She answered it, feeling confused.

"Is this Mrs. Morey?" the voice on the other end said.

"Yes. Who is this?"

"I'm calling from the hospital. Your husband is here. He's had a boating accident."

Emily was on her feet in a second. She clapped a hand over her mouth. What the hell was Daniel doing out on his boat? He was supposed to be at work!

"Are you sure?" she stammered. "My husband's name is Daniel."

"That's what it said on his ID," the woman replied.

Emily couldn't believe what she was hearing. "Is he okay?" she cried, her hand clutching her cell phone so tightly it felt like she could snap it in two. "Please God tell me he's okay."

"He has hyperthermia but other than that he's looking good. You might want to come down here, though."

168

Emily didn't need telling twice. She hurried out of the nursery and thundered down the steps of the inn. Lois was at reception and looked panicked when she saw Emily's stricken expression.

"What's happened?" she asked, concerned.

"It's Daniel," Emily told her. "He's in the hospital."

Lois gasped. "Emily, wait," she said as Emily headed for the door. "You can't drive like this. There's a storm and you're really upset. Let me call you a cab."

"There's no time," Emily said, grabbing a jacket from the hooks and her keys from the bowl by the door. She yanked the door open and was lashed by rain. But there was no time to stop and think. She had to get to Daniel.

She hurried down the steps. Behind her she heard the sound of Lois calling her name, her voice swallowed by the now howling wind.

Emily got into her car and threw it into reverse, moving at speed through the parking lot and along the lane. She reached the road in record time and turned. That's when she heard the sound of a blaring horn.

She slammed on the brakes. The car juddered to a halt. Panting, Emily looked out her driver's window and saw dazzling headlamps. She'd pulled out right in front of another car.

The door of the other car opened and a figure ran toward her, covering their head with their jacket to protect themselves from the rain. Emily wound her window down.

"I'm sorry," she began.

But then she realized it was Raven Kingsley. She tensed. There wasn't anyone worse she could have run into really.

"Emily?" Raven said, surprised. "What are you doing?"

If she'd been planning on biting Emily's ear off she'd clearly changed her mind.

Without even thinking, Emily blurted out, "Daniel's in the hospital." Then she broke down in sobs.

A second later, Raven had heaved open the driver's door. She started tugging Emily by the arm.

"Come on, I'll drive," she said.

Emily was so consumed by anguish she didn't even protest. She let Raven guide her through the rain to her car, with its heated leather seats and tinted windows. She was relieved that someone had taken command.

"I was on my way to school to pick up Laverne and Bailey," Raven said as she swung the car back around the way she'd come. "I'll call Yvonne."

Emily felt stunned to hear her friend's name. She realized then how long it had been since they'd properly spoken. The whole Laverne issue had really put a dampener on their relationship and with everything going on in Emily's life at the moment she hadn't had time to deal with it.

Raven was tapping at a computerized screen on the dashboard of her car. The sound of a ringing phone filled the space.

"Yvonne, can you pick up the girls after all?" Raven said when the call connected. "Oh, and Chantelle, too?"

There was a pause before Yvonne spoke. "Chantelle Morey? But why?"

Emily spoke next. Her voice came out like a tremble. "Daniel's in the hospital," she said. "Raven's driving me there now."

"Emily?" Yvonne said. Then a wave of compassion was suddenly audible in her voice. "Of course. God, I'm sorry. Is he okay?"

"He had a boating accident," Emily said, and she started shivering.

"I'll bring Chantelle to the hospital," Yvonne said. "Don't worry, okay, hon? It's going to be okay."

Emily felt reassured for the first time since she'd received the call from the hospital. She let Raven's state of the art air conditioning warm her to the bones and sat back, relinquishing control, as the car sped along the rain-drenched road.

*

A horrible sense of déjà vu raced through Emily as she hurried along the corridors of the hospital. It had been a matter of days since she'd been racing along with her father on a stretcher. Now it was Daniel who was the object of her deep anguish.

She reached his ward and rushed in, searching for his bed. Then she saw him, tucked up in a white blanket looking pale and disheveled.

"Daniel!" she cried, running forward.

He looked up at her, tears glittering in his eyes, and reached out. Emily grabbed his extended hand. He was as cold as ice.

"What were you doing?" she cried, falling into his arms. "Why were you out on the boat in this weather?"

"I'm so sorry," Daniel said, choking as he spoke. "It was an accident. I just needed some space to get my head clear."

"I don't know whether to slap you or kiss you," Emily stammered.

170

Daniel let out a strangled laugh. "You can do anything you want to me," he said. "Whatever you need to do to forgive me."

She pressed her lips to his, over and over. They were as cold as his hands and somewhere in Emily's mind she felt like her kisses were breathing life back into him. She sat back, finally, holding his cold face in her hands.

He gripped them tightly where they were pressed against his cheeks. "I don't know how many times you're going to keep allowing me to let you down," he said through his gasped sobs.

Emily shook her head. "An infinite amount," she said. "You know that. I'm committed to you through thick and thin."

As she spoke, light caught the diamond on her wedding ring, making it sparkle.

"I don't deserve you," Daniel murmured. "I'm the luckiest guy alive."

"Tell me about it," Emily joked, her eyebrows rising sympathetically. "Lucky you got rescued! Who was even out there at that time?"

"It was the guys," Daniel said. "Stu. Clyde. Evan. I thought they went to look at marble, but turns out they were transporting a load of materials to the island so had taken a bigger boat. They saw the whole thing happen."

"Are they here?" Emily said.

"I think they went to get coffee."

As if on cue, Daniel's three rubbish best friends clattered into the ward, bringing with them their loud chatter. Emily turned, tears falling from her cheeks, and collected all three in her arms.

"How can I ever thank you guys?" she said.

Stu spoke gently, his hand patting her back a little awkwardly. "You know we'd die for that guy, Em."

"Thank you," she said, breathless.

She moved out of their arms, squeezing each of their hands.

"God knows why," Clyde added. "He isn't half dumb sometimes."

"I know, right," Evan quipped. "What an idiot!"

Emily laughed, feeling relieved that someone had cut through the tension of the moment. Then she saw at the entrance of the door a new person appear. Chantelle.

The child caught Emily's eye and ran full pelt at her. Emily caught her just as she saw Raven, Yvonne, Bailey, and Laverne reach the ward. They looked out of breath, like they'd been running to follow Chantelle. The child must have made a run for it the second they entered the hospital.

"Thank you," she mouthed at them as she pressed Chantelle against her.

"Mommy," Chantelle cried, clutching at Emily.

Emily held her close, hugging her hard. She led her to Daniel's bedside.

"Daddy, you're in so much trouble," Chantelle scolded him.

Daniel let out a melancholic chuckle. "I know."

"You promised you'd be careful on the boat," she added.

"I know," he repeated. "I'm sorry."

Chantelle tutted and shook her head. "I think we're going to have to ground you. Aren't we, Mommy?"

"I think so," Emily agreed.

Daniel nodded. "That's for the best."

Finally, Chantelle flung her arms around him. Emily saw Daniel sag with relief as his arms closed around his precious daughter. He was lucky to be alive, to have this chance at reconciliation. Unlike the rest of his thoughts and emotions, he didn't need to say that aloud. Emily could see it in his eyes.

CHAPTER TWENTY EIGHT

Emily hurried up the steps of the town hall. The wind outside was frigid, but once inside she found the place filled with people and humidity. It looked like every single person in Sunset Harbor had come for the meeting.

To her surprise, she noticed Amy amongst the crowds, and remembered the time her friend had crashed the town meeting held when she'd first arrived here, about whether she ought to be allowed to open her own inn. How times had changed.

She went up to her friend. "What are you doing here?" she asked.

Amy looked embarrassed. "I'm here for you. If Raven tears down that beautiful property and builds a swanky new inn it will damage your business. Not to mention the character of the town."

Emily raised a skeptical eyebrow. "I can't believe you care about the character of the town, Amy! How far you've come. Does that mean you're planning on staying here indefinitely?"

Amy brushed the comment away. "I haven't made any final decisions yet," she said. "I'm just looking out for my best friend."

Emily smirked and pressed her lips together. A hush fell over the room as Mayor Hansen took to the stage and walked up to the small podium. Emily found a strange rush of nostalgia as she remembered how it had felt to be on the other end of this process, to be the one being judged and evaluated. Now she was as much a part as Sunset Harbor as anyone else. Now she had the power to judge and evaluate others.

"We're here to discuss the beachfront property," Mayor Hansen said. "The old Ocean Breeze Inn, for those of you who've been here long enough to remember it as such." He nodded to Rico in acknowledgment. "Or the mansion in disrepair for those of you who don't. Now, Raven Kingsley is proposing to tear the place down and build a new inn on that space." He gestured to Raven, who was sitting next to him, doing herself no favors dressed in a black fur coat and oversized shades. Mayor Hansen cleared his throat. "May I open this out to the floor?"

There was an instant hubbub.

"I oppose," Birk from the gas station said, standing. "A new build would ruin the character of our town."

"I agree," Karen added. "What about the plans to open a museum for Trevor?"

"We've not been able to find the money for it," Mayor Hansen explained. "The museum is definitely not going to happen. It's either a case of leaving the property as it is, or tearing it down. It's unsafe to merely remodel it."

"What about Emily's inn?" Vanessa added. "Can the town handle two places?"

All heads turned to Emily. She knew the entire room was against Raven. She hadn't made many allies in Sunset Harbor. But after everything they'd been through, Emily couldn't help but feel compassion toward her.

"I don't mind a bit of competition," Emily said.

She saw every expression on every face turn to bemusement.

"Emily," Cynthia stage-whispered. "This one is in the bag. You just have to say no and it will be turned down."

Emily just shrugged. She knew everyone disapproved. But she remembered being where Raven was. Disliked by everyone in town. Them all being suspicious of her motives. Thinking she was a New York City type just here for the money. She hadn't gone as far to say she was out loud but that was everyone's first impression of her. Raven had made things even worse for herself, talking about how Sunset Harbor was in fashion at the moment. She'd shown no support of the town, and no love for it or its people. But Emily knew there was more to it than Raven would let anyone else know.

"Raven, why don't you explain to everyone what your plan is with the inn?" Emily called across the hall. "I think there may be some misconceptions about what you want to do."

Raven removed her sunglasses. "You know my plan," she said, shortly. "I'm tearing it down and building a new hotel. I want it modern, with space for conferences."

The whole room collectively cringed.

"And your family?" Emily said. "What about them?"

A look passed Raven's eyes. "We'll be living onsite," she mumbled.

This surprised everyone, Emily could tell by the increased volume of whispering.

"Now my divorce has come through," Raven added, "I'd like to put some proper roots down."

"So you wouldn't just be making a quick buck and then moving on?" Emily asked.

Raven shook her head. "Not this time. I'm looking for a home."

The hall erupted with conversation. Emily knew that Raven had played her cards close to her chest, and in reality she wasn't particularly into the idea of the woman opening a rival business, but she also knew how the townsfolk's minds worked. Raven deserved as much of a shot as she'd had. It was only fair.

Mayor Hansen hit his gavel on the podium for silence. "Emily, are you really saying you're not in opposition?" he asked.

"I'd prefer the house to be restored rather than torn down," Emily explained. "But like you said, that's not an option anymore. It's not safe. It can't be salvaged. What's the point of leaving it to languish?"

Mayor Hansen looked completely flummoxed. This clearly had not gone the way he was anticipating.

"I think we ought to adjourn this meeting for now," he said. "With the new information about Mrs. Kingsley—"

"*Ms.* Kingsley," Raven clarified.

"Sorry, Ms. Kingsley," he corrected, "moving here as a resident."

He banged the gavel again and the meeting was dismissed.

With a grumble, people began to stand and leave the hall. Emily was relieved the meeting had been postponed, even though she knew everyone was frustrated with her for not calling what they so obviously had wanted to hear.

"Oh, guys," she called. Everyone stopped and looked over at her. "Before you go. Remember we're having an open invitation Thanksgiving this year at the restaurant. Raven will be there so you can all ask her questions about her plans for the inn if you want."

She caught Raven's expression out of the corner of her eye. For the first time, there was a smile on her lips. Emily had known she'd be spending Thanksgiving alone now that her husband was out of the picture and the thought troubled her. No one should be alone on Thanksgiving.

The rest of the congregation looked a bit guilty at their ungrateful attitudes earlier. They turned their grumbling dissatisfaction into kind words of gratitude to Emily for hosting the event.

She smiled to herself as everyone left, wishing them well and saying she couldn't wait to see them tomorrow at the meal. Her conscience was clear and that was what mattered to Emily. She'd done the right thing by her fellow human.

CHAPTER TWENTY NINE

The restaurant had never looked so beautiful. Each table was covered in a hessian-blue tablecloth and had a floral bouquet filled with camellias and amaryllis. Beside each placemat was a sprig of red berries. There were candles everywhere, on the tables and all around the restaurant, making it sparkle like it was filled with stars.

Amazing smells emanated from the kitchen. They were serving a special menu just for the night consisting of all the dishes they'd cooked in Greece for Roy on their early Thanksgiving meal.

Emily was filled with excited anticipation for the evening.

Just then, Owen arrived, his sheet music under one arm. He greeted Emily in his usual shy manner.

"I have some news," he told her. "This will be my last concert. I'm leaving Sunset Harbor."

"Oh!" Emily exclaimed. She'd miss Owen. He felt like part of the family he was here so often. "Where are you moving to?"

"Singapore," he replied, and Emily suddenly remembered Serena's artist scholarship. She must have decided to go for it after all. She turned to Owen and smiled. "I'm really happy for you," she said.

Owen thanked her and then took his seat at the piano and began to play, ready for the guests to arrive.

Emily stood at the doors beside Harry, feeling a little wistful as the cold fall air rushed past her.

"Are you okay?" Harry asked.

Emily smiled and nodded. "Just thinking about how things always change," she said. "The world keeps on turning. Life keeps on moving forward. Do you ever wish you could just pause things?"

Harry looked at her with contemplation. "Do you know what, I don't think I do," he said, finally. "I like the way life changes. Because even when you hit rough spots you know you'll get out the other end. Even when things are tough it won't be like that forever. I like knowing that everything can always change, that people can come into your life that you'd never expected and shake everything up."

Emily could see in his eyes that he was thinking of Amy, of how he'd never predicted someone like her coming into his life. She smiled, comforted by his glass half full approach to difficulties. She decided to follow in his footsteps. Tonight, of all nights, she needed to remember all the good in her life, not think about the hardships.

The first of their guests arrived, and Emily and Harry greeted them warmly. Soon, more and more townsfolk came streaming in. This was the most elaborate event Emily had ever thrown, not to mention the most well attended.

She looked around the busy restaurant at all the friendly people. There was a table of school parents, including Raven and Yvonne, as well as Holly, who was making her first outing since the miscarriage. Tilly and her mom were in attendance, and even Mrs. Doyle had made an appearance with her equally sour-faced husband.

There was a table of Daniel's friends and Emily laughed as she saw they had already popped open their champagne and were taking sips of it then pulling faces. The three of them were much more into their beer, and she remembered she'd have to stock up if they did indeed take up her offer to stay at the inn and work on the island until the renovation work was complete.

Roman had come too, and he sat at a table with Astrid, who was now employed as his fitness instructor, and George, who it looked to Emily like was now her new boyfriend.

Just then Emily saw Paul Knowlson, the guest who'd been staying in apartment four of Trevor's house, coming down the stairs. He was carrying his cases and seemed to be heading out, going against the flow of people. She stopped him at the door.

"Are you checking out?" she asked.

He nodded. "Yes, my booking is over today."

"You should stay for some food at least," she told him.

Paul looked touched. "Thanks, maybe I will." He put his case down at his feet. "You know, I should think about buying a B&B in Maine sometime. There's something about this place."

Emily smiled. "There certainly is. And I don't mind a bit of competition." She cast her eyes across the room to where Raven was chatting with Yvonne, looking more relaxed and happy than she had yet. "But you might have a run for your money with that one." She pointed Raven out to Paul and chuckled. "She is one shrewd businesswoman."

Paul looked intimidated by Raven immediately. "Yeah, I might wait a little while in that case. I've gone head to head with people like her before. I'm not sure I'm ready for a war."

Emily laughed and showed Paul to a table, placing him in the spare seat beside Bryony.

When she turned back to head to the door, she realized with surprise that there were two people there who looked extremely out of place, more so than Raven in her head to toe black. The first person was Jayne, dressed in a power suit like she was heading to the office rather than a Thanksgiving meal. Beside her was Emily's mom.

Emily was so stunned she lost her breath entirely. She wended her way through the tables and hurried to the main door.

"Mom, what are you doing here?" she gasped. "Did you drive up with Jayne?"

Patricia turned to her, her usually sour face a little softer.

"She let slip she was heading here," Patricia said.

Emily caught Jayne mouthing sorry out the corner of her eye. But there was nothing to apologize for. Emily realized that her mother was very much welcome. She wanted her here for the first time in her life.

"Come on," Emily said, taking her hand. "I'll find a space for you at the family table."

She led Patricia through the restaurant, clasping her hand like a little girl. When Daniel saw them approaching, his eyes widened. He leapt from his seat.

"Patricia," he gasped. "You're here."

"Don't look so stunned," Patricia replied. "I'm not moving in or anything. It's just dinner."

"Of course," he spluttered, pulling her chair for her.

"Thank you, dear," she said as she sat.

Over the top of her head, Daniel gave Emily a look. She just shrugged, feeling as bewildered herself as he clearly was.

"Who are you?" Chantelle asked then, turning to the unfamiliar woman suddenly sitting beside her.

"I'm your grandmother," Patricia said.

Chantelle paused, as if pondering the words for a moment. "Cool," she said finally. "On which side?"

"Your mom's."

"So you used to be married to Papa Roy?"

Emily tensed then, worried her mom might be triggered by the mention of her ex-husband and make a scene. But to her surprise, she just smiled.

"Yes. A long time ago."

"Are you sad that he's dying?" Chantelle asked.

"Very sad," Patricia replied.

"Me too," Chantelle said, glumly. Then she suddenly gasped. "I forgot to look for the hidey hole!"

Patricia frowned with confusion as Chantelle hastily pushed her chair back.

"What's the matter with her?" she asked Emily.

But Emily couldn't stop from laughing. Chantelle certainly did know how to make a scene. She watched as the child ran out of the restaurant.

Patricia continued her bemused questioning. "Where is she going?"

"Just wait," Emily told her.

A little while later, Chantelle hurried back into the restaurant. In her left hand she was holding a brick. In her right was a bag.

"What did Papa Roy leave you then?" Emily asked as she took her seat again.

"Seeds!" Chantelle cried. "To grow watermelons!"

Emily laughed. That was a very typical gift from her father. Something poignant, small, but packed with meaning. Watermelons like the ones they'd eaten in Greece. She wondered when during his visit he'd stashed them there, and whether he'd known at the time he did it that Chantelle would one day join him in Greece.

Just then, Emily heard the sound of someone tapping their glass to get attention. The room became quiet and everyone turned to see that it was Harry who was standing.

"I just wanted to thank you all, from the bottom of my heart," he said. "Opening a restaurant was always a dream of mine. And now I've done it! I never imagined it would be this successful, and that's all because of you guys and your support, and Emily and Daniel for giving me this chance, and of course, my gorgeous Amy for always putting her faith in me and encouraging me to reach for the stars."

He turned then, looking at Amy. Emily felt a sudden hitch in her chest, as she realized what was about to happen.

"Which is why," Harry said, and his hand reached for his pocket.

Everyone gasped. Amy's hands flew up to cover her mouth.

Harry produced a small box and got down onto one knee. "Which is why I'd like to ask you to marry me," he said finally.

The whole room let out a roar of excitement. Tears blurred Emily's vision. She felt Chantelle's excited hand on hers, squeezing, as the girl bounced excitedly in her seat.

Through her misty vision, Emily just about made out the sight of Amy nodding. The room erupted with applause, a standing ovation. Emily stood and clapped, too, and watched with utter joy as Harry slid the ring onto Amy's finger.

When she sat, Daniel reached for her across the table.

"I've made my mind up," he said. "About the shop. I'm going to do it. I'm going to do what you suggested, make bespoke children's furniture."

"You are?" Emily gasped. "What changed your mind?"

"What Harry just said," Daniel replied. "I didn't realize you just wanted me to succeed and live my dreams. I thought you were pushing me for more money and I was so stressed with the workload at the time it seemed impossible. But I can see now you were only ever trying to support me."

Emily smiled, glad, and filled with gratitude. "Now. Let's eat!"

They all tucked into the myriad dishes, eating until they were stuffed. Once the main meal was over, they went to the inn for spiced rum cocktails and dessert.

Emily caught up with Amy and hugged her. "Congratulations. I guess that means you're staying now."

"I guess it does," Amy replied. "You'll be seeing me at more town meetings, sticking my nose in and ordering everyone around!"

Bryony came over, looking excited. "Emily, did I tell you? The island's been booked!"

Emily's eyes widened with astonishment. "Really? All three rooms in the cabin?"

Bryony nodded eagerly. "Yes, but it's called a chalet now, darling." She winked. "All three rooms. So it had better be ready for April!"

"Let's go and see the progress!"

EPILOGUE

A magical sunset hovered above Daniel's boat as he rode it carefully through the gentle ocean. In the boat, Emily was huddled beside Chantelle, Patricia beside her. Amy and Harry were snuggled up together at the stern, Clyde, Evan, and Stu taking up the rest of the space.

"This is definitely the most people we've had on the boat," Chantelle said. "A grandma, two parents, a pair of fiances, three amigos, one kid, and an almost baby!"

Everyone laughed.

They reached the island and Daniel helped them all get on shore.

"I honestly have no idea what to tell the girls about this," Patricia said, referencing her friends in the DA. "I mean an *island*, Emily. How audacious."

"Can I start the bonfire?" Chantelle asked Daniel.

"Actually," Daniel said, "I have a surprise. We're not having a bonfire tonight. We're having a real log fire."

Emily looked at him, surprised. He led them to the cabin. Though it was still just a shell, with only a few rooms complete, one of them was the main living space. It had wonderful floorboards and ceiling beams, looking every inch the luxurious chalet Bryony had marketed it to be. And there at the far end was a gorgeous fireplace made of marble.

"Daniel," Emily gasped. "You made this?"

Daniel nodded. "Do you like it?"

"It's incredible!" Emily cried.

He crouched down and got the fire going. From his basket he produced all the ingredients to make s'mores, and they toasted the marshmallows on the fire.

With the fire glowing and filling the room with warmth, the sun setting through the empty window frame, Emily felt so filled with gratitude for everything she had. Though life was fleeting, and her father would not be in hers for much longer, there was a lot to be thankful for. Friends, family, and unforgettable moments like these.

Emily thought of Daniel, of the determination she'd seen in his eyes over dinner. And she thought of Stu, Clyde, and Evan, his three amigos, his trusty companions. She had every faith that they would get everything finished in time for April.

She thought of Daniel, opening his own shop. She thought of her baby, coming soon. She thought of Chantelle, getting older each day. And for the first time in a while, she was able to look toward her future in the way that Harry looked toward his—with the glass half full, with anticipation of change but not fear of it, with wide eyes, eager.

Ready.

CRISTMAS FOREVER
(The Inn at Sunset Harbor—Book 8)

"Sophie Love's ability to impart magic to her readers is exquisitely wrought in powerfully evocative phrases and descriptions….This is the perfect romance or beach read, with a difference: its enthusiasm and beautiful descriptions offer an unexpected attention to the complexity of not just evolving love, but evolving psyches. It's a delightful recommendation for romance readers looking for a touch more complexity from their romance reads."
--*Midwest Book Review* (Diane Donovan re *For Now and Forever*)

CHRISTMAS FOREVER is book #8 in the #1 bestselling clean romance series THE INN AT SUNSET HARBOR, which begins with For Now and Forever (book #1).

35 year old Emily Mitchell fled her job, apartment and ex-boyfriend in New York City for her father's historic, abandoned home on the coast of Maine, needing a change in her life and determined to make it work as a B&B. She had never expected, though, that her relationship with its caretaker, Daniel, would turn her life on its head.

Christmas and New Years are fast approaching in Sunset Harbor, and Emily Mitchell is nearing her third trimester. While they continue to develop their new private island, a new business opportunity arises—one Emily had never anticipated, and which could change everything.

Roy's time left to live is running out fast, and as Christmas looms and all are busy preparing, Emily knows that this will be the most meaningful one of her life. It will be an inspirational holiday season, one that changes their lives forever.

CHRISTMAS FOREVER is book #8 in a dazzling, wholesome romance series that will make you laugh, cry, keep you turning pages late into the night—and make you fall in love with the contemporary romance novel all over again.

Sophie's new romantic comedy, LOVE LIKE THIS, is now also available!

"A very well written novel, describing the struggle of a woman (Emily) to find her true identity. The author did an amazing job with the creation of the characters and her description of the environment. The romance is there, but not overdosed. Kudos to the author for this amazing start of a series that promises to be very entertaining."

--*Books and Movies Reviews*, Roberto Mattos (re *For Now and Forever*)

Sophie Love

#1 bestselling author Sophie Love is author of the romantic comedy series THE INN AT SUNSET HARBOR, which includes eight books (and counting), and which begins with FOR NOW AND FOREVER (THE INN AT SUNSET HARBOR—BOOK 1).

Sophie Love is also the author of the debut romantic comedy series, THE ROMANCE CHRONICLES, which begins with LOVE LIKE THIS (THE ROMANCE CHRONICLES—BOOK 1).

Sophie would love to hear from you, so please visit www.sophieloveauthor.com to email her, to join the mailing list, to receive free ebooks, to hear the latest news, and to stay in touch!

BOOKS BY SOPHIE LOVE

THE INN AT SUNSET HARBOR
FOR NOW AND FOREVER (Book #1)
FOREVER AND FOR ALWAYS (Book #2)
FOREVER, WITH YOU (Book #3)
IF ONLY FOREVER (Book #4)
FOREVER AND A DAY (Book #5)
FOREVER, PLUS ONE (Book #6)
FOR YOU, FOREVER (Book #7)
CHRISTMAS FOREVER (Book #8)

THE ROMANCE CHRONICLES
LOVE LIKE THIS (Book #1)
LOVE LIKE THAT (Book #2)
LOVE LIKE OURS (Book #3)